Minor Adjustment

Prologue

"I'M SORRY?"

Winston was not a slow man, nor was he hard of hearing, as his uncle Lewis had become after a few too many bar fights with a particularly unpleasant steelworker named Ian who, through years of practice defending himself against two older brothers and one unusually large younger sister, had a nifty left cross. It was more the events of the evening, perhaps even his life, which led Winston to genuinely question whether he had accurately understood the large man standing over him with cold eyes and an expensive suit that was partially engulfed in flames.

"What in the hell are you doing?" the large man with his suit on fire repeated testily.

Winston had not misunderstood, but it was simply a little beyond him to answer such a question after he had set fire to, as police and fire department estimates would later reveal, over six-hundred million dollars worth of property. Inadvertently set fire to, as his defense lawyer would later frequently repeat at the trial.

"Your sleeve is totally on fire, man," Winston responded matter-of-factly.

The large man slapped at his arm repeatedly until the flames died down. A sharp pain sprung up the side of Winston's head and he reached to remove the offending obstruction from his hair only to realize he no longer had hair on most of his head, save for a tiny patch near his right ear. *I must look ridiculous*, Winston thought, as the pain began to increase markedly.

"Just what in the hell are you doing?" the large man said yet again.

Winston was about to answer when a serious case of the giggles overtook him.

"What?"

"Dude, your sleeve is totally on fire again."

The large man looked down and saw that the fire had indeed leapt up with renewed energy.

"Goddammit," he sighed.

Chapter 1

IT WASN'T as if she had killed him.

That, Susan happily conceded, would warrant an investigation, or a cursory examination at the minimum. Reports would be filed, and rightfully so. Public curiosity would be aroused and who could blame them? It isn't every day a suspect is shot while in police custody.

Robbery homicide detective Susan Ciarelli shifted uncomfortably on the hard wooden bench outside her captain's office. The benches in North Hollywood's seventh precinct were in need of serious repair or, better yet, replacement. She made a mental note to take immediate action, lest she ever have the misfortune to sit on one again.

A full decade had passed since Susan had applied for the forty-two thousand three hundred and sixty-two dollars a year legal possession of a gun, nightstick and handcuffs would grant her. She went ahead and accepted her societal obligation to protect and serve along with it. Her parents, not particularly pleased with her decision, pressed gently for an explanation.

"What the hell are you thinking?" her father asked with as much civility as he was capable.

"Thanks for the support, Dad. Is Mom home?"

"I'll see if she's recovered. The paramedics seemed

optimistic about her recovery since your proclamation."

Susan rolled her eyes.

"Even funnier the twentieth time, Dad. Is Mom home?"

Her father was a physics professor at Hillard University, a quaint little liberal arts college situated on the northern edge of the Finger Lakes in Upstate New York. Having attained a measure of fame within the cozy confines of the classroom walls for a series of articles on quarks, including '*Leptons versus Quarks*', '*Flavors of the Rainbow*' and his most recent, '*Disputing the Seventh Quark*', Leland Ciarelli was firmly ensconced as department chair and ran his household with similar aplomb. Befitting a child of such a luminary, Susan was never allowed to roll her eyes as a child. 'Young ladies do not roll their eyes' was a fairly common refrain in the Ciarelli household. 'No', 'Don't' and 'What were you thinking' were not far behind. Her most enjoyable form of teenage rebellion had been rolling her eyes at anyone and everyone, the most common recipient being her high school physics professor. Susan tried hard not to think too much about that.

Her mom, loyal and reliable as an old Siberian Husky, was far worse. A few sarcastic jibes were nothing compared to the awesome scythe of guilt her mom wielded with freakish skill and strength. She breathed deeply in preparation for the ensuing battle at the sound of the phone exchanging hands.

"Susan?"

"Hi, Mom. How are you?"

"What were you thinking?"

"Thanks for the support, Mom."

"Well, what would you have me say? Congratulations? Best of luck? We're proud of you?"

"Heaven forbid."

Both had mellowed as the years passed, but the underlying expectation of failure had never left. Her parents never really believed their daughter, a straight-A student her whole life save for one unfortunate B in high school, the result of a strenuous disagreement with her freshman English teacher who to Susan's chagrin felt it necessary to extol the virtues of Jane Eyre, was capable of success away from a stack of books. Two dates with a psychiatrist from Toluca Lake brought about the suggestion that Susan's lightning fast move through the ranks of the LAPD was the result of her subconscious desire to gain her parent's acceptance. With staggering insight like that, a third date was completely out of the question.

Chiropractic care had, in recent years, gained a measure of acceptance in the medical world. Referrals from a M.D. were not uncommon. The New England Journal of Medicine even published a flattering review of a new form of chiropractic involving spinal decompression. With all of this, Bob still couldn't get past the unsettling notion that he was a quack. Maybe it was because his patients referred to him as Dr. Bob.

Your left leg is an eighth of an inch too short. Your hands are hanging at an oblique angle. The pain in your pinky toe is caused by a slight crick in your neck. Who believed such claptrap? Apparently, people like Mr. and Mrs. Carpenter.

The sale was the worst. Telemarketing as a teenager for a long-since defunct time-share outfit in Jacksonville had been painful, but this was excruciating. A two-day seminar in Vegas that came with a free lobster buffet in 2000 taught the basic principles of sales. Immediately establish the upper hand. The seller must always appear to be smarter than the potential buyer. Press the issue. Always be closing. That one was stolen from David Mamet, Bob later learned. Good advice, though. People have an amazing ability to be manipulated, he had found, even more so with a chiropractor.

"I want my wife to be out of pain. Whatever the cost." Mr. Carpenter said this earnestly, as if leaning forward in his chair denoted a more intense appreciation of his three-hundred pound wife.

Bob restrained himself from laughing out loud. *Until I show you the bill, right?*

"What can we do about it?" Mrs. Carpenter inquired.

"Three times a week is the best-case scenario." Three times a week was industry standard. He was so very, very ashamed to be in business.

"How much will it cost?" Mr. Carpenter asked.

"Do you have insurance?" *Please have insurance. Don't make me take your money.*

"We have an HMO."

So you don't have any insurance. "Well, what I can do for you, as a special arrangement, is take fifty percent off my normal fees, if you agree to a certain number of visits, say, seventy-two." *I should rot in hell.*

"If you think it's best."

"I do." *God help me.* "Debbie up front will sort all this out and schedule your first visit."

"Thank you so much, Dr. Bob."

"You're welcome." *Thank goodness my mom is dead. Seeing me like this would've killed her.*

Susan shook her right leg in an attempt to wake it. How much longer was she going to have to sit here? She cast a bored eye around the room. The office was slower than usual this morning. Boys in blue moved like old ladies under siege from arthritis until their café mochas eased them into the day on the best of days, and this clearly did not fall into that category. She dreaded the crime spree that was sure to unfold should Starbucks employees decide to strike.

When Susan was eight, she had been, quite unfairly, blamed for breaking a violin in art class. Sent to the vice principal for a punishment her eight-year old mind was positive would be life threatening, she was subsequently forced to wait outside his office for forty-six minutes. Staring at the clock, Susan pondered the untold torture and suffering that surely awaited her with every passing second. When she was finally admitted into the office, the supremely kind albeit leathery-skinned vice principal asked for her side of the story and, seeing that a lie was clearly something beyond such a charming girl, sent her quickly back to class with an apologetic smile. A valuable lesson had been learned that day. Expectation of punishment was far worse than any actual penalty that could be handed down.

She had been waiting outside Captain Baker's office for twenty minutes. It felt longer and was starting to wear on her. She felt like Kafka's most famous literary hero, Joseph K., not so calmly awaiting his fate.

A particularly lurid incident in her second year with the LAPD that had yet to be forgotten in the nine years since kept running through her mind. The exact details surrounding the vice cop with a heart of gold, as the Daily News touted her, became a more rousing story with every passing day until the district attorney, himself rumored to have a soft spot for bucking tabloid sensationalism and undercover female operatives, made headlines when he dismissed all charges. The department still caught flak for that little humdinger.

For the record, at least as far as Susan was concerned, it was not the fault of the police department. What bureaucratic industry funded by taxpayers isn't rife with human frailty? It's the city, really. L.A. is at fault; the damn place is just made for scandals. The entertainment industry in all its sickeningly opulent glory had imbued the entire town with an endless blood thirst for a juicy sound bite every fifteen seconds. Not that she was immune to that sort of thing. More issues of *The Enquirer* littered her bathroom tile than she would care to admit, or to be more accurate, than her parents would ever be willing to admit.

The whole silly incident had been blown way out of proportion. It wasn't even her fault. Not really. Had she attempted to rob a liquor store? She had not. Neither had she threatened to kill eight people with a .357 handgun. She was a police officer and had acted accordingly.

Her ill-timed response to a reporter's question had not helped matters. She probably should have looked to see who had posed the question before answering. She definitely should have seen the camera crew tromping around the entrance. For weeks now, newscasts had replayed her snarling answer to an admittedly innocuous question. When it hit the AP wire, the situation only worsened. The heat from within the department went up a thousand degrees the first time CNN ran the story and had increased every day since.

"Fuck, yeah, I shot him. Who the hell are you?" did, she was forced to admit, have a certain sensationalistic flair to it. The fact that she was half-naked and covered with blood probably didn't help matters any. But still. It wasn't as if she had killed him.

She glanced behind her. Baker was still yakking on the phone. *Dear God, man, teenagers don't spend this much time on the phone.* The impending conversation was not going to be fun. Even the best-case scenario was not a pleasant thought. There was an outside chance she would be charged, and although there was no way she would go to prison, her career as a police detective might very well be over the moment she left the office.

She liked being a cop. Her parents would have preferred she make some use of her bachelor's degree, but really, what good was an English major in Los Angeles? Language was not the friend of plastic Southern California. Her mom had been somewhat mollified when she rescinded her threat to quit the force and become a stewardess. The respected social order of the world is apparently professor, then cop, and finally flight attendant.

Being a police officer was fun. She didn't tell people that. Not anymore. She'd tried to explain to Beatrice, a friend's elderly aunt she had the pleasure of meeting at a New Year's Ever party, the sheer joy one could find driving a hundred and twenty miles an hour in pursuit of a suspect. Beatrice had been so outraged, she lodged a complaint with what she thought was the North Hollywood sixth precinct. Beatrice dialed the numbers without the aid of her glasses and with great gusto regaled a hapless Korean grocery clerk with tales of police excess. Having fun is apparently not allowed on the job. It was a good thing Susan had stopped short of discussing the finer points of a legal chokehold.

She looked away from Baker in time to see a grinning Archie Polk making a beeline for her. Archie, blessed with wavy hair that would make a movie star jealous, was always grinning, a trait that equally unsettled criminal and colleague. The rumor mill was split on over-the-counter medication or mild mental instability. Susan tended to think a healthy mix of the two.

"Susie, baby. That skirt would make Ally McBeal blush. Did you wear it for me?"

"That show has been off the air for ten years now."

"What, you're not happy to see me? No warm hello?"

She loved Archie. Chauvinism wasn't as rampant amongst police officers as most people might think, but neither was it a figment of a hack screenwriter's imagination. To the uninitiated, Archie was the worst purveyor of misogynistic crapola this side of Henry the Eighth. To the select few, of which Susan was a card-carrying member, his constant assault against decorum was an amusing jab at everyone else's hang-ups. Archie was the sort of guy who could make an airplane crash survivor smile while still in sight of the wreckage.

"Hi, Archie."

"Why so glum, Sugarplum?"

"Don't call me that." Susan loved it when Archie called her

sugarplum.

"You see the game last night?"

"You hate sports, Archie. You don't even know what offside means."

"It was a doozy."

"Nobody talks like that, Archie."

"I was thinking about you last night while I was naked."

"Stop trying to cheer me up."

"Waiting for the captain, huh?"

She leveled a withering stare at Archie, but he paid no heed. He sat down unnecessarily close to her. Susan smiled and rolled her eyes.

"You want me to go in with you? Soften him up a bit, maybe say a few nice things about your legs?"

"I'm good, thank you. Is it necessary to sit so close?"

"I'm fine, thanks for asking. Doctors say it's not contagious, just so you know."

The blade, it turned out, was only four inches long.

"What the fuck is this?" Julio inquired.

John did his best to maintain an even voice. "It's fifty dollars."

"It's the size of my baby son's dick."

"It's thirty bucks." John was not taking another dive. His wife was still going through the roof about the time he failed to sell their grill to their neighbor Faunia an hour before her Fourth of July party. Still, can't show any weakness. "Take it or leave it."

"Fuck."

Julio thought it over. Mugging people wasn't easy. You didn't just run up and tackle people and wrestle away their valuables. You had to be smart about it. Rule one was to avoid physical contact. To that end, a weapon was necessary, especially with so many people carrying pepper spray. Even guys. Julio didn't truck with no sissies, but he had to admit, it was an effective tool.

Guns were out of the question. Case of bad luck gets you dragged before some judge and he hears the words 'assault with a hand cannon' and you're looking at five years bunking with some kiddy fucker from Guam. No, a pig sticker was the way to go. Flash that shit in some college fuck's eye and he'll pass over his wallet and his girlfriend's panties faster than Gary Sheffield can throw a baseball game.

Four inches, though? He didn't want to get laughed at. John saw the look on Julio's face and saw his sale waving bye-bye.

"Twenty-five. That's as low as I go."

"Twenty-five?"

"Twenty-five."

Julio took the knife.

Reflecting on the day in question caused Susan to grimace. She knew better than to play the lottery. She made fun of people who played the lottery. Why had she chosen that day to win seventy million dollars? She'd told her parents the whole dirty debacle, save for the real reason she went into the store. She could handle being chastised for shooting an unarmed man, but the mere thought of her parent's outrage and quiet indignation at the realization their only daughter played the lotto jackpot was beyond imagination.

She had waited until the perp's back was turned before drawing her weapon. She had clearly identified herself as a police officer and ordered the man to drop his gun. Coked out of his mind, he whirled and fired without even looking. The shot missed her head by at least eight feet. Training and a sense of self-preservation returned fire. One shot was all she needed, as the bullet buried itself into his right shoulder and he went down like the proverbial ton of bricks.

Two of the customers fainted. The clerk vomited. The others fled in hysterics. Susan was momentarily stunned by the amount of blood. The plexiglass was covered with it. More seeped out from under the robber, whose name she later found out was Keith. Recovering her wits, she stepped over him, her gun still at the ready. Ignoring his screaming complaints, Susan rolled Keith over and handcuffed him.

She stood up, holstered her gun, and smiled. She was more than a little proud of what she had done. She considered asking the clerk to call an ambulance, but he was otherwise occupied dry retching on the lotto tickets, one of which might have been her lucky winner and ticket to a higher tax bracket and a condo in Malibu. Instead, she reached for her cell phone.

It was at that moment her gun went off. Susan reacted more strongly than Keith, despite his left shoulder being on the receiving end of the blast. She wasn't even sure he had been hit until her boot, still firmly planted on Keith's arm, turned a dark red. She hadn't remembered even touching the trigger, but she knew instantly she hadn't clicked the safety on. She might have burst out in tears if she wasn't so angry with herself.

Punching the numbers into her phone, she had a hard time keeping her voice steady.

"Officer involved shooting at…" Susan trailed off. She looked to the clerk. "What's the address?"

He stared at her like a lost little puppy. Susan repressed the urge to shoot him. She tried a calm approach. "Listen. I need the address or this man might die. What's the address?"

He blinked a few times, his attention given more to the blood covering his store than Susan snapping her fingers, begging for his attention.

"What is the fucking address?! Now!!" Susan screamed at the top of her lungs, a giant fissure appearing in her rational nature and on her forehead.

The clerk snapped out of it. "Uh, it's…Ninth South Brand."

Susan repeated the address to the operator and hung up. She lowered her gun.

"I need a towel or he is going to bleed to death." The clerk stood motionless. "Something, gimme something! Anything!"

The customers who hadn't fled numbered two, both unconscious on the floor. The clerk had waited until Susan looked away and then hastily retreated into the restroom. Susan rolled her eyes in utter frustration and looked around for anything to slow the bleeding. Seeing nothing, she stripped off her shirt, tore it in half, and pressed it against Keith's wounds. She hadn't realized how much blood had transferred onto her body until she saw the newscast that night.

Sweaty and covered in blood, Susan had been preoccupied with pressing her torn shirt into Keith's wounds. She barely heard the question coming from behind her. She paid it no heed until it was asked again. A valuable lesson had then been learned. The only silver lining was that she had worn her favorite bra.

So here she was, sitting outside her captain's office, awaiting her fate. Prepared for the worst. Her captain was, all things considered, a good guy. She had arrived in robbery homicide four years ago to a single sentence of advice. "Try not to screw up too bad in front of other people." The grammatical question of using 'bad' instead of 'badly' aside, up until the 21st Amendment fiasco, she had done a pretty good job of following that simple philosophy. Now she was going to lose her job because of one tiny little mistake.

A passing detective greeted her with a smile. "Hey, Shooter."

Susan let it go. She was used to that sort of thing by now. Half the time, the teasing was good-natured fun. The other half was barely hidden resentment and anger at the torrent of bad publicity unleashed on every cop in the city as a result of her shooting an unarmed, handcuffed suspect. 'Hey, shooter' was the current greeting of choice.

"Ciarelli, get in here." Baker's voice forced Susan to bend over and pick her stomach up off the floor before forcing herself inside.

His office was an oasis in a police station filled with photocopies of Dilbert comic strips and she never tired of it. The first time she'd stepped inside, her jaw had practically hit the floor. Posters of Clark Gable were everywhere. Still photographs from *Gone With the Wind*, *It Happened One Night* and that movie he did with Marilyn Monroe were plastered on the walls. His screensaver rotated between Gable as a young man and Gable as a 'distinguished elder gentleman,' as Baker was often heard to say. His wife, Claire, had taken him to a double feature at a local revival house on their first date. There was even a bust of Clark above the doorway. Everyone was careful not to say word one about the subject within his earshot.

She took a seat in front of Baker. He crossed his arms and leaned back in his three thousand dollar leather chair, another gift from his beloved Claire.

"Listen—", Susan began.

He cleared his throat, cutting her off. Susan's eyes narrowed. Surely he didn't want to do this now.

"Baker, I'm not in the mood-"

He cleared his throat again. Susan rolled her eyes. She leaned forward, holding Baker's gaze with her own. If it's a staring contest you want, then a staring contest you shall have.

It had started almost as soon as she had been assigned to the 14th. After one particularly long day involving an attempted kidnapping, two murders, and a mistakenly hijacked truck of live bait, Baker sat down across from her and bored holes into the back of her head.

"What are you doing?" she asked.

He just kept staring. Susan looked around for the cameras, sure her face would appear on a new Fox reality show within the week.

Off and on for the next four years they would have themselves a little staring contest. It was a surprisingly good way to relieve stress. He would usually let her win.

She blinked this time. Baker sighed, taking no pleasure in the victory.

"You let me win," he said.

"Never."

"I've got the committee recommendation here. Stop looking at me like that, it's not as bad as all that."

"How bad is it?" Susan managed to ask.

"Four months suspension, with pay."

"Four months!?"

"With pay."

Susan wanted to be angry, wanted to protest the unfairness of it all. But she was keeping her job. And she had shot a man.

"No other reprimands? No recriminations when I come back?"

"Four months and it'll be like it never happened."

"The past is never gone, Baker, it's not even past."

"Aw, quit your whining," he said, not appreciating nor likely recognizing the nod to Faulkner. "You should be kissing my hand in gratitude, not moaning and complaining."

"I'm not kissing your hand."

"I'm not kissing your hand and…"

"And thank you."

"My pleasure."

"Baker, what the hell am I going to do for four months?"

"Think about how you'll have a job to come back to. It could have been a lot worse, and you know it."

Well, that was certainly true.

"Four months." Saying it out loud didn't lessen the blow a bit.

"It's a tough beat, I know. It's not as if you killed him."

"That's exactly what I've been saying."

The office door closed behind her with a solemn thud. Susan looked out at the bullpen. The pace was picking up. Calls were coming in, paperwork getting filled out and filed. Loud voices filled the air where smoke once resided. An avowed non-smoker, she still felt fascist influences at work with every new no-smoking designation.

She couldn't help it. She was going to miss this. It was her life. What the hell was she going to do for four months? And dear God, what would she do if she never came back? A straight job? Academia? She shuddered at the thought.

Alex, one of the desk junkies caught her staring off into space and waved a friendly hello. Alex was always friendly, but rarely helpful. He had a knack for saying the wrong thing at the most inconvenient of moments. Perhaps that was why he was stuck behind a desk. Alex was also a liar. Not in a bad sense, not really. She hadn't even noticed for the first few years. His cunning façade was destroyed when he related to her an amusing anecdote about taking a box of donuts home to his pregnant wife on his daily commute down Burbank Boulevard. Several weeks later, Susan discovered Alex drove home on the freeway, was a confirmed bachelor at thirty-seven years of age and after a particularly bad experience in college, had opted for a vasectomy.

Alex cut her off before she could make it to the stairs. She did her best to be polite.

"Hey, Shooter. What's the good news?"

"Suspended. Four months."

"Have fun."

"Thanks." Susan smiled her goodbye as politely as she

could and started down the staircase.

"Ciarelli?"

She turned. "Yeah?"

"Try not to handcuff anybody and then shoot them. You're a civilian now. It's looked down upon in high society."

Then again...

Chapter 2

"DO YOU see anything to your liking?" Tony asked, noting that the elderly gentleman had been browsing alone for ten minutes.

Karl smiled disarmingly. It was a well-practiced maneuver, perfected over the last seventy years. It had gotten him his first job, his first free meal and his first wife. If anything, it had only increased in power as the years passed. Society was ill equipped to deal with an eighty-one year old man with a smile like his. Karl glanced quickly at Tony's nametag.

"Just looking, thank you, Tony."

The salesman nodded and scurried off in search of a higher commission. Using the name was always a clever touch. Familiarity puts the mark at ease. His greatest fleece had been preceded by a pleasant five-minute conversation with a young lady about her aspiring acting career. Caught moments later red handed with a ruby the size of an oyster, Karl had flashed the smile and pleaded ignorance to the young clerk, Patricia. Maybe I was mistaken, she remarked to the store security officer. He had walked out of the store with a bounce to his step, aided by the small emerald tucked securely in his elastic waistband.

Ripping off department stores was a step down, to be sure. In his heyday, he had rarely stooped below high-end jewelry stores. Diamonds were his favorite, but the resale value was far below virtually every other precious gem. Amethysts were the way to go. More bang for the buck, so to speak. Karl sighed. If only there was some way for him to pass his knowledge along to the younger generation.

A pair of fashionable, darkly tinted sunglasses disappeared in his pocket. The first of many that day, he was sure.

Charles saw the young woman from afar. He elbowed his cousin Fred in the ribs. Fred looked up irritably from his hot fudge sundae.

"What?"

"I'm gonna go talk to her."

"Whaddya need my permission? Go talk to her." Fred returned to his sundae, wondering not for the first time why he bothered to hang out with someone with no appreciation for dessert. Charles tucked in his shirt and marched over to the young woman, trying to formulate his opening line.

At seventeen, Charles was tall for his age. It wouldn't have been so bad were he not so horribly uncoordinated. Trying out for the basketball team had not been his idea, and it showed quickly, but his mom was quite insistent on the subject. He had always thought it nice of the other players to hide their laughter until they reached the locker room. For reasons that were beyond him, though, he was very popular, especially with the girls of Fairfax High School. Even seniors wanted to date him. Not for him to wonder why. Get while the getting's good, his father told him, the only good advice the old man had ever shared. Not long after imparting such words of wisdom, he ran off with a coffee shop waitress and her son of Charles' approximate age. Not that it mattered much to Charles. The old man wasn't around much before he left, either.

Upon closer examination, Charlie determined the young woman was not so young. She was very pretty, maybe twenty-five, with the beginnings of dark circles forming under her eyes. She looked tired. Straight blonde hair accentuated an oval face, with a nose that seemed out of place, but all the more attractive for it. Charles was especially enamored with her rack, which was far more impressive than the high school girls he was used to having.

Nina could have screamed. She had been standing at the counter for four minutes. Didn't customer service have any place in modern society? She just wanted her takeout lasagna and a Valium, but that seemed a more remote possibility with every passing second. *Surely somebody must care that I'm starving, dehydrated and clinically depressed.* God, who did she have to fuck to get a Diet Coke around here?

Nina saw the young man with a prominently placed zit subjugating his lower lip drawing a bead on her. She looked longingly to the kitchen. Her food was on the shelf, under the warmers. The waiter was also visible, smoking a joint with the cooks in the kitchen. That's probably not endorsed by the FDA, Nina thought. She could smell her lasagna. So close. Charles was fast approaching. She could see the look in his eyes and would have run had she not been so hungry. *Please let me be wrong. I don't have the energy for this.*

"Excuse me, miss, is there some reason you're alone?" Charles asked.

"How old are you?"

"Old enough, babe."

"Several state laws spring to mind, kid. I'm going to take a pass."

"You're way too beautiful to be alone."

"Is that a fact."

"Sure is. Maybe I can help you with that."

"How so?"

"Well, maybe we could slip off somewhere, you know, and be alone."

"What would we do alone?"

Was she serious? She looked serious.

"Why don't we go off and I'll show you."

"You know what? I thought this might be fun for a second, but that second has come and gone. I'm married. Unhappily married. My husband is a mobster. Not a rich, successful mobster, mind you. But he would kill you if he knew you wanted to take me in the back and fuck me. So why don't you waddle on back to your table and we'll both pretend we have lives to look forward to."

It was a strange thing, this disaffecting boredom. She hadn't felt it since college and had attributed such feelings largely to alcohol. Massive quantities of alcohol. She'd heard rumors that frat boys were the binge-drinking champions of the ivory tower, but within the confines of her dorm, nobody had nothing on the English majors. And when you stopped to think about it, it made perfect sense. Hemingway and intoxication went hand in hand, regardless of reader or writer. And who could sit through Moliere, Euripides, Beaumarchais and Joyce without needing a shot of something hallucinogenic? Sea Breezes were the late teen and early twenties beverage of choice. She had since graduated to apple martinis, and occasionally single barrel bourbon when she wanted to forget everything about everything in the world.

Two days. It had only been two days and already she was at her wit's end. There really was only so much Maury Povich a woman could take before she started yearning for a phone call reporting a multiple homicide. Worse still, she knew exactly how long it was until tomorrow's eleven AM showing of Jerry Springer. Eighteen hours, forty-two minutes on the dot. As if this self-effacing knowledge was not gut wrenching enough, there was the crushing weight the next one hundred eighteen days was already heaping upon her. It was intolerable and worse still, it had only been two days.

Susan rolled off the couch onto the floor, her empty can of

Sprite tumbling harmlessly to the floor. The impact did nothing to alleviate her sense of self-loathing. How could she have gotten suspended? After all, she could quote the first eighty-eight lines of Keats' Fall of Hyperion. It was the eighty-ninth line that always gave her fits. Something about death, she was sure. She should have mentioned that when the civilian review board asked her if she had anything to say in her defense.

Maybe she should get dressed. But then what? The carpet was surprisingly comfortable. Maybe she should clean. She could hire a maid. Four months, with pay, after all. She could go see a movie. Read another book. Perhaps what she needed was a new hobby. Oh! She could learn Russian.

The phone was ringing in the other room. Please let it be somebody in dire need of assistance. Susan tripped over the coffee table in her hurry. She pressed the talk button while massaging her shin.

"Hello?"

"Is this Mrs. Gionelli?"

"It's Ciarelli. Miss."

"Mrs. Ciarelli, because of your outstanding credit record, we'd like to reward you with a Visa platinum card. Zero percent interest for the first six months and a low APR of nine percent. Plus, if you act today, we'll guarantee no annual fee for the life of the card."

"I appreciate it, but I'm not really interested."

"All right, well, we appreciate your time, Mrs. Ciarelli. Thank you for—"

"Wait, wait. That's it? You're giving up already? Give me your sales pitch. Tell me more."

"Tell you more?"

"Yeah. Sell me."

"It's a Visa platinum card with zero percent interest for the first six months and a low APR of nine percent. No annual fee."

"Yeah, I got that. Why should I get one?"

"Uh, well, there's no annual fee."

"How is it better than other credit cards?"

"I…this is my first day. It's not really in my script. I just read this page and then people hang up on me."

"Aren't you allowed to ad lib? What's your name?"

"Marcie. I mean, Alice."

"Which is it?"

Alice. Marcie is the name I made up for the job. It's also the name on my fake ID."

"I'm a police officer."

"Shut up."

"It's true. Ten years. Robbery homicide. Badge number eight three nine—"

The line went dead. Susan smiled and hung up the receiver. Please ring again. Make my day and ring again.

The phone rang again. She laughed out loud as she lunged for the phone.

"Hello?"

The first thing Veronica noticed was the pair of pants on the sidewalk. Chinos. Leather belt. Nice. The second thing she noticed was the naked man standing on the sidewalk. *I'll bet those are his pants*, Veronica thought. Her second thought was to call Susan.

Veronica whipped out her cell phone.

"Hey, Susan."

"I thought you'd be a telemarketer."

"Sorry to disappoint."

Susan was disappointed. Oh, well.

"So, listen," Veronica continued, "I'm staring at a naked man on the sidewalk outside my building. What's the protocol on this sort of thing?"

"You mean a ten-nineteen?"

"There's a number for it?"

"I'm kidding, Veronica. Aren't you?"

"Should I talk to him?"

"Call the police."

"You are the police. Why do you think I called?"

Fair enough.

"He's probably on something," Susan said. "Meth, maybe."

"Meth?"

"Crystal meth. Methamphetamines? Didn't you used to be a nurse?"

"Shut up. He looks cold."

"Stay away from him. Hang up and call the police."

"What did you mean you're not the police? Did you quit?"

"No."

"You could, you know."

"I didn't quit."

"I'm just saying. Just because your parents would like it doesn't mean it's the wrong thing to do. Now he's staring pretty intently at his elbow."

"Call the police, Veronica."

"Did something happen?"

"Veronica—"

"Oh my God, something happened. What happened?"

"What's the naked man doing?"

"He's scratching himself. Pretty hard, too. Do you think that's bad? Oh, the police just got here. Hey, are you thirsty? We should get a drink."

Veronica could handle her liquor, of this Susan had not the slightest doubt. Susan was a drinker. She had put more than a few men under the table in college and rarely reached her tolerance limit, even on dollar margarita night at La Carbon Casita Mas, the best Mexican restaurant in the San Fernando Valley. Susan was a perennial contender for the middleweight title. Veronica was the reigning and undisputed heavyweight champion, all the more impressive given her five-foot tall one-hundred pound frame.

As if on cue, Veronica downed the last of her Long Island iced tea and looked thirstily for the waitress in the pink push-up bra. Susan looked Veronica up and down and had to admire how someone who drank as much as she did maintained such a trim figure. Or balance, for that matter. She had to exercise twice a week just to fit into her dress blues, and it was becoming more of a pain with every passing year. Veronica's idea of exercise was working the gas pedal.

"Hot women in need of alcohol on table five! Anybody?!" Veronica yelled out at no one in particular.

Susan had friends. Most were police officers and if she was being honest, or extremely inebriated, she would be the first to admit that police officers are kings among men, but make for pretty lousy friends. Susan herself was a lousy friend. It certainly wasn't her fault. It came with the job, and the reality of being a police officer meant that people could, within a margin of error not exceeding plus or minus two, fit into two categories. The first, and most popular, was the live the job workaholic type, of which Susan was a card carrying member. The problems with which are readily self-evident. The second group consists of men and women for whom a job is just a job and police officer is any other civil service profession. These two groups do not relate well to one another, which eliminates a third of the Los Angeles Police Department for the purposes of socializing. For those within Susan's species, intermingling with those outside the force was a difficult proposition. Susan never had enough time for her friends and when she did see them, she was invariably preoccupied by some case she had once worked on years earlier. Within this group, however, police form a very tight bond, but it is a bond that sadly does not extend far beyond the police corridors and hallways.

This is why so many cops get married to one another. Incest within the department was rampant. Of course, the ridiculous stress the job creates is why so many of these same couples get divorced. Joseph Heller would have loved the social scene inside the LAPD.

Veronica accepted that Susan was awful at returning phone calls, worse at initiating conversation, and reluctant to talk about the details of her job. Veronica never asked Susan about her day, she never pried for information. Everything Veronica knew about Susan, she had gladly and gratefully shared, usually over a bottle of something eighty proof. Everyone needs a friend like Veronica.

"I'm having doubts about being a police officer, V. It's been a while coming and this latest incident just brings everything to a boil. I'm burnt out, exhausted. I'm edgy all the time and I don't know why. I mean, I know why, it's because I'm so freaked out I shot a guy in a Quickie Mart and I could just pass out and cry all at the same time because of that little debacle. But I don't know, it's what I do, maybe it's become what I am. You know? Veronica?"

"I'm sorry, what? I was checking out this guy over there playing pool. Is that a ten on the Richter scale or what?"

"Veronica—"

"I heard you. Do you want me to tell you what to do with the rest of your life?"

"Of course not."

"You want me to listen and nod?"

"No."

"Well then?"

"I want you to tell me what to do with the rest of my life."

"Ah."

"I'm feeling lost, V. I am lost."

"You know what I do at moments like this?"

"I'm afraid to ask."

"I order another round and charge it to Hotpants at the

pool table. In this particular case, I am going to order several rounds and you and me, Miss Missy, are going to have ourselves a fun night."

"Not to bring down the house, in a depressing manner of speaking, but how is that going to solve my early-thirties life crisis?

"Drinking solves everything. Don't you know anything?"

The end of evenings with Veronica tended to be a bit of a production, akin to the last ten minutes of La Boheme or the big shootout ending of *The Wild Bunch*. Tonight's festivities included, but were certainly not limited to, Susan carrying/dragging Veronica to her car.

You may look trim, sweetie, but carrying you constitutes my exercise session for the week. She propped Veronica up against the car door and fished around for her car keys.

"Wait." Veronica looked poised to make a profound statement, but the words clearly escaped her.

"What?" Susan asked, with as much patience as she could muster.

"I'm forgetting something."

"It wasn't the two drink minimum."

"That's not it. Oh, hello."

Susan turned around, coming face to face with an irate little Hispanic man holding a tiny knife. He was jittery, his eyes darting to Susan's purse and Veronica's necklace, a cheap knock off she had acquired from a loud-mouthed businessman from Toledo intent on having an affair.

"Hand it over."

He said it almost in a whisper. He looked scared.

"I'm a cop."

"Bullshit. Gimme your shit or I'll slice you open."

"I'm going to be sick," Veronica said. "Oh, God."

Veronica let loose and held nothing back, certainly not the

eight Long Islands she'd consumed over a three-hour period.

Julio looked aghast, his face ashen at the sight of vomit dripping off Veronica's chin. Susan tried to pat Veronica on the back, but it was difficult to watch both a man waving a knife at you and a woman in a cheap dress vomiting on your suede shoes.

"The penalty for assaulting a police officer is double the norm. Walk away."

Julio thought about it. She didn't look like a cop, but who the hell could tell these days? He sure as hell didn't want no trouble with the LAPD. But the puker was holding a fortune. Her jewelry alone made his heart race. Maybe she was one of those ultra-rich broads who carried wads of hundreds everywhere they went. He looked around the tiny parking lot. Only a few cars left, but someone was bound to come along in a minute.

"Show me your badge."

"What?"

"Show me your badge. If you're a cop, I'll go. If not, you give me everything you've got."

"You have got to be kidding."

He was clearly not kidding. Susan fished around in her bag before remembering she'd left her badge in her locker.

"I don't have it."

Julio grinned victoriously. "I fucking knew it! Hand it over."

Julio grabbed at Susan's arm. As she twisted free and struck out with her palm, she hoped she would have the opportunity to express to Veronica her gratitude at a night out. That very morning, she had been positive she wouldn't be able to beat anyone up for at least three months and twenty-seven days. Susan slammed her elbow into Julio's ribs, ending his night but wrenching her back in the process. She caught a glimpse of Veronica, slumped over and asleep against the car. Susan would thank her later.

Chapter 3

BEFORE LUNCH Bob had a quick word with Debbie and at the end of their one-sided conversation announced he was quitting chiropractic forever. It was nothing new. She had heard such declarations many times. Today was a bit more vociferous, but Debbie attributed his demeanor to Dorothy, a particularly unpleasant patient with a lisp who treated the office as a restaurant. Who asked for Pepsi with a wedge of lime in a doctor's office?

It was no surprise when Bob came back from lunch exactly at two o'clock, as he did every day. The man was nothing if not a creature of habit. Debbie felt a little sorry for him and secretly hoped he would fold up shop. Her husband had been pressing for her to go back to college for over a year. Her first attempt had not gone well. She'd spent a month at a tiny junior college in Arkansas before the administration had advised her that continuing at their school was not in her best interests. One little fire and everyone is against you. The office closing up shop for good was the best excuse she could think of to shake up her life.

It was a surprise that a woman was in his office. She had insisted on filling out the new patient paperwork in his office instead of the waiting area, and something about the inflection in her voice convinced Debbie not to argue. She debated telling Bob whether or not the woman was in his sanctuary, as he liked to call it.

On one hand, it was her job. On the other, she'd probably have to listen to him vent about his life's woes if she brought the subject up. Lately, any and all subjects had given rise to self-loathing soliloquies that would make an angst-ridden teenager do a self-reflective double take.

Bob walked in. Debbie decided she could take no chances. She was in a delicate frame of mind today.

"I've got to use the restroom." Debbie said as she hurried past him.

Bob sat down at his desk across from Susan. She was perched on the edge of the chair, clearly in discomfort, though whether that was from some ailment in her back or from reading his framed accreditation from Cleveland Chiropractic College on the wall was hard to tell. He reached over the table and shook her hand.

"I'm Doctor Bob Kessler."

"Doctor?"

"Yes?"

"No, I mean, you're a doctor?"

She'd been looking at the wall. "Yes."

"I thought only medical doctors called themselves doctor."

"I'm a doctor of chiropractic."

"So you're not really a doctor."

"Tell me about your back."

"It's near my side, but you have to turn left and eventually you'll run into it."

Bob waited patiently, barely reacting to Susan's attempt at levity. *That's interesting*, Susan thought. Usually people laughed at her jibes or took offense. It was not at all uncommon for people to do both. Rarely did she fail to receive a response. She pressed on, minus the sarcasm. "It hurts a lot."

"Were you in an accident?"

"Yes."

"Rear ended? Sideswiped?"

"Attempted mugging."

That got his attention, she noted with satisfaction.

"Oh. Are you all right?"

"My back hurts a lot."

"We can help."

"We?"

"The royal we. I can help."

"How lucky I'm here then."

"Do you have insurance?"

"I'm with the city."

"What do you do?"

"Public servant."

"Are you being intentionally coy?"

"I haven't been coy since college. I'm a police officer."

"Really." Bob paused and took a long look at Susan, who tried her best to cover her face without appearing too obvious. "Have I seen you on television?"

"No."

"I know you. Yeah, I knew you looked familiar. You're—"

He stopped short.

"Back hurts a lot, yes. Can we do something about it, or do you want to sit here and chit-chat some more?"

She said this more aggressively than she had wanted to, but Bob did not appear to be bothered. He shrugged and stood up.

"Come with me."

It was comforting to Bob that he did not think of himself as a professional.

"Oh my God that feels great."

The neck massage wasn't really therapy in the strictest interpretation, but it went a long way towards making the customer happy. Normally, Bob spent his time rubbing people thinking about what movie he would see or which life he wished he was living, but with Susan, he couldn't seem to take his attention away from the three freckles at the base of her skull, or the way her hair curled up when he ran his thumb across it. It was, all in all, disturbingly inappropriate. Good thing he wasn't a real doctor.

Bob looked at the clock. He'd been massaging her neck for seven minutes. He usually stopped after five. Debbie, who had just now returned from the bathroom, did not seem to notice anything amiss. He should stop.

"This is amazing. I didn't even realize I was in any pain back there."

A few more minutes wouldn't hurt.

The first time Karl faked a heart attack did not go particularly well. The ruse had been flawlessly executed, but Karl could not have foreseen the trouble an overeager med student in the cafeteria would cause. Instead of bodies helping him to a table for a breather, which was the desired result, a circle of spectators formed around him and the kid desperate to put his CPR training to the test. The young man, who carried no wallet and a paltry two dollars in his pocket, forcibly kept the crowd at bay and cut off every escape route. Karl was forced to endure an ambulance ride, a series of tests and a painful hike in his insurance rates.

Minor setbacks like that aside, acting was an awfully fun way to lift wallets. Sadly age had sapped a measure of his energy. Most often when the mood to steal struck him nowadays, he was forced to 'trip' on a bus, or bump into somebody in a shopping mall, something simple. No skill involved there, the margin of error was too high for it to be a real challenge, and it could be accomplished on the way to and from the doctor's office. It cut down on the cravings, but there was nothing like the real thing, and more and more, those moments were just memories, growing more distant by the hour.

Still, every now and then, Karl found a day when his aches and pains took a holiday, his head would clear and the drive was back, the same desire to get out and pick the world's pocket he had felt ever since he was old enough to remember. On those days, feigning imminent death and thievery was a match made in heaven. If he felt truly adventurous, he might sift through a young woman's purse with his left hand while his right clawed at his chest. That required more time, and as age advanced, time became increasingly more of a factor. Happily for Karl, he woke up on this particular morning feeling better than he had in years. It was like someone had jammed a B-12 shot into him during his dream of finishing second in a baking competition. Carefully stirring his oatmeal for fear he would break the spell, he discovered breakfast only increased this glorious feeling, and he was determined not to waste it.

He decided on a restaurant, and the place was bustling, plenty of suckers just begging Karl to lighten their load. He had finished with his meal of corned beef on rye with lots of mustard. It was his second favorite dish behind roast beef and Yorkshire pudding. He paid the check with cash, as he always did, so he would be less memorable should anything unforeseen occur. Now, he was ready for business.

Karl looked around for a suitable target. He found it almost immediately in the guise of a ridiculously large man with an abundance of hair gel plastered across his head, alternately spiking up and plastering down his graying black hair. Hair Gel let loose a volcanic sneeze that turned every head in the room, and Karl got a chance to take stock of his victim without raising an alarm.

Too good to be true was the line. The man was alone for starters. When he fished out his handkerchief, the bulge of his wallet was prominently displayed for all to see. The suit was Armani and clearly tailor made. The man tipped very well and did it slowly enough so anyone who might be looking could denote the ten-dollar bill, rather than the usual single or two people would typically bestow upon the help. Ostentatiously generous people never failed to help a soul in need, especially with an appreciative audience in attendance.

Too good to be true was an expression that had never made such sense to Karl. Too good was ripe for the plucking always seemed more apropos. Karl got up from his seat and moved towards Hair Gel. Waiting until he was close enough to be caught, Karl clutched at his shoulder, wobbled his knees, and crumpled to the ground.

The place was in an instant panic. Several customers yelled for someone to call 911, one woman fainted, and a busboy dropped a tray full of dishes. Hair Gel, right on cue, leaned over Karl.

"It's all right, old timer. You'll be all right."

Karl's hands were old and weathered, and they weren't what they used to be, but they were still fast. His fingers slipped inside Hair Gel's jacket and lifted his wallet with precision and skill. Only as the wallet disappeared into the lining of his jacket did Karl notice the gun nestled in Hair Gel's shoulder holster. *Funny I didn't see that earlier*, he chuckled silently. *Must be getting old. I hope he's not a copper*, Karl thought. If he had looked very closely, the deep scratches over what used to be the serial number would have allayed that particular fear, but the truth was Karl knew precious little about guns. He'd never felt the need for one himself, such a clumsy and artless tool for a man of his stature.

Just to be safe, I'd better be on my way, Karl thought. He propped himself up on his elbows, and allowed Hair Gel to get him into a chair. The crowd, hovering in anticipation of death, murmured and grumbled their way back to their seats.

"Feeling better?"

"Yes, I am. I don't know what happened, but I feel my strength returning."

"Good, good. Gave everyone a scare, old timer."

"Myself included. Thank you for your help, young man. Please tell me your name."

"Paul."

"Thank you Paul. I feel my breath returning."

"You gonna be okay if I leave you for a minute? I want to get cleaned up."

"Of course, please. I will be fine."

Karl waited until Paul had disappeared into the bathroom, then beat a hasty retreat to his car. Unable to help himself, Karl took a peek at the goods. Fourteen crisp new hundred-dollar bills stared back at him. Well now, my glossy haired friend. Aren't we traveling in grand style this day.

Karl snuck out to the parking lot feeling most pleased with himself. Fourteen hundred dollars was a nice take, especially for a Tuesday afternoon. Maybe if his good health continued he would treat himself to a show tomorrow night. Karl unlocked the car door.

"Hey, old timer!"

Hand still on the handle, Karl turned. Paul had not come alone after all. Three men stood behind him, none of whom appeared friendly. All used too much product, Karl noted, though none was as dressed nattily as Paul.

"Feelin' better, huh?"

"Quite. Again, thank you for your assistance."

"I didn't catch your name."

"Karl."

"Karl, I got to the bathroom and couldn't help but notice my wallet is missing."

The three tough guys moved on Karl. There was no way he was getting away in the car, might as well start talking his way out. In all his life, he'd only been forced into violence once. During a stopover in Pittsburgh in 1956, Karl had gotten his hand caught in the lining of a very poorly made overcoat and was subsequently throttled by the much larger man. Never too old to get beaten to a pulp, Karl supposed. He stepped away from the car and flashed the smile.

"Gentlemen, I'm sorry if there's been some confusion."

Paul's smile held none of the charm of Karl's. "Confusion? You ripped me off, old man. I don't like getting ripped off."

"An error in judgment." Karl tossed the wallet to the nearest man, who caught it with ease. "Please accept my apologies. I'm just an old man, as you say."

"I don't like getting ripped off."

Karl's smile faltered, but only for a moment. It returned with all the radiance he could muster.

"None of us do. Why, when I was not much older than you, I suffered a swindle that relieved me of eight thousand dollars and change. I myself was most irate until I considered the skill and talent it took to loose me of my fortune. At which point, I found it impossible to be angry. I shrugged my shoulders and wished the man well."

"Is that a fact?"

"It most certainly is. Might I receive the same courtesy from you tonight?"

"Hey, Pete, anybody see us come out here?" he asked one of the other men, his focus never leaving Karl.

"Nah."

"Good. It's nothing personal, old-timer. You see, I just don't much like getting taken."

Paul took out his pistol and stepped towards Karl.

This would be interesting, Karl thought. *I've never been shot before.*

Chapter 4

BOB GOT the message his father had been shot and killed at three o'clock Wednesday afternoon. It was a very polite message.

'Hello, I'm attempting to reach Doctor Bob Kessler. This is Sergei Alekhov of the Los Angeles police department. I've left a message at your home number. I'm terribly sorry to inform you, but your father was shot yesterday afternoon. He passed away last night at the hospital. Please call me immediately on my cell phone. Thank you.'

He replayed the message twice, not quite believing his ears. Surely it was a prank phone call. Terribly sorry to inform you? Who would leave a message relaying a loved one's untimely demise? And surely if they were to do so, they would leave the cell phone number on said message.

Unable to reach his father, Bob placed a nervous call to 911.

"911 operator, what is the nature of your emergency?"

"I'm trying to reach a detective. Alekhov. He called and told me my dad died."

"This is an emergency line, sir."

"He left a message on my answering machine telling me my father is dead. This is an emergency."

"Sir, I can't help you."

"What falls under the definition of emergency with you? Is

there a guy named Alekhov? That's all I want to know. Does he even exist? If he doesn't, I'd like to find the son of a bitch who left me the message and if he does exist, I want to find the son of a bitch who left me a message like that without a goddamn return phone number."

"You can dial the non-emergency line, sir, and they can direct your call." And with that, the line went dead.

Later that night, he went home and erased his messages without listening to them. In doing so, he missed the one-hour cleaners behind his apartment calling to inform him they were going out of business and as such, he had only one week to pick up his charcoal gray suit before it would be unceremoniously tossed in the garbage. Three weeks later, Bob came face to face with a gutted strip mall and a large sign reading, 'FUTURE SITE OF EARL'S UNDERGROUND PARKING'.

More cars are sold on Sundays than all other days combined. This was one of the many industry facts Stanley Musselman knew by heart. Long ago he had memorized which demographic was most likely to purchase a particular type of vehicle, what role children under the age of eight play in influencing their parents and how to make payments of three hundred and eighty-five dollars a month for thirty-six months seem more fiscally responsible than four hundred and twenty dollars a month for thirty-one months. Selling luxury cars in Los Angeles granted riches beyond compare thanks to a populace with an elitist sense of greed and generally poor math skills.

Sundays had become a series of rituals for him. Up at four AM, shower, shave, dress in immaculate black suit with red power tie, light breakfast of mixed fruit, at work by five. Spend fifteen minutes alone in his cubicle, mentally preparing for the day ahead. Visualize the customer. Anticipate their needs. Always stay three steps ahead. Next came the coffee. One cup, no cream no sugar.

Mentally reevaluate the stock. What needed to go? Where was his highest commission? If a family of five came in looking for legroom, which buttons must be pushed to sell the optional DVD player and sunroof? At five minutes to six, slip away to the back room for a quick snort of coke. Not too much, just enough to get the engine revving. Check mirror, smile at reflection.

When the doors opened at six AM, he was rip roaring ready to go, as he liked to tell the other sales associates. He was the consummate professional and saw no reason to change his approach, though others, most likely jealous of his success, call him 'Easy Sleazy Stanley' behind his back. Secretly pleased, he quickly made the phrase his newest Gmail address.

Everything was exactly as she had left it. Not that anything should have changed in three days, but her irrational and vivid imagination pictured a gigantic purge of everything Ciarelli. Susan frowned. She couldn't help feeling a little disappointed. Isn't the world supposed to come to a grinding halt without me? What the hell.

Baker tromped up to her, none too thrilled. "You're on vacation. Drive up the coast and buy knick-knacks."

"I'm on suspension. And I have to be here. I'm making a statement. And would a smile and a how the heck are you be out of line?"

"What did you do?"

"Nothing," Susan said with as much innocence as she could muster. He crossed his arms and gave her a withering look. "Put a kid in the hospital with a broken nose."

"Jesus," Baker sighed.

"He started it."

Any sympathy Susan might have hoped for vanished instantaneously. "You think that's cute?"

"Maybe a little. He did attack my friend and me with a knife,

I feel compelled to point out."

"So, what, you're here to make a statement?"

"Yup."

"Are we going to get sued on this?"

"I might."

"But we're in the clear?"

"Yes, you're fine. Thank you for the concern."

"And what do you do, Pete?"

"He's a mobster," Nina interjected, cutting off her husband's response.

Stanley laughed appreciatively, expecting a similar reaction from Pete at his wife's jest. None was forthcoming. He toned the laugh down to a gentle chuckle and pressed on.

Pete's manner of speech was more of a grumble than anything else. He had never enunciated particularly well, and had grown worse as he had gotten older. When he went into extortion and collections full time, he had found his baritone growl quite the motivator, a nice change of pace from his previous work of supervising the non-union night shift at a grocery store in Tucson.

"Free-lance contractor," Pete said, his eyes flashing angrily at his wife.

"Are you looking for something recreational? Perhaps something you and your wife can both drive?"

"Just make sure it has a big trunk and tinted windows," Nina snickered.

"Would you excuse us for a sec, Stanley?" Pete asked.

"I'll wait right here."

Pete pulled Nina aside with more force than was necessary. She acted as if it didn't bother her. He exerted his physical superiority on everyone he encountered. It was his way of compensating for a staggering inability to relate to anyone on a personal level. Probably a miserable childhood, but that was only speculation. The one and only time Nina had brought the subject up had been the one and only time Pete threw her in the pool with her six-hundred dollar Manolo Blahniks on. From then on, Nina made sure to act as if his brutish behavior never bothered her in the slightest and she delighted in the knowledge it drove him crazy. The first year was all in good nuptial fun. She carried on with it now still strictly out of spite.

"Are you still pissed about last night? I said I was sorry," he simpered apologetically.

"It's not about last night." she said. It's about every night except Tuesdays, which Nina spent with her parents. Not that her parents were much better. Nights with Steve and Irene were spent watching reruns and playing gin rummy. Her mother was an incorrigible cheater, her father suffered from narcolepsy and their pet poodle had a grudge against Nina's clothing. Tuesdays were her favorite day of the week.

"I'm sorry, all right? We can do it when we get back to the apartment, if you want," Pete said without a trace of sarcasm.

How could she have married a man so horridly and utterly clueless? At least he was without a sense of humor or a shred of personality. If she stabbed herself with an ice pick, he'd probably grunt and ask if she was hungry.

"I didn't want sex last night, I sure as hell don't want it after you buy an extension of your penis."

"You didn't?"

"No."

"Then what was all that blubbering about?"

She hated crying in front of Pete. He didn't understand, he couldn't help, but he was her husband, goddammit. If you can't break down and sob in front of your spouse, why bother getting married at all? Granted, he was the reason she was teary in the first place, but the very least he could do was sit in silence and pretend to listen.

"I wanted to talk to you about—"

"We'll talk when we get back home. I can't deal with this shit right now, Pudding. Jewtopia here is gonna try and hash one over on me. I gotta concentrate."

"He's not Jewish."

"Look at his haircut."

"You're an idiot. Can we talk about that when we get back?"

Stanley saw a lot of fights. Two had ended in fisticuffs, one had led to an arrest. Most disappeared in a puff of bluster. These two looked fairly tame. She was a looker, probably ten years younger and a hundred and fifty pounds lighter. Typical L.A. story, she likely married him for the money, he wanted a trophy to park upstairs from his Porsche. Now, a few years after the novelty wore off, she was pining for true love and he for a new Porsche.

He would have been half right.

The details were hazy. No amount of repetition helped. Only the most painful portion was clear. Shot three times, mortally wounded, no eyewitness reports. The two detectives had been kind enough to give Bob a five-minute break after an hour and a half of the same questions. What was Karl like? Did he have a normal routine? When did you last see him? Did your father have any enemies?

"Did your father go to Jerry's Deli on Ventura often?" Detective Ortiz asked.

"I don't know, maybe." Bob answered.

"What did—"

"He was a thief, you know."

"What was that, Mister Kessler?" Detective Alekhov asked, slightly taken aback.

"My dad was a thief," Bob explained. "A professional. All his life. Hell, it was his life."

The two detectives exchanged a look. Ortiz looked through

the folder on his desk. "He never did any time."

"Why would he? He was a very good thief."

"Our records show he was a locksmith, owned and operated a place near Woodland Hills for forty-one years."

"That was a front. He thought it was a funny little joke. You know, locksmith, thief?"

"What did he steal?"

"All kinds of stuff. Jewelry mostly. He stopped that in eighty-nine, something about not tempting fate in five decades. That's when he started lifting wallets."

"Wallets?"

"Wallets, cash, purses, whatever he could take off people in crowded places."

"He became a pickpocket in his sixties?" Alekhov asked incredulously.

"Well, he dabbled with it before then, but it became a more full-time thing in the nineties. He still does that." Bob caught himself and winced. "Did that, I mean."

"I'm going to stretch my legs," Alekhov said, getting up and walking away.

"Anything else?" Ortiz continued, ignoring his partner's abrupt exit.

"Petty stuff, mostly. Shoplifting, walking out on checks, volunteering change to people and then shorting them. That kind of thing. I know it sounds awful, but that's dad."

"How do you know this?"

"He told me."

"You never saw it?"

"I never saw him do it, if that's what you mean. Mom wouldn't let him take me out with him on jobs. He stuck to that even after she passed away."

"Mister Kessler," Ortiz said with as much tact as he was capable, "it is very unlikely that someone who has been stealing for fifty years would never get caught."

"He was very good." Bob paused for a moment before asking, "Do you think that's why he was killed?"

"We'll look into it," Ortiz said, though it was perfectly clear to Bob that he would do nothing of the sort. "Now, did your father go to Jerry's often?"

"You write me a check right now, Pete, for ten thousand dollars. If you do that, here is what I am willing to do for you. I will knock off two grand right off the top, and that's on top of our four thousand dollars cash back or one point five percent. If it were me, I'd take the four K. That's just me. Fully loaded, over forty-eight months, that'll be nine twenty-eight a month. You wanna cut that down, no problem. I can get you out of here in thirty-six months for twelve thirty-nine. I can't stand the monthlies, so I'd recommend the forty-eight month. What do you say?"

Stanley said it all in one breath and hardly paused in the process. Nina nodded appreciatively at the skill of the pitch, if not the content of the offer. Pete was less impressed. He leaned forward and spat on Stanley's shoes. Stanley, too shocked to react, stared blankly at the couple before him.

"You people are all the same," Pete venomously declared in Stanley's general direction.

"You people?" Stanley asked, genuinely perplexed. Did he spit on salesmen often?

"What's the rate for your kind?" Pete sneered.

"Is it the monthly that's bothering you? I can get it down a little. Can you put twenty-five on the table?"

"I want to take a test drive."

"All of our test cars are in use at the moment, sir," Stanley lied, not wanting for a moment to leave the showroom floor with a worm so firmly on the hook. "Is it the monthly that's giving you trouble? Maybe we can work on that a little."

"We're going to take a test drive. Now."

Pete took out an envelope from his pocket. Nina stifled a yawn, but Stanley never saw. His attention was focused on the stack of bills clearly visible inside the wrinkled manila envelope. *There must be fifty-thousand dollars in there*, he surmised. Arrogant prick probably just wants to look like a badass in front of his wife. Stanley could play the wimp, he'd done it plenty of times. What could a little car ride hurt?

"Get out."

"Excuse me?" Stanley asked, not sure why they'd pulled over to the side of the road and genuinely unsure whether Pete was talking to him.

"Out of the car, smart guy."

"We're not supposed to do that."

"I'll bet."

Pete got out of the car, slamming the door shut violently. Stanley recoiled a little and felt a twinge of fear for the first time. Maybe this guy is really crazy. Men had tried to intimidate him plenty of times, several had tried the insanity route, but he would always hold his ground and he always collected his commission. He turned to Nina for reassurance, but she was too busy attempting to light her cigarette.

Reflex kicked in. "I'm sorry, you're not allowed to smoke, Ma'am."

"I'd lock your door," Nina advised.

"What?"

The passenger door flew open and Pete dragged a surprised and increasingly terrified Stanley from the car. Pete, easily five inches and a hundred pounds heavier than Stanley, tossed him to the ground with ease. He landed on his backside and looked up at Pete with a mixture of fear and astonishment.

"What's the monthly payment for forty-eight months?" Pete

asked.

"Nine twenty-eight."

"Wrong!"

He punctuated his emphatic denial with a kick to Stanley's midsection. Stanley had been sucker punched in the gut when he was in high school and that had left him breathless. This felt like an eighteen-wheeler just lodged itself in his ribs. He gasped for breath, pain shooting up through his body at an exponential rate.

"What's the monthly rate for forty-eight months?!"

Reflex earned Stanley another vicious kick. "Nine twenty-eight."

"Wrong, motherfucker! Try again! What's the fucking payment on forty-eight months?!"

Stanley clutched his side in abject misery. Clearly a different figure other than nine twenty-eight was needed here. Still, he had to be careful. If he cut the payment too much, his commission would suffer and he'd spent three hours of his Sunday on this deal already.

"Eight ninety-five."

"Eight ninety-five. You believe this guy?"

Pete looked to Nina for commiseration, but she was too busy trying to shake a little butane loose in her lighter. She gave up and reached for the lighter in the car. He turned his attention back to Stanley, who looked unsure whether or not to stay on the ground.

"Do I look like I'm playing around? What is this, a fucking joke?" Pete yelled to no one in particular.

Eight hundred and fifty meant two hundred and seventy-two dollars less in commission. Stanley weighed it against a cracked rib. Ribs heal, he decided.

"Eight seventy-five. I can't go any lower."

Pete snorted derisively. "Eight twenty."

"I can't."

A kick to the face opened a cut under Stanley's left eye. He coughed, his entire body in agony. Eight twenty? He'd lose almost a thousand dollars.

"I can't do eight twenty."

Pete reared back, poised for another blow. Stanley held out his hands defensively.

"Wait, wait! Eight forty-seven. I'll lose my job for sure, but if you take it off my hands this afternoon, I'll do eight forty-seven for forty-eight months, twenty thousand up front."

"Twenty? You said ten, you miserable fuck."

Stanley was ready for the next series of kicks. They mostly glanced off his arms. Feigning serious injury, he mustered up some tears. Al his training, all his preparation went into high gear. You're a fucking salesman, Stan. This guy is begging to buy. You can do it.

"All right, all right. Fifteen thousand. I'll do fifteen. I can't go any lower, I can't!"

"All right. Fifteen. Eight forty-five."

"It's a deal."

"You want a hand up?"

"Sure."

Pete pulled Stanley up as if he weighed nothing, then clapped him on the back, knocking Stanley off balance.

"Let's get out of here. I wanna be driving my new S series yesterday."

She waited until they were home before confronting Pete about his latest transaction.

"Did you take the cash back?"

"Four thousand, you believe it? Those suckers never knew what hit them."

"You do realize that with fifteen up front and eight forty-five a month, you're paying them over fifty grand for the life."

"So."

"So, with ten up and nine twenty, you're still paying over fifty. You actually lost a hundred and forty-four dollars by beating the hell out of that guy."

"Fuck you." Pete thought about it. Nina had a pretty good head for numbers. "Really?"

"Good salesman, huh."

"Fuck. Scuffed up my loafers for nothing."

Chapter 5

"DEBBIE, YOU can head to lunch, I'll schedule Miss Ciarelli."

Debbie shrugged and searched for her timesheet. She was glad Bob was finally going to ask Susan out. He needed something to take his mind off his dad. It was strange he didn't take any time off work, not even for the funeral. Not that she knew what he was going through. Her parents and both sets of grandparents were all alive and kicking. Maybe she'd see it differently when her folks passed on. He looked fine, he even spent most of the morning complaining about the dreadful state of network television. Still, Debbie hoped Susan said yes. She didn't relish the post-lunch rant if she declined his invitation.

"I'll see you this afternoon," Debbie said to Bob, already halfway out the door.

Susan set her purse on the counter and took out her palm pilot. "I'd like to come in a little later on Friday. They're wrapping up a plot thread on *Dark Shadows* this week."

"Do you have a minute?"

"Too many of them. What's going on?"

"It's about my father. Mostly. He was shot and killed two weeks ago."

Susan was taken aback, both by the horrifying news and the fairly matter-of-fact manner in which Bob delivered it. "I'm so sorry," she said, recovering quickly.

"He was eighty-one. I hope to live as long."

"That's terrible. What happened?"

"He was murdered in the parking lot outside Jerry's Deli on Ventura."

"That's horrible. Bob, I'm really sorry."

"I'd like you to find out who did it."

Susan stopped herself short. She had been ready to launch into her oft-used sympathy and revenge speech. Polished over the years, it usually managed to ease the anger of the victim's family and convey her genuine sorrow over their loss. It was a good speech, but usually she delivered it to those who were crying or breaking beloved household valuables in a rage.

It wouldn't be appropriate if he asked me to solve his father's murder. I must have misheard him, Susan thought.

"I'm sorry?"

"I'd like you to investigate my father's murder. I'll pay you, of course. Whatever you think is fair."

"You're not serious."

"Do I sound serious?"

"That's why I asked. The police handle this sort of thing."

"You're the police."

"Policemen who haven't been suspended with pay do this sort of thing."

"I've spoken with the police many times, they're completely stymied."

"Well, I'm not sure why I would fare any better." Susan paused. "Mostly."

"Mostly?"

"You said it was about your father. Then you added the word mostly. What is mostly?"

"I'd like to have dinner with you."

"You mean like a date?"

"Exactly like a date."

She stared at Bob, who looked back with an even expression, devoid of any emotion. He had what might be the smallest traces of a smile playing at the corners of his mouth, but she couldn't be sure. No question he was a good-looking fellow, and he kept up with her banter well enough. A homicide witness had awakened from a four-day coma the doctors were evenly split on being permanent and asked her to marry him within ten minutes of his miraculous awakening. This was similarly disconcerting.

"I'm not sure what to say," Susan said cautiously.

"Yes or no is the norm. Every once in a while I get a maybe, but I prefer the yes or no response."

"You want me to find your father's killer, services which you're willing to pay for."

"Yes."

"And you want to take me out to a romantic candlelit dinner."

"That I will also pay for. The place I had in mind doesn't have candles. It's really nice, though. Italian."

"Bob—"

"We could go somewhere with candles. I know a great Lebanese place with tons of candles. Do you like Lebanese food?"

"Are you all right?"

"Sure. I was just thinking it would be fun if we could go eat something ethnic sometime. Together. Perhaps Friday night. Are you busy?"

"No."

"Then we should go."

"No, I mean no, I don't think it's such a good idea."

"Okay."

"I mean, you're my chiropractor. Isn't that a conflict of interests?"

"Not really."

"And your father, and I am truly sorry, I don't think I can help with that either."

"I don't know where else to turn."

"If you're convinced the police can't help, maybe you should try a private detective."

"But you're a cop. A homicide detective. Who would know better than you how to investigate a homicide? Is there some rule that says you can't do that sort of thing while you're suspended?"

"It's not that, exactly."

"Then what?"

Susan opened her mouth to respond, then closed it with the knowledge she had not the slightest clue where to begin answering the question. She certainly wasn't going to go with the truth; that never got anybody anywhere. The ridiculous nature of the request didn't make refusal any easier. If anything, it was far more difficult. Telling someone you aren't going to go into the kitchen and get them a bowl of ice cream doesn't really involve much explanation, nor is refusal likely to invite an inquest. Asked, answered, move on, but when your chiropractor has the nerve to ask for assistance investigating his father's murder, a simple no just doesn't seem to suffice. Misdirection is the key, Susan decided, like the time in second grade when she convinced the boy with spiky hair who had a crush on her in the front row to pull the fire alarm when she had nothing to present at show and tell.

"How did you know that?"

"That you were suspended? I read it in the paper."

"Great," Susan sighed, deflated. There was a strong likelihood her mom had seen and clipped the article, a favorite pastime that began harmlessly enough when Susan was in grade school and continued unabated into adulthood. It didn't matter what the nature of the piece was, if Susan's name was mentioned it was heading straight into the scrapbook, the limits of which were tested a few years back when she had been mentioned in passing as a bridesmaid in a vanity piece the bride had paid the L.A. Times an exorbitant amount to run in the guise of human interest.

"Maybe you should think about talking to someone," Susan offered gently. "It might help."

"I'm talking to you."

"I mean a professional."

"My father was a thief."

"Excuse me?" Somehow the conversation had managed to take a turn for the increasingly bizarre, despite heavy odds.

"I don't know if it matters, I mean, it may mean nothing, maybe he was shot by some asshole hopped up on pills, but my dad was a thief. I tried telling the police, but they don't believe it. Mom always said robbing people would end my father, maybe it did."

"He was a thief?"

"A pro. He officially retired a while ago, but he still liked to rob people for fun. He would get bored just sitting around the house."

"I certainly understand that."

"Help me, Susan. My father and I didn't have the greatest relationship ever, but I loved him."

"I'm a little overwhelmed."

"Understandable."

"I'll talk to a few of my friends. See what's happening." Did she just agree to help? What the hell is going on here?

"Thank you."

"I'm not promising anything, you understand."

"Of course, I understand. Thank you. I can't tell you how much I appreciate this."

"You're welcome."

"I'll give you a rain check on dinner, and we'll see you Friday at three," Bob said, letting her off the hook for the moment.

She was almost out the door when his voice stopped her. "Oh, and Susan?"

She turned back, wondering what else could possibly be in store for her today. "Yes?"

"Remember to do your exercises."

It had been two years, three months and sixteen days since Paul had murdered anyone. Ben Kaplan had been the poor sap's name and it was the man's misfortune to be in the middle of a dispute not of his making. Mason Cole was a ten-cent hood living a dollar-twenty lifestyle and time had finally caught up with him. Using Paul's name to intimidate and threaten people, Mason would go out and skim drugs and cash off anyone he could. Quite rightly shot by one of Paul's boys, Mason was rushed to the hospital where he made a full recovery despite bullets lodged in both lungs, a rarity even for the emergency room in South Central Los Angeles, and a boon for Alice Bennett, a nurse in dire need of a new used car who went with the long shot and won over four-hundred and fifty dollars in that week's 'Survival of the Luckiest' office pool. A week later, Mason was back on the street, engaging in the same self-destructive behavior. Deciding to take no chances, Paul strapped on his .44 and tracked the man down in his three-bedroom townhouse.

For a ha-ha, he decided to let Mason beg and plead for a few minutes. When the tears stopped flowing, Paul pulled his gun and shot Mason dead. Or, rather, he shot the man he thought was Mason dead. The newspaper reported the bizarre circumstances surrounding the execution style murder of Ben Kaplan the next day. It turned out Mason lived next door and upon hearing the news and learning of his miraculous good fortune, left town and reportedly became a cab driver in Boston. Truth to tell, Paul had felt a little bad about the whole thing.

Two years, three months and sixteen days. An eternity, really, when he stopped to reflect. It had gotten to the point where he genuinely questioned whether he would ever have the opportunity to kill someone again. It wasn't that he didn't want to kill people. He most certainly did. It was just such a time consuming proposition, and his position as head of a citywide crime syndicate didn't allow much time for personal initiative. He'd grown accustomed to giving the order instead of pulling the trigger.

Last week had been a revelation. Forgotten had been the surge of adrenalin and the rush of power. It all came flooding back every time he let his mind wander back to the old man in the parking lot. He had a bounce to his step even his wife had commented on, and this from a woman who was in a perpetual drug induced daze.

Work was important, sure. But make time for the essential stuff, Paul. Get out there and live a little.

Archie was on the telephone when Susan entered the police station. She hopped up on his desk, knocking over several files in the process. Trying to distract Archie was endlessly amusing and invariably frustrating all at the same time. She'd once tried pouring lukewarm coffee on her head while Archie was receiving a commendation from the mayor. He looked right at her and didn't bat an eyelash. The man's train of thought just could not be deflected. Not surprisingly, he was a great detective.

Archie hung up the phone and pushed Susan off the desk with a smile.

"Sugarbritches."

"I am in need of lunch and your company, Arch. One will not suffice."

"Well, you've come to the right place. I was just thinking about something greasy and covered in chili."

"There's something I need to talk to you about."

"Give me a sneak preview. Of anything you like."

"Archie, I need to be serious."

"I'm always serious when it comes to you."

"I need to ask a few questions."

"Shouldn't we go downtown for that?"

"We are downtown, you goombah. I want to know about Karl Kessler."

"Mugging victim at Jerry's Deli, yeah, I remember. How come?"

"I'm curious."

"You're suspended is what you are."

"Come on, let me buy you lunch and you can fill me in."

"Lunch I can do."

"Archie, don't make me beg," Susan said, pursing her lips and giving her most pouty expression.

"Sweetie, normally I'd melt at the sound of that voice, but I can't do it. It is strictly frowned upon and you know it. Plus, it's not even my case, I don't know how helpful I can really be."

"Whose is it?"

"Ortiz and Alekhov."

"Good."

"Yes they are."

"And you won't…"

"Nope."

"Police on television always help the rogue agent."

"Appalling how television has lied to us, I know. Where are we going for lunch?"

"You really won't help me? Just a few details, an update, something."

"Sorry, Susan, no can do. Let's get back to the subject of lunch. I'm famished. Where shall we dine?"

She had tried. No one could say that she had not tried. And by no one, she meant Bob. She felt bad and that knowledge cut right through her. Ridiculous requests came to her ten times a day, from bereaved and criminally insane alike and all manner in between. *'Could you find my puppy?' 'I'd like to confess to killing a Kennedy.' 'I need a visa for my second cousin from Krakow.'*

The reply had become standardized with so much use. I'm sorry, but I can't help you. Then, if the situation warranted it and Susan was in a good mood, she would add, 'but you might consider trying so and so'.

It wasn't so much telling Bob she couldn't help. It was caring way too much about his reaction. Not a good sign. She was a professional, though. Reflex would take over and carry her through it. Now was just not the time to start a relationship. Relationship? Who the hell said anything about a relationship? What the hell is wrong with me? Focus, Ciarelli. Focus. Give him the line, get the back cracked and go home to watch reruns of reality television. A solid plan. Lunch first.

"You choose as long as I like it," Susan said. "But you're giving me all the gossip or I'm sticking you with the bill."

"Deal. Phillip from auto's wife is having an affair with some tall guy from legal aid. They're getting a divorce."

Susan's jaw dropped. "No."

Chapter 6

WHEN SHE was nine, Debbie had read a newspaper with a front-page caption reading, 'Man with a full head of hair on one side of his head' and an accompanying photograph. The caption had made her laugh out loud, the image doing little if anything to help her giggling subside. Whenever she was desperately bored, depressed or stoned, this happy memory would invariably pop into her mind and life would brighten. She thought of it now.

"Please say something," Bob implored.

"You're closing the office, effective immediately. I'm fired."

"You did hear the part about a month's severance and a glowing recommendation, didn't you? And we're going to finish out the week."

"Why?"

"I need a change, Debbie. I'm sorry for dropping it on you like this—"

"Are you kidding? This is great! Husband wanted me to quit anyway and now I can tell him I gutted a fish on your desk and gave you the finger and still managed a month's pay. I can go back to school now."

"What was stopping you before?"

"Inertia. But you got the ball rolling, didn't you? This is just the bestest news ever."

"Happy to oblige. You want to take the rest of the day off?"

"Paid?"

"Of course."

"Best day ever," Debbie decreed, and with that, she was out the door and on her way home to finish smoking the joint she'd started before breakfast.

"How was *Dark Shadows*? Did the forces of good prevail?" Bob asked.

"Of course. Though there may be evil stirring in the shadows. The dark shadows," Susan added.

"Gotcha."

She'd come prepared. She'd rehearsed in front of the mirror for ten minutes. Something about rules and procedures and professionalism and that was to be the end of it. But he looked like a lost little puppy. A cute little lost puppy, and now she couldn't remember how the speech was supposed to go. Not good.

"I tried, Bob, but I can't help you." She could have stopped there. Nothing else was required. "I really wish I could. Really. They won't tell me squat. I know the people working the case. They're very good. Let them handle it. Give it time." Susan forced herself to stop babbling. Dammit. She should have just given the stock answer and had done with it.

He nodded and scrunched up his forehead, as if contemplating a question he knew better than to ask.

"What would you do?" Bob asked.

"I'd let the professionals handle it. As I just said."

"No, I meant what would you do if you were the one investigating this?"

"Why?"

"Curious?"

"You're not qualified to do what I think you're thinking. It's stupid and dangerous and most likely unlawful. A very, very bad idea. In the realm of bad ideas, this particular idea reigns supreme above all others."

"I can't let it go."

"Bob, think about this. Please."

"How about dinner tonight?"

"Your mind works, or doesn't, in mysterious ways."

"I'm great company. Full of fun facts and interesting figures. It's great food. And I'll pay."

"I'm a patient, you're a doctor. Sort of. Doesn't this cross all manner of ethical lines?"

"I meant to tell you earlier, the office is closed, as of today. You're not a patient anymore."

"You're kidding." Bob kept an even stare. Susan rolled her eyes. "Oh my god, you're not kidding."

"I know a good guy in Torrance who can work on your back more if you like. He loves billing the city, too, so he'll be thrilled to have you come down."

"Bob."

"I can't let this go. I just can't. I know it's idiotic, I know it's dangerous, and I know I am spectacularly unqualified to do any semblance of this sort of thing, but I'm going to do it anyway. I'm going to find out who killed my father. Now, should I pick you up or do you want to meet there?"

Women. You love them, you buy them things, you tell them they're gorgeous even when they're not and what does any of that get you? Pete wished he had an answer to that question, but Nina would have to start making some sense first and that didn't seem very likely. The last few months had been downright painful. If he so much as opened his mouth, she bit his head off. The other night he had asked her to pass the mashed potatoes and sailors came rushing out of her mouth.

The first year had been great. He'd never had a woman like Nina. She was smart and classy, but in a good way. He had introduced her to the gang, the first woman he'd had the nerve to see in public since the first ex Mrs. Pete, Allison. Allison had gained damn near forty pounds within three months of the 'I do's' and he had justifiably kept her confined to quarters from that point on. Miffed, she had run away to Detroit with a furniture delivery truck driver who had a thing for the big and beautifuls. The second ex Mrs. Pete had been the result of a psychotic two-week bender that ended in a chapel in Carson City and then definitively ended with an unfortunate incident in the swimming pool. Nina was a strong swimmer so there was no real chance of her becoming a carbon copy of number two. She had an unbelievable body that hadn't gained an ounce of flab in the three years he'd known her so he felt pretty confident in that regard as well. But she was the first woman to treat him like an embarrassment and Pete was completely flummoxed.

A fatty he could deal with, who would miss that? Death you could get over. But rejection? That just flat out hurt.

"Why'd you become a keeper of the peace?" Bob asked in typical first date fashion.

"It's complicated," Susan answered honestly.

"We've got at least two more courses on its way. Plus, that's Henry back in the kitchen tonight and he's a bit of a perfectionist. It's going to be a while."

"You know the chef's name?"

"I come here a lot. Why'd you become a cop?"

"A good question."

"I thought you stopped being coy in college."

"The definition of a good question, in my mind, is one that does not lend itself to a simple answer. Why does anybody do anything? Why don't the Cubs win a world series? Why is it commonplace to use a comma after a dependent adverbial clause when it precedes a main clause?"

"English major?"

"Born and bred," Susan answered with a smile.

"So why'd you become a cop?"

"A good question."

"We don't have to talk about work."

"We can talk about your work. Former work."

"What would you like to know?"

"Why'd you become a chiropractor?"

"Susan, I could lie to you right now. Make up something, tell you an amusing anecdote and some such nonsense in an attempt to entertain you. I'm not going to do that. I want you to know I respect you too much to do that."

"Duly noted."

"We make choices, roads take turns, life works in mysterious ways."

"So why did you become a chiropractor?"

"I don't know. I mean, I think about it sometimes and I really have no idea."

"We have a lot in common."

"You weren't in it to do great deeds? Serve the public, be a productive member of society?"

"The world kills those it doesn't break, the good and brave impartially."

He raised an eyebrow at that.

"Hemingway," Susan explained, suddenly a little self-conscious.

"I really liked *Catcher in the Rye*," Bob said.

"That's Salinger," she said automatically, more than a little disappointed. Doesn't anyone read anymore?

"Really? I thought he was the guy who did *Raisin in the Sun*."

It took a beat, but Susan did a double take. Who confused

Salinger with Langston Hughes? Wait, was he messing with her?

"Would you like an appetizer?" Bob asked, a smile tugging at the corners of his mouth.

Pete had asked her to come tonight. In a rare flash of insight, he questioned her commitment to their marriage. Not in so many words, of course.

"What the fuck is wrong with you?" he asked, not unkindly.

"Nothing."

"Are you hungry or something?"

"You're going to be late."

"What is with you lately? You need to see a doctor?"

"I'm not sick." Well, that was debatable. "I don't need to see a doctor, Pete. The mafia is waiting for you."

"I hate it when you call us that."

"Then stop committing crimes in an organizational capacity with an Italian last name."

"You can be such a pain. What do you think you're living on? Fairy dust?"

Nina would have liked to argue, but it was true, at least up until the fairy dust part. She knew what she was getting into when she agreed to for better or worse. Nothing had changed, which was probably why she felt like screaming all of the time. Moral objections to drug use kept her from getting high. Her family, save for her parents, lived two-thousand miles away and didn't like her much anyway. She couldn't tell her friends her problems, they couldn't relate and probably wouldn't believe her anyway. She hated working, so a job was out. What was left but to antagonize and ostracize the hubby?

"You want to come with me tonight?" Pete asked, never expecting for even a moment she might say yes.

Nina thought about it. She could spend the night watching season three of *Vampire Diaries* for the second time or she could congregate with thieves and murderers.

"I'll get my coat," she said.

The room smelled of stale donuts, which was oddly comforting. Pastry denotes a certain level of normalcy and thereby safety, Nina had always felt. She had never once read, heard, or seen an atrocity committed when fried dough covered in glaze was present. Black metal folding chairs rested in haphazard fashion, the only furniture present. Several men, all of whom Nina recognized as Pete's core associates, were chatting amiably when she and Pete entered.

Conversation abruptly ceased. Nina, enjoying her husband's discomfiture, cheerily waved hello to the band of thugs and felons that comprised the room's population.

"What's going on, gents?" Nina asked with a conqueror's grin.

A half-hearted smile and a few grunts formed the entirety of the response. Pete sulked off to the bathroom leaving her alone with three men charged collectively with armed robbery, assault, assault with a deadly weapon, misdemeanor drug possession, felony drug possession, identity theft, pandering, attempted murder, extortion, possession of stolen goods, sale of stolen goods, shoplifting, parole violation, arson and racketeering.

Harvey, the shortest and most direct of Pete's co-workers, was the first to break the silence. "Nina, what in the hellfire are you doing here?"

For ten years Harvey had been foreman for the Birmingham division of Lassa Construction, one of the most corrupt companies to ever grace the fine state of Alabama. The game was fairly simple to play and he had proved a quick study. Orders funneled in from Earl in the deputy governor's office. He then sent his union operatives (Harvey had bribed half of the Republican party, seduced a liberal federal investigator and once kidnapped a whistleblower's two daughters for an afternoon but could never get around employing the fucking AFL-CIO) to lay the groundwork. Within a week, construction would begin and sixty cents of every dollar 'spent' was routed back to the main office. In his last year, he made just shy of half a million dollars.

When Earl was arrested, Harvey felt it prudent to retire from the hustle and bustle of the South. Los Angeles seemed an ideal change of pace, but after several months of stargazing and fake breasts, the allure had quickly evaporated. Paul had been a blessing. Tired of being his own boss, Harvey relished the opportunity to relinquish the reins to anybody else. The work was easy, occasionally fun and it came with full medical, full dental and flexible hours. The money was less, of course, and he wished twenty times a day every day of the week he had invested his laundered fortune in something other than strippers, but it was, all in all, not an uncomfortable or unpleasant lifestyle.

If only he could rid himself of the damn accent. Harvey had hired one of those Hollywood speech therapists, but the drawl was still thick enough to draw a second look from virtually everyone he came into contact with, not exactly the quiet level of anonymity the career criminal desires. At least he no longer said y'all all the time.

"Pete asked me to come. I hope it's okay with you guys." Nina lowered her head a tad and shrugged with as much nervous modesty as she felt would be believed.

She found her innocent Little Red Riding Hood impersonation extraordinarily beneficial when dealing with Pete's friends. None of them had children, and their paternal instinct, long dormant, came out in spades with Nina, the youngest of the wives. The other wives, exhibiting characteristics ranging from drug-induced paranoia to drug-induced lethargy, did not have her youth or bubbly personality, either. To ensure maximum hospitality from Pete's friends and maximum hostility from Pete, Nina would always manage to rub her breasts up against everybody at least once an outing. She decided to start with Alan.

"Alan, have you lost weight?" If anything, he had gained several pounds around the midsection and chin. He smiled, pleased and embarrassed.

Terrified of aging, Alan celebrated his thirtieth birthday by paying an obscenely underweight man with a thick mustache fifty dollars in ones for forged documents thereby reducing his age to twenty-seven. Three years later, he'd repeated the process, shelling out five-hundred dollars to a pretty girl at the Burbank DMV on that occasion.

Then that jerk Rick had gone through his wallet, purportedly for change for a diet soda. Upon finding his fake ID, Rick went ahead and announced it to everyone. Now, not only did he have to suffer the indignity of everyone treating him as if he was thirty, he was actually thirty-seven. Adding insult to injury, he'd just been diagnosed with arthritis. He'd nearly passed out when the doctor started writing a prescription.

"I don't think so, Nina," Alan said. "It's probably the shirt. Black is slimming, you know."

His smile grew as she brushed her breasts against his arm. Alan was ninety percent sure Nina acted the way she did to antagonize Pete, but if there were even a ten percent chance she would sleep with him, there was no point in burning any bridges. He couldn't help it, she made him feel young, and nothing in the universe was worth more than that.

Nina wondered if flirting with non-criminals was as easy. It had been so long she wasn't really sure what normal people were like. Her advance through the room brought her to Harvey, an inch shorter than Nina and ever receptive to her advances.

"Hey there," she cooed. "How are you?"

"You shouldn't be here tonight," Harvey intoned, his brusqueness betraying his frayed nerves.

He's usually cool as a cucumber, Nina thought. Maybe this was a mistake. Every once in a while, someone would be killed. Pete tried to avoid discussing it with Nina - he was surprisingly squeamish about that sort of thing - but she knew it happened. She had even extracted the information that he had pulled the trigger, or to be more accurate, wielded the big club, twice in his time as an associate of Paul and his blue-collar criminals.

"What's going on?" she asked.

"Don't know. All due respect to Pete for wanting to make our time family time, but why don't you go wait out in the car like a good girl?"

Rick took Nina's silence as an opportunity to throw his hat into the ring.

"Nothing personal. Why don't you come out with us this Wednesday, have a couple drinks?"

Rick was under the delusion that Nina was madly in love with him. It stemmed from a misunderstanding at last year's Christmas party. A handwritten note promising a multitude of lurid and obscene acts had found its way from Nina's pen to Rick's jacket pocket. The note was intended for Paul's wife as a joke and had begun during Nina's second margarita and was finished after her sixth. Fortunately for Rick, he had been unable to sneak away from his wife to make good on the offer and had since been too embarrassed to make a move.

"Of course, yeah, sure," Nina said, beating a hasty retreat. Harvey and Alan resumed their huddled conversation.

Rick walked her to the door, unable to make up his mind whether to put his arm around her. He settled on a gentle pat on the back.

"What's going on?"

"I don't know. Paul's been a little off lately."

"What does that mean? Off?"

"Your guess is as good as mine. I wouldn't worry about it,

though. I'll see you later, okay?"

He smiled and closed the door on Nina, leaving her alone in the short hallway. She stared at the door for a good thirty seconds, mulling over her options. On one hand, she could walk out the door, sit in her husband's new S series Porsche, and listen to the radio a little. It was an all 80's weekend on KYSR 98.7. Pete would come out, they'd drive home, and another day too depressing to contemplate would come to an end. Or she could press her ear up against the door and eavesdrop. Only one option could lead to a bullet behind the ear and she was only surprised that it took her more than thirty seconds to kneel down, pretend to lace up her pumps, and wait for Paul to arrive.

Meetings were held twice a month and lasted anywhere from twenty minutes to two hours. Very little was ever accomplished. Most of the time was spent listening to Paul and then nodding in agreement. Pete treated it like high school, where he managed to graduate despite arguably leaving school knowing less than when he entered. He was pretty sure the other guys tuned out Paul's rambling monologues, too.

Nobody had bothered to mention this to Paul, less in fear of recrimination than for the sense of apathy that comes with enjoying the comforts of middle-class life. None of them were rich, to be sure, but the mortgage was paid each month with plenty left over. Who rocks the boat when land is constantly in sight?

Supposedly, he had something special planned tonight. The last time Paul deviated from the script, he announced his intention to branch out into prostitution. Pete had zero interest in being a pimp, and despite his relatively low stature in society as a thug, the mere thought of standing on a street corner arguing over the hourly rate of a hand job with some pissant suburbanite kid was enough to contemplate working a nine to five in a cubicle. The experiment lasted a grand total of four days before Paul realized whores were a bad long-term investment. It was a quick return to their bread and butter of loan sharking and extortion.

"You watch the fucking Lakeshow last night, Pete?" Alan asked.

Pete hated the Lakers and had ever since they refused to offer Byron Scott a contract back in 1993. He maintained a diplomatic silence about the issue with his friends in L.A.

"I missed it."

"Fucking amazing. Clark at the buzzer with a bank shot over Duncan. Fucking amazing."

Rick felt it necessary to add his voice to the discussion. "One dribble and up, place was going gonzo."

"No shit," Pete said with as much enthusiasm as he could muster.

"Fuck yeah, you kidding? It was like a college game, people trying to climb over the seats to get to the court. Cops had to push 'em back to get the players out of there. Unbelievable."

"Paul showing up anytime soon?" Pete asked.

Alan wasn't letting go anytime soon. "You think we can take the West this year?"

"I don't know. Sure."

"If we can get the home court, there's no way anyone is taking us. Not with—

"I just wanna get Nina home, you know?"

"Sure, yeah, of course." Alan checked his watch. "He should be here any minute. So, you think we can make the finals, huh? Me too."

Paul's arrival was signaled by the roar of his custom-made engine. Purchased not long after his arrival in Los Angeles, Paul had paid the mechanic to loosen the something or other (Nina had been informed of the technical term but had forgotten it before the end of the description) so the engine would be louder. Nina had ridden in 'Blacky', as Paul christened his two door trans-am, once, and her hearing had taken a few weeks to recover.

Nina hid behind the staircase and shook her head in wonder. What was it with guys and cars? In walked Paul, dressed immaculately in his blue three-piece pinstripe suit. The man simply refused to be seen in public with a hair out of place. Nina stole a quick glance, then ducked out of sight. No reason to take any chances. She waited until the door opened and shut, then resumed her position on the floor, ear pressed to the door, relishing the opportunity to break up the tedium of her week.

He lived for moments of sheer, unadulterated power. The group before him comprised men of staggering ability and an almost complete lack of scruples, yet each man hitched his fate to Paul's will. *This must be what the king of England feels like.*

"Gentlemen. I'll make this short and sweet. The times they are a changing. Things are working, but I want them to work better. We're going to start doing some things different, starting from the top down."

Pete did not like the sound of this. *Do things different? Is he insane? We're making money hand over fist, why the hell should we change anything? You don't mess with success. Look what happened when the* Dukes of Hazzard *got rid of Tom Wopat and that other guy. This cannot end well.*

"What are you thinking?" Pete asked with as much composure as he could muster.

"A lot of guys owe us money. It's time to collect."

"You want us to round up a few guys, make an example out of 'em?" Harvey asked, jotting down something in his notebook.

"No. I want you to round up every low-life piece of shit thug who has been yoking us lately and bring them to me."

"Gonna scare the money out of 'em?" Alan asked.

"Gonna kill every last one of them. Let's see somebody take

a goddamned thing from us ever again after we wipe the earth clean of every thieving motherfucker on the streets."

Paul savored the shocked looks coming his way. This is living, goddammit.

She woke at five till five to the rhythmic pulsing of the neon green alarm clock. Bob was fast asleep next to her, his arm at an impossible angle behind his back. *Hope he knows a good chiropractor*, Susan thought.

Getting out of bed, getting dressed and getting out of the house after a tryst was a challenge Susan had never mastered. Of course, she'd only attempted it twice before. The first time was in 1991 at Amherst. A nice young Republican with a bit of a toe fetish had been very nice to her after a particularly bad day that included a scolding from her Renaissance history professor, a row with her roommate's boyfriend about used macaroni and cheese dishes and a slightly sprained ankle, the result of her innate clumsiness. Sex with a Republican seemed the logical conclusion to such a day. She'd tried to escape his room with her dignity intact, but after gathering her clothes and subsequently tripping and falling on the floor, that hope was dashed. At least he called her Sarah when they hugged goodbye.

The second time was much better. Not successful, mind you, but better. A taxidermist with a smooth tongue had his alarm set for three-thirty for reasons Susan was never able to ascertain and just as she got her first heel strapped on the damn thing went off like a tornado warning and Susan's sneaky and evasive exit was made less sneaky and evasive. He forced her into small talk for ten minutes until Susan complained of an impending stomach virus. He did manage to get her name right.

Bob shifted position, the color slowly returning to his arm. Susan would have laid odds he was a snorer, but the only indication he was even alive was the rhythmical movement of his chest. She shouldn't have slept with him. That was so going to give him the wrong idea. Maybe it was because she was suspended. Perhaps she felt bad for his father passing. Or, to be more accurate, she felt bad his father was brutally shot to death. Maybe she felt guilty for not helping. She had tried to help. What more could she do? Besides sex.

She knew the lead detective, but was reluctant to approach him for a favor. Ortiz had been her training officer back in the day. They wouldn't be mistaken as friends on their best day, but he had never failed to give her a sterling recommendation from day one. Plugging him for information might not be a bad idea. Certainly couldn't hurt. Just because Archie has standards doesn't mean every policeman does. Bob had paid for dinner.

There was no hard and fast rule that she couldn't stay the night. Dinner had been nice. A little too much garlic, but nice. He was funnier outside of the office.

She rolled her eyes. How could I break the cardinal rule of dating? Do not sleep with people with severe emotional instability. It cannot end well.

"Hey."

Susan jerked upright, startled at Bob's groggy greeting. She smiled and put her hand on his arm.

"You're not leaving, are you?"

"I was just going to get some water."

"Hurry back, yeah?"

"Of course."

Great. Now she had to stay and drink a glass of water.

"How do you like your eggs?"

A chef in training who went by his middle name Javier had made Susan the single greatest breakfast she had ever eaten. Grapefruit, cheddar cheese strata (with a dollop of sour cream), molletes, which she later found out was basically French toast but at the time she would have sworn before a jury of her peers it was pure decadence in food form, and for dessert, a homemade almond crusted croissant. The relationship had lasted two months, solely on the strength of that breakfast.

"Whatever's easy."

"They're eggs. Everything is easy."

"Over easy, then."

"Coming right up."

"So, listen," Susan began, with every intention of being brief. "The thing is, I like you. Obviously. It's just, and I don't mean this to come out the wrong way, but, and here's the thing, I don't really think we can do this. And by this," Susan said quickly, cutting off any chance for Bob to reply, "I just mean us having a relationship. Not that I think you want one, I don't. I mean, I don't know what you want, not really. I mean, for me, and I know I can't really know what you're thinking, it's just, for me, it's not really worth it to me. Not that you're not worth it, because you are. I think you're great. Fantastic. Last night was great. Fantastic, really. It's just, and this is just me being all me, which I'm working on, I promise you, I don't really know what 'it' is."

Susan actually used air quotes while saying 'it' and wanted to hit herself over the head for doing so, but she had the momentum and nothing was going to stop her now.

"I was with this guy. David. Not that you need to know his name. Not that I was thinking it last night, either, I don't want you to think it wasn't amazing, because it was. Fantastic, really." She already said fantastic. Shit. "It's just, well, you remind me an awful lot of him and that didn't end well, and it's not so much that I think you're like him and you'll end up screwing around with some flight attendant from Chicago, it's just that if you're like him, then maybe I'll end up being like me when I was with him and I didn't like that particular me and I so do not want to go back to being that me and so, I really think that the best thing to do would be to end us before one of us gets hurt. Unless, I don't know, maybe we could move back from this and try being friends, and I hate using that word, I don't think of you as a friend, not that we couldn't be great friends, because I'm sure we can, but with everything you're going through, and clearly, the mess I am, I just…I don't know exactly, and that's really it, if you know what I mean."

Susan forced herself to stop. She could have gone on, but what would be the point? At some point, you've caused yourself the maximum embarrassment allowed under the law.

He was staring at her, his spatula filled with eggs poised above her plate. He wanted to run screaming from his own apartment, she could see it in his eyes. An insane woman has invaded his home and delivered a rant while this nice man who doesn't snore tries to serve her eggs. Susan had friends who complained with energy and enthusiasm to anyone within earshot of the sad state of affairs surrounding single life, due exclusively to men's numerous and alarming deficiencies. Never again would she be able to join in those discussions.

Bob set Susan's eggs down on her plate and moved over to the toaster.

"You want toast with your eggs?"

"Yes, please."

Chapter 7

FAKING AN addiction to prescription drugs was surprisingly easy. What was not surprising was how much fun such an act could be. It was a three-pronged process, and application could be undertaken in no particular order. Symptoms must be exhibited, and these can range from mild depression to hallucinations, the entire spectrum necessary for public consumption at least once for the illusion to take full effect. Two must be pushed to the front and be ever-present. Amy had opted for loss of appetite in conjunction with stinging pain from a fall (fake, of course) down the stairs. This provided the opportunity for actual medication to be prescribed, which led to part two, procurement of real pharmaceutical drugs, such as Demerol or Percodan. Once prescribed, subject must then 'accidentally' take too many pills for an excessive period of time, thus becoming addicted.

It was important to avoid fake addictions to such illegal substances as heroin or crack cocaine, in part because more difficult physical transformations were necessary to maintain the plausibility of the ruse, but also because society looked down on such people with distaste. Take a few too many Vicodin and the world can't rub your feet enough. Injecting some potentially life-threatening (another definite downside) solution into your veins and people become supremely prickly. No, prescription addiction was the way to go.

The perks were varied and many. For instance, social obligations were optional. Family could be avoided with less guilt. Odd behavior becomes par for the course. The best part, the reason everyone should engage in such activity as far as Amy was concerned, was the ability to slowly but surely withdraw oneself from public and/or private life. Personal responsibility was a thing of the past, a relic from a bygone age. Sympathy was constantly pouring in from friends and family without the distasteful reciprocation that marred most familial relationships. It was deceptively simple, and until recently, completely foolproof.

It had, as far as she was able to tell, only one potential shoe in the wheel. A caring and supportive spouse was the fly in the ointment to her well-oiled machine, a possibility she had immediately discounted upon the completion of her honeymoon, but one that had become more and more of a reality.

She had noticed a definite change in Paul over the last few weeks. Gone were the long silences and the furrowed brow, replaced with giggling (giggling!) and an increased appetite for everything life could offer. She had long since grown tired of life in all its vast glory and joy. Been there, done that, ready for retirement.

Everything was different all of a sudden, and anything different was bad. It had started with a renewed interest in his appearance. Paul was always a little vain, but now he was spending forty minutes a day in front of the mirror, preening every which way and that. Then came exercise. She had never seen him exercise a day in his two-hundred and forty pound life. Now he was doing sit-ups while watching the Discovery Channel. She couldn't be completely sure Paul had sworn off all things intellectual long before puberty, but it seemed likely. The logical conclusion was an affair, but that was precluded by the strangest behavior of all, a renewed sexual interest in his wife. This bothered her most of all.

The front door slammed, a defect the contractor had

sworn would disappear after repeated use but was, if anything, significantly worse with every passing year. Paul was home. Dumping a few baby aspirin (the fake pharmaceutical grade drug of choice) on the floor, Amy steeled herself for the impending confrontation. It was high time she let him know that enough was enough and nip this whole situation in the bud. She loved her life. It was vacuous and decadent and utterly pointless. There was no way she was giving it up without a fight.

"How are you?" Paul asked upon entering the kitchen. To Amy's disappointment, he paid no attention to the carefully spilled pills, instead looking her in the eyes.

"Fine, I guess."

"No, I mean, how are you, really? How was your day?"

"It was fine. What is going on with you?"

"What did you do yesterday?"

This was unexplored territory, which made Amy extremely nervous. Personal questions had hardly entered their discourse before they were married, let alone afterwards. Maybe he was setting down a bear trap. It would be just like Paul to lay down the twigs, cover them with pine needles and crouch behind a tree with a giant mallet in hand. She had to play this carefully.

"I had a bit of a headache, so I took a few extra."

"A few extra what?"

"Blue ones, I think."

"You look beautiful, today."

"Are you all right?" Amy blurted out, unable to stop herself. The last compliment Paul had paid her had come at the beginning of her Wonder-bra experimentation period. Who was this man who looked so much like her husband but was clearly his doppelganger?

"I'm great. Better than I have been in a long time. The last couple weeks have been a revelation for me." Paul stepped over, taking his wife's hands in his, his voice soft and gentle. "Now, honey, I'm going to need you to stop taking your pills. They're not good for you."

Amy stared incredulously. A look of innocence graced Paul's face, something perhaps never before seen on God's green earth. It looked to Amy almost like…love. *Oh, sweet Jesus,* Amy thought. *This is not good. This is so terribly, horribly not good.*

"It's not that simple, Paul."

"I know, but I'll get you all the help you need and I'll be there every step of the way."

Amy grabbed him by the shoulders, determined to nip this bizarre behavior in the bud.

"What is going on?"

"Nothing. Hey, what are you doing right now?"

"What am I doing right now? I'm trying to figure out what the hell is going on with my husband." Amy paused, her mind backtracking in the conversation. "Wait, why?"

"Let's go to Disneyland."

Amy could not have been more surprised if Paul had invited her to take a walk on the moon.

"What in the hell are you talking about?"

The average American changes jobs at least four times throughout his adult life, and that statistic, alarming in and of itself, does not even take into account the myriad of minimum-wage jobs one suffers through during school and retirement. Leafing through the Los Angeles Times classifieds provided Bob with a likely explanation. Who in his right mind would ever settle for a forty-year life sentence nine to fiver when any bloke off the street can become a truck driver with only three short weeks of training and a desire to travel the open road?

"Ah, but, Bob, correlation is not causation, is it? And you just said that out loud. Which you've been doing a lot lately. You should stop talking to yourself, it's getting a bit creepy, and not in a good way."

A satisfying and enriching career, in any sense of the word, was not exploding off the printed page. Part-time bartender and resident nurse seemed the best options, but they required school and training and there was just no chance of Bob stepping inside the classroom ever again, even if it was one filled with the prospect of alcohol and morphine.

He had tried once, really tried, and it had just not gone well. After four years of undergraduate and two years of chiropractic college, he should have known higher learning wasn't for him, but he couldn't help himself. A master's degree practically earns itself, what with one short year of commitment. His first assignment took him four days to complete. Some sort of obsessive compulsive disorder had kicked in and draft after draft had yielded no discernible results save for the concisely worded comment the professor had written in lime green marker in the margins, 'Are you kidding?' Confidence shot, enthusiasm reduced to a negative number, Bob threw away his class notes and never looked back. It had been an in-class assignment to boot.

An advertisement for the LAPD caught his eye. I could be a cop, Bob thought happily. I'd have a gun, I'd get to solve crimes for up to forty-two thousand dollars a year. That's probably after you've completed a year or two. Of course, I'd have to be a beat cop, that won't be fun. I like driving fast and police are always doing that on the news. Blue isn't my best color, though, and I'm a pacifist. Well, a coward anyway. I'd have to get in shape, and exercise isn't really my thing.

I wonder how Susan does it. Good question. A phone call seems in order. Bob promptly picked up the phone and dialed the number.

"Susan, how do you become a policeman?"

"Who is this?"

"It's Bob. How do you become a policeman?"

"Okay."

"I'm flipping through the classifieds. You people get paid pretty well, work is interesting, certainly a one-eighty from what I've been doing. Society would thank me, I'm fairly certain. So what's the process? Fill out a W-2 or two?"

"There's a test. And a physical. And a psych evaluation. And a crash course, sort of like basic training. And that's pretty much it."

Bob felt she had laid a bit too much emphasis on the psych evaluation portion of her description, but he didn't want to get sidetracked. "That's what?"

"You're in the secret society, handshake and everything. You don't really want to be a policeman, do you?"

"Either that or drive a truck. I suppose I could be a nurse, but white's not really my color, either."

"What would you want to do?"

"Come again?"

"As a policeman."

"I don't know. Chase people, I suppose. What else is there?"

"What else is there. Lots, you goombah. You could have a desk job, be a paper pusher. You could be a detective, like myself, and there's lots of possibilities from there, like robbery homicide, grand theft auto, vice, whatever your speed.

"Options galore. I don't know. How did you choose robbery-homicide?"

"What about a prison guard? They make as much as police, but they'll let anybody do it, which means you'd probably qualify. Probably."

"You're avoiding my question."

"I'm sorry, you're breaking up, I can't hear you."

"Susan."

"You could be a longshoreman."

Bob laughed. "I suppose I could. Is their screening process as rigorous as you all?"

"More."

"Really."

"Well, there's fish involved."

"Makes sense. Okay, thanks for the input."

"Anytime."

Bob hung up the phone. He mentally crossed off the LAPD as a future employer, and decided to make a grilled-cheese sandwich instead. It was a good decision.

"Excuse me, I'd like to speak to somebody about this ride."

"Is everything okay, Sir?" asked the grown man in the Goofy costume.

"No it isn't. My wife did not spend an hour in line to go on a ride that crummy. I'd like to speak to someone."

"I'm sorry you didn't like it. I'll go get someone right away."

"Good."

Amy smiled, relaxing. This was more like it. Paul taking her to an amusement park, asking her about her feelings and then actually listening to her response was a certain sign of the apocalypse. Paul berating a mascot and yelling at his supervisor was more in keeping with the man she had married. Not a moment too soon, either. She was getting genuinely worried that he had been stricken with leukemia or worse, saved by Jesus.

A young man not more than thirty, dressed in a sharp black suit that seemed to thumb its nose at the noonday sun, strode up to Paul and gave the trademark Disney smile. His name was Scotty, or at least, that was the name written on his Finding Nemo nametag.

"Sir, I am so sorry your wife did not enjoy the ride. Please, accept these two passes to come back and visit us again at your convenience."

Paul took the tickets, looked them over, and then politely handed them back to Scott. Amy looked away and smiled. Here it comes. He's going to make a scene. Everyone will look at us and after a lot of yelling and threatening, Paul will get tired and drag her home where she can pretend to pop pills and read a magazine. Or security would throw them out and he would bitch and moan all the way home and then she would pretend to get loaded and watch TV. Either way was fine with her.

"That won't be necessary," Paul said amiably. "I just wanted to make a couple of suggestions. First, it takes a long time to get to the boulder coming down at you. I love the drop, that's fantastic. But it drags a little before that. Is there anything you could do to strengthen the first half of the ride?"

Scotty looked a bit startled that his offer of free passes had been refused, but to his credit, quickly recovered his wits and engaged Paul in discussing the merits of the Indiana Jones ride.

His surprise was a mere Three Mile Island compared with Amy's Chernobyl.

"Well, sir, to be honest, we don't get a lot of complaints. This is one of our most popular rides."

"Oh, I loved it. But my wife just thought it could be spiced up a bit, if you know what I mean. You know in the third movie when the tank is scraping him against the side of that rock, and he's hanging on for dear life?"

Scotty's eyes were bright. "I love that part."

"Maybe you could incorporate more stuff like that."

"Well, the problem there is our ride doesn't really deal with *The Last Crusade*. It's more just the *Raiders of the Lost Ark* and a little of *Temple of Doom*."

"Well, why not expand to cover all three? I mean, the third one is better than the second, anyway."

Scotty arched his eyebrows, appearing to genuinely consider Paul's idea. Then it hit her, and she could have started crying right there on the spot. He was genuinely considering the idea.

"Just between you and me, Sir, we've been throwing around the idea of expanding the ride. But up until now, we've only really considered adding more from the first two." Scotty leaned in conspiratorially and whispered, "We've been thinking of adding that part where they're on the rope bridge, you know, when Indy cuts it and Shortround says, 'Hang on Spielberg's wife, we going for a ride!'

"That's Spielberg's wife?"

"Kate Capshaw? Oh, yeah."

"I didn't know that."

"No one has ever mentioned the third or fourth movie before, but I'm going to be honest with you, I really like the concept. Do you have any specific ideas?"

"A few. I was thinking the part with the boat and the propeller—"

"Wait, wait. Would you mind if I called in my boss, I think he ought to hear this. And really, I insist you take the passes since I'm taking up so much of your time."

"Well, if you insist."

Amy almost fainted on the spot.

Chapter 8

SUSAN TOLD herself she was plugging Ortiz for info in order to relieve herself of the massive embarrassment her rant would cause untold future generations. Bob, God bless him, had listened without interrupting, and as if that miracle had not been enough to convince her of all things wild and unimaginable, he had proceeded to eat breakfast with her and engage in quasi-normal conversation. He even walked her to her car and kissed her on the cheek while saying goodbye. Clearly, the man has serious psychological impediments to a relationship that need immediate attention.

Then he had the temerity to call her and be nice and funny. He didn't even get huffy when she pointedly refused to answer a perfectly reasonable question about her vocational selection. No two ways about it, this guy was not what could in any way be considered normal. Anybody who witnesses behavior such as hers and does not apply for a passport in order to escape the country and pursue odd jobs under an assumed name to elude pursuit is in need of a qualified mental health professional. Since he clearly didn't have the marbles necessary for such action, Susan would be forced to do the running and hiding. It was for the best.

Still, the least she could do was make a second effort at unmasking his father's killer. All she had to do was wrangle confidential information out of a man who had once called her a pretentious blowhard who wouldn't amount to jack shit in a badge. Susan sighed. Dating was such a pain in the ass.

"Ortiz, I need a favor."

"I really wish I could, Ciarelli, but I just got done covering up for a Venice Beach boy in blue who shot an unarmed suspect in handcuffs. It'd be awkward if I had to do it twice in the same week."

She resisted the urge to reach out and smack him on the back of the head.

"Subtlety always was your strength."

"What was your strength, again?"

"I wonder myself sometimes."

That got a smile out of him, Susan noted with satisfaction. Ortiz was prickly, and many a fellow officer had stepped out of line with deleterious consequences to follow. His ability to hold a grudge was legendary. He had once blacklisted a social worker who changed his testimony on the stand, ensuring the release of Ortiz's collar. Unable to make a living, the social worker eventually gave up and moved to Idaho to manage an apartment complex.

"So what's the favor? Though I feel compelled to tell you I'm probably going to say no, whatever it is."

"Karl Kessler."

"Who?"

Susan rolled her eyes and fought back the urge the slug Ortiz in the shoulder.

"Just fill me in. I'm going to be back in a few months and we're going to have to work together. Think of this as a minor concession in the ongoing peace process."

"No," Ortiz replied, in an offhand, casual manner that made Susan wish she was armed. She took a deep breath, as her high school driving instructor had taught her to do when faced with a stressful situation, and proceeded to try again. Once more into the breach, dear friends…

"Ortiz, you nincompoop, cut me some slack."

"Don't get agitated, Ciarelli. I did warn you."

"Brass tacks here. What'll it take?"

He thought about it. "I get first dibs on your docket for a month after you come back."

"Fuck you."

"Two months."

"A week. A week is too much, but what the hell, I'm in a good mood."

"Three months."

"Two weeks. My final offer."

"Three months."

"A week."

"Which one of us has no clue what they're doing?" Ortiz asked, a smile tugging insistently at his mouth.

"Is it possible it's both of us?"

He laughed out loud and slapped the desk in delight.

"Two weeks, Ciarelli, but only because you're funnier than usual today. And you have to buy me a bear claw on your first day back."

Susan gritted her teeth. Giving up cases was tantamount to bending over in prison or at a frat party. Never fun. But buying a donut for a cop? That just plain hurt.

"Deal," she said reluctantly.

Ortiz smiled triumphantly, relishing the moment. "What do you want to know?"

"Everything."

"Won't take long."

"That bad?"

"Flimsy would be a kind word to describe our case. Nonexistent might be more appropriate."

"Suspects?"

"Zero."

"Witnesses?"

"Zero."

"What do you have?"

"We've been able to recreate the crime scene. Forensics tell us the shooter was tall, probably right-handed. The gun was an oldy but goody, a thirty-eight revolver. No prints anywhere. And by no prints, I mean no prints we can tie. The lot has over four thousand sets, not even counting the partials. The whole thing was like an execution. Pretty quick, brutally efficient."

"Who heard the shots?"

"Half the staff. One of the busboys, Daryl, was closest. Having a smoke in the kitchen, which is a crime that itself needs investigating. He heard the shots, he found the body, he called it in."

"Darryl's in the clear, I assume?"

"Crossed my mind for a second, but he is one-eighty off from the profile and the timeline doesn't work. There's no way."

"The staff?"

"Hey, I don't wanna say never, but my opinion says no. My guess is it's some fuck who was waiting outside, saw an opportunity, ripped the man's wallet and for whatever reason decided to plug him."

"Robbery."

"We think so. Wallet's gone, no apparent motive, scene is consistent with a jacking MO."

"Tell me about Karl."

"Retired for fifteen years or so. Lived at a convalescent home, but everyone there says he was pretty active for an eighty-year-old guy. Surviving son, only relative. Modest savings. No animosity from anyone who knew him, but frankly, that's not a lot of people."

"A loner."

"Definitely. Staff didn't recognize him, so he probably hadn't been to Jerry's much before, which backs up the random theory."

"The son?"

"Robert. Rock solid alibi. He's clean. Weird, but clean."

"Weird?"

"He kept telling us his dad was a professional thief."

"Really?"

"Said he was a jewel thief, stole millions. Apparently moved on to petty theft when he 'retired'."

"It's not possible?"

"It's crazy. In, what, sixty years, not a blemish on this guy's record. Nobody is a criminal for a lifetime without taking a hit somewhere along the line. Nobody is that good."

"You're right, pretty slim."

"Why the interest?"

"Do I get my case load back?"

"Hell no."

"Then my motivations will have to remain mysterious."

It was Ortiz's turn to roll his eyes.

"Get out of here, will you? Real cops have work to do."

"Always a pleasure," Susan said, standing to leave.

"Oh, hey, wait a sec. There is one thing."

"Yeah?"

"Man made a commotion not long before he was shot. He had a bit of a heart condition and suffered a bit of an episode before going to his car. Made a scene, bunch of people came over to make sure he was fine."

"Thanks, Ortiz."

"The pleasure is all mine. See you and the bear claw soon."

A neutral location was crucial for this, the official second date, doubly so since they had slept together and Susan was planning to break up with him. She had called and asked to meet him to discuss her rather meager findings. He agreed and suggested a coffee shop near his house. Susan countered with a dive diner off Vermont Street. They settled on the House of Pies. Susan did not especially care for pie, but felt more secure if Bob was taken out of his comfort zone. It would make breaking it off so much easier.

That he knew the greeter was a bad sign. That the waitress gave him a hug hello spelled certain doom for Susan.

"You should try the chocolate cream," Bob said.

"Not a big pie person," Susan replied icily. Who gets a hug from the waitress? A sense of dread flooded her senses. Maybe they're dating. Do I care that they're dating? Oh, dear God, I need help.

"Cheesecake is pretty good."

"I spoke with the lead detective about your dad."

The gratitude practically bled from his face.

"Thank you so much. I know that can't have been easy for you."

"No biggie," Susan demurred, a little embarrassed by Bob's heartfelt thanks. "I wish it had yielded better results, though. The investigation is pretty much stalled."

"Anything?"

She proceeded to tell him the details of her conversation with Ortiz.

Sickles was an honest man, in that steadfast way only a lifelong criminal deviant can be. A grade school victim of a torturous bully named Andrea, referred to as 'angryangryandrea' (all one word, no capital letters) whenever safe proximity allowed, Sickles had found solace in making other kid's lives as miserable as his own. Violence, however, was not his thing. He despised physical aggression. Intimidation and coercion were the way to go. All the benefits of punching somebody in the nose with none of the bruising and societal repercussions.

A smart kid with a predilection towards Elizabethan drama, the principal felt it would better serve the school population to part ways sooner rather than later with a boy who threatened three teachers in one day with decapitation but who charmed his way to an A in English through his love of Shakespeare. Sure the fun would cease after expulsion from high school, Sickles found that such tactics were, if anything, more effective. Secure in the knowledge that life had let slip its major secrets, Sickles wreaked havoc on the civilized world for the next sixteen years. Petty theft led to muggings, muggings to extortion, extortion to mid-level drug czar and pimp. It was a good life.

Not that there weren't roadblocks on the path to success. The eighteen months he spent in jail for car jacking was intolerable, in part due to his innocence, and in part due to the completely ineffectual manner in which his style and tactics were received inside prison walls. Threats of violence without the corresponding violence were downright dangerous, and Sickles had adopted a Switzerland-like policy of neutrality that had enabled him to escape incarceration with major vital organs still intact, but without any discernible improvement in his lifestyle. Going back to jail was simply not an option. Those people could not be reasoned with.

That was the start of what Sickles called the 'borrowing phase' of his professional life. He got the idea after an outstanding medical bill resulting from an unfortunate meeting of his forehead and the dresser was sent to collections and then summarily dropped when Sickles steadfastly refused to pay on the high moral ground that he didn't want to. The idea hit him like a thunderbolt. Why is it necessary to ever pay for anything?

This profundity still needed practical applications to make it useful in Sickles' daily life and he found it through borrowing large sums of money and then refusing to pay it back, save for the threat of bodily harm. If such a case arose, and it did about twice a month, he would simply borrow more money, pay off the outstanding debt, and go about his day. Initially afraid the well might dry up, Sickles found there was an unending number of lowlifes who would lend any amount of money for eight percent on the spot. Sickles would have agreed to twenty, what the hell did he care? He was never going to shell out his own money for it.

Stunned that he was the only man ever to think of such a brilliant scheme, Sickles lived quite well for a man who didn't finish high school and never filed a tax return. Not that he didn't still engage in drug dealing and prostitution. After all, a man has to fill his days. But it was just for fun, never profit. That, Sickles was a thousand percent certain, was the key to enjoying life. Do what you love.

Today's meeting would be no different than a hundred others he had been forced to sit through. The mark would demand his money. Sickles would plead poverty and promise to pay it back as soon as he possibly could. There would be raised voices, harsh words, occasionally threats and if Sickles was pushed, he would promptly go out and borrow enough money to pay the outstanding bill, plus a little to take the little lady out and buy her something pretty. All very civilized, all very profitable. He hoped he'd make it out in time to see the late show at the Egyptian Theater in Hollywood.

Harvey opened the door and ushered Sickles inside. Paul stood in the center of the room, his six-foot two, two hundred and forty-pound frame an imposing sight to the five-foot nine Sickles.

"Paul! How the hell are you, man?"

"Never been better."

Sickles was forced to agree. The last time he had seen Paul, the man looked tired and depressed. Now, the man looked positively reborn to Sickles. Doesn't matter, he told himself. The game is still the same, emotional makeover or no.

"You owe us a little money, Sickles."

"I do, yes. I do."

"Alan, how much is it?"

"Four thousand, three hundred, twenty-seven dollars and forty-eight cents, as of this morning," Alan recited in a flat tone. "It's probably a little more by now."

"That's four grand you owe us, Sickles."

"I know, I know. I feel real bad about it too. Whatcha say I roll on down here in a week or two and pay you then. I know I'll have it by then."

"You don't have it now?"

"Four grand in cash in this neighborhood? Hell no. But I can get it. A week. I just need a week."

Harvey locked the door behind Sickles, to which Sickles raised a questioning eye.

"I have a confession to make, Sickles. I've brought you here under false pretenses."

"Okay. So a couple weeks is cool?"

"We're having a bit of a reorganization. Changing priorities, shifting around responsibilities, that sort of thing. Anyway, your name came up and we decided to call you on down here to chat about it."

"So the money…"

"We don't care about the money."

"You want me to do a job for you? You want to hire me on?"

"No, friend, I think it's best if we both get out of this business. You know what they say, after all. Neither a borrower nor a lender be."

Sickles had a snappy comeback on the edge of his tongue, but sadly was unable to deliver it, as he was quickly shot five times before he could invoke Shylock, far and away the most appropriate Shakespeare character to invoke in a meeting such as this.

"That's it," Bob declared triumphantly, standing up in the middle of the restaurant for, as far as Susan could tell, no discernible reason. She desperately wished he would sit down, certain every patron in the place was staring at Bob, and if not him, certainly at her. Making mention of it would only draw more attention, better to simply move the moment along.

"What's it?"

"Heart condition? My dad didn't have a heart condition, and if he did, that doesn't even matter."

"Do you want to sit down?"

"Why?"

"Your last sentence made no sense. And you're standing up."

Bob sat down. "It was one of his patented bits. He would tell me about it with this sort of malevolent glee, he enjoyed it so much. He would get up in a crowded place, malls, bars, restaurants, wherever and then keel over. Somebody would come over and try to help. Then he'd lift their wallet."

"Bob, it's not that I don't believe you."

"What is it?"

Susan pondered her reply, then shrugged and decided on the truth.

"It's that I don't believe you."

"Thank you for that."

"Ortiz doesn't think he was a thief, and he's got a pretty good bullshit detector. It does seem a bit far fetched."

"This is it. He tried to rob somebody and it went bad. Can we arrest everyone who was in Jerry's that day?"

"Not unless the Constitution is taking a constitutional."

Susan thought such a comment extremely clever and was disappointed when Bob seemed to pay it no heed. She was fond of saying extremely clever things and quoting the great works of literature and very rarely did anyone give her the appropriate credit for raising the level of discourse, which was shamelessly low in Los Angeles. She tried to dumb down her lexicon, it truly made day-to-day interactions function more smoothly than they would otherwise, but sometimes she just couldn't help herself. Like her friend's annual Halloween party when she told the guy dressed as an atheist the real reason all dogs go to heaven is because God's a dyslexic and then followed up the silence with a line from The Iliad. She had not been invited back the next year.

"He was a thief. I think this is something we should pursue."

"We? What is this bizarre pronoun you keep using?"

"You made it clear the police aren't getting the job done. It's up to us."

"There it is again, another bleeping pronoun in the wrong context."

"You and me. Us."

"I'm trying to make a point."

"I got it."

"Did you? Because you're still doing it."

"I'm optimistic."

"You're loony. You want us to be vigilantes?"

"Good use of a pronoun. We're private citizens investigating a criminal act. I see nothing wrong with that." Bob paused, cocking his head slightly. "Susan, are you sorry we slept together?"

Susan's eyes went wide. The rest of the restaurant did not seem to hear, to her everlasting relief. In college, a boyfriend had let slip his venereal disease history in an ice cream shop well within earshot of Timothy, the editor in chief of the school newspaper. She was gun shy about public revelations since then.

"Uh, no, we…am I what?"

"Sorry to switch gears like that. You seem uneasy."

"Not at all." A more blatant lie had not been told since Coleman Silk in Philip Roth's shitheap of a follow-up to his Pulitzer Prize winning epic. She should amend.

"Well, yes. A little." What do you say at a moment like this? There was no precedent for her to reference, which was probably for the best. After all, awkward moments between people arguing over the proper role of the private citizen's role in matters of law enforcement was less common than, say, well, almost anything else. Or so she fervently hoped.

It took a moment for Susan to realize Bob was waiting for her to say something else. For the life of her, she had no clue what the appropriate response was in such a situation. She could make things more awkward, and maybe that would relieve the tension. She could ask him if he saw marriage in the future. He'd run for the hills. But what if he didn't? What if he's excited about the prospect of holy matrimony? How would she get out of that thorn bush? Oh, God I could use a drink.

She settled on, "I think I will have pie. Are you having pie?"

"Chocolate cream."

"Taking us off the table," Susan said, pressing on despite suddenly vivid memories of her and Bob on his kitchen table, "I still have to veto the whole investigation thing. If you're right, and that's a big if, it's insanity to even consider it."

"Just because we're tracking an armed murderer?"

"Caution springs to mind."

"We could go to the scene of the crime. Look around, interview the staff. See if the fuzz missed anything. Where's the harm in that?"

It sounded reasonable and that scared Susan more than the gigantic slab of pie that was suddenly before her.

"All of this is contingent on the notion that your father was a crook. And don't call us the fuzz."

"Listen to me. I am clearly not a normal person. Neither are you, which I like immeasurably, by the way. But I am telling you, beyond a shadow of a doubt, Karl Kessler was a thief and a robber and a pillager."

Susan smiled. "That's a good word. Pillager."

"Underused, I find."

"Yes, indeed. This is usually the part where you tell me you can't prove it to me, but I have to trust you."

"Not exactly. This is the part where I have to trust you and then I can prove it to you."

"What does that mean?"

"If you knew of someone, and this is of course hypothetical, who had in their possession certain stolen goods amounting to several million dollars in value, would you feel obligated to turn over said items, and perhaps said individual, to the authorities?"

"You cannot be serious."

"Hypothetically speaking."

"You're the recipient of your dad's loot?" Susan practically shouted.

"Not all of it. And could we use our inside voices?"

"Are you insane?" Susan whispered violently across the table.

"What is your obligation in this, again, strictly hypothetical situation?"

She buried her head in her arms. It was not supposed to go this way. Not this day, not this encounter, not this relationship, not this life. She should be gainfully employed, happily married to a wealthy financier, with a condo somewhere far away from her parents. Yet here she was, discussing contraband and professional ethics with a former chiropractor who may or may not be crazy, indictable, or both. Maybe she should have listened to her parents and become an academic.

"Susan?"

Her head did not come off the table as she replied, "Yes?"

"What are you thinking over there?"

"Hypothetically speaking?" she asked sarcastically.

"I know this is a lot. But I will buy you your slice of chocolate cream pie if you won't turn me over to the authorities for possession of stolen merchandise."

"Oh my dear God in heaven."

Chapter 9

IT WAS radiant. Slender and ornate, the necklace was framed with tiny diamonds lining the rim in perfect precision. Amethysts shone out from the clustered center with uninhibited joy, the splendor and craftsmanship captivating Susan in a way she never expected a piece of jewelry ever might. She found her hand outstretched but hesitant, unsure whether or not to touch such extraordinary beauty. How would one even begin to describe such a thing?

"Sparkly."

Bob grinned. Hers was not an uncommon reaction. His mom had screamed so loud the neighbors phoned the police. Upon their arrival and query, Karl took great pleasure describing to them in exquisite detail the enormous mouse that scampered across the living room at the exact moment she was attempting to balance a pile of clothing in one arm and a bottle of merlot in the other. The story was too preposterous and elaborate to possibly be false, and the officers stayed for a glass of merlot, of course, just eight short feet away from a prize valued at over a million dollars in 1964. Whenever his mom took the necklace out, she would recount the story with as much pleasure as she took wearing the piece. Like all of his father's lies, it was told with such flair and panache it was hard not to get swept away.

"It was my dad's favorite. My mom's too, I think. He gave it to her thirty years ago and then to me when she died. I'll never sell it, I won't make a cent off it, the insurance paid the company more than its value a long time ago, and yes, I know that doesn't make it right, but I can't help it, I'm not giving it back. Is that wrong?"

"Is that wrong? It's stealing. Did you miss that day in kindergarten? Of course it's wrong."

"My dad was a jewel thief."

She couldn't take her eyes off it. "Bob, I believe you."

"Can we set about solving his murder then?" Bob asked, setting the necklace back in its box and shutting the lid, disappointing and shocking Susan back to reality at the same time.

"Do you listen to yourself when you say things like that?"

"We could have a plan, if that would make you feel better. An action plan."

"An action plan?" Susan asked derisively.

"Or not. Criticism should be constructive whenever possible seems a good guideline for us, by the way."

"Sorry. Wait. Did I just apologize to the crazy man who should be in jail?"

"Susie, what does your gut tell you?"

Her gut was telling her to help him, but there was no way she was going to admit that. Evasion was necessary. Maybe she could try starting a fight.

"Don't call me Susie."

"How about Suz?"

Her uncle on her father's side, Vincent, called her Suz. She saw him rarely, which was a shame since he felt about her father much the same way she did. She liked being called Suz. She liked hearing Bob call her Suz even more. Dammit. Clearly, starting a fight is not the answer. Still, must keep things orderly.

"Susan is good."

"Susan. Don't change the subject."

"I suppose we could talk to a few people, see if my

colleagues missed anything."

"Excellent."

"But then we're turning it over to the police, understood? We're not obstructing justice here?"

"The information, or the prized family heirloom I cherish above all else?"

"I never saw this. Don't ever show it to me again, don't ever tell anyone else, ever, and so help me if I see it listed on eBay."

"Totally with you."

Nina was sitting in the living room, staring into space. Pete watched her while he took off his coat, shaking his head in disbelief. Her behavior was getting stranger by the hour. Why didn't she turn the television on or read a book? Who just sits and stares?

He would have given anything to avoid conversation with her at this moment. He wanted to go upstairs and forget about his part in today's bizarre and useless murder. Who goes around shooting people for four grand? I could piss four grand by tomorrow and we wouldn't have to worry about getting a needle jammed up our arm under the watchful eye of the governor. Just up and shot the fucker.

What made the whole thing really irritating was cleaning up the mess afterward. Every week until he was seventeen, Pete's dad forced him to mow the lawn, take out the trash, mop the floors, dust the mantle, vacuum the carpets and clean the bathroom. And that was just for starters. Pete hated each and every task, with the notable exception of dusting. For some reason, that duty never frayed his nerves. As a child, he could never imagine a more hellish fate than a life spent performing household chores. Spending two hours sopping up blood and wrapping a body in cellophane, for four-thousand dollars no less, made doing the dishes seem altogether palatable.

She was just sitting there. Pete wasn't the type to pretend

everything was hunky dory when it was plain to any eye blessed with sight that the situation was anything but. He wished he knew how to fix things. Maybe talking to her might help.

"What did you do today?"

"Sat around the house, like most days," Nina answered, never taking her eyes off the wall. "I drank more than usual today."

"Great."

"What do you expect me to do all day, Pete?"

"Anything you want!" he yelled, angrier than he wished. "I'm not keeping you here."

"That's where you're wrong. Just, go away and let me alone."

"To stare at the fucking wall?"

"Yes. To stare at the fucking wall."

Storming away was the move, Pete would have bet anything on it. Just like the poker player who folds when confronted with a pair of aces on the flop, stomping away in furious indignation was the percentage play. The odds had not been paying out of late, though. Perhaps one more try, and for fuck's sake, Pete, don't yell this time. And stop saying fuck, you know she hates that.

"What did you drink?"

She stopped staring at the wall and turned to him in surprise.

"Excuse me?"

"You said you drank more than usual. What did you have? Scotch?"

Not sure how to respond, Nina decided upon the truth, minus the usual snide glance and cutting barb.

"Whiskey. And a little cognac."

"Was it good?"

"I liked the cognac."

"How come you only had a little?"

Nina looked for a hidden agenda behind Pete's question,

but it seemed genuine. *What the hell*, she thought, *I'll play along*.

"I'd already had too much whiskey, but it left this aftertaste, so I had a sip of cognac to smooth it out."

"I do port for that, sometimes."

"I'll have to try that next time."

"Okay. Well, I'm going to take a shower. Can I get you something first, babe?"

Silence of this magnitude had not enveloped their house for over a year, and that was when termites forced an evacuation. Pete had not made a blank check offer such as this in such a long time that Nina was unable to remember the last time it had occurred. She was sure it had happened, though. Pretty sure.

"No, thanks. Thank you, though."

"Sure."

Nina watched Pete walk up the stairs, still stunned. When the shock wore off, hunger pangs struck and she made a mental note to have him make her a sandwich the next time he was feeling benevolent. She hoped it would be before she was forced to get off the couch and make something herself.

"We need to set some ground rules," Susan declared authoritatively. This whole bizarre situation was already getting out of hand, and a firm hand was needed to set the world to right.

"What are you thinking?" Bob asked.

"First. Let me take the lead. I'm a detective, I've been around the block. You're an idiot. Let's not forget this."

"What's second?"

"No threatening, no misrepresentation. If people don't want to talk to us, we can't make them. Understood?"

"Third?"

"In keeping with number two, there will be no illegal acts of any sort."

"What sort of illegal acts are you anticipating?"

"I don't know exactly what, but in anticipation of some request you make down the line, I want to be able to point to rule number three and say, Bob, remember rule number three."

"Seems fair," Bob said, moving a little closer to her.

"I also reserve the right to create rule number four from now through infinity at my discretion including but not limited to the duration of the following proceedings, however long or short they may last."

"I accept your terms. Shall we seal this bargain with a kiss of some sort?"

"Handshake will do. I also think we should postpone any and all physical anything until after we're done doing whatever in the hell it is that we're doing. I hope that's all right."

"As long is it's just postponed."

"And let's avoid clichés, too, all right? I get enough of those from work and television's version of my work."

"You really think he's going to kill him?" Alan asked, more for himself than to hear Rick's opinion on the matter.

"No way."

"What the hell makes you so surefire sure?"

"Trust me. Besides, does it matter?

Alan considered it. "Yeah, you're probably right. Work is work."

"This the one?"

The apartment was without a number adorning its door, but it was the only apartment door not currently boarded up. Rick knocked politely.

Derek answered, dressed only in his boxers. He was eating an apple, and regarded Rick and Alan with open hostility.

"What do you two want?"

Chapter 10

CLEANING UP refuse was the best job Daryl ever had. There was not a single aspect of the work he disliked, and he made sure to tell everyone who would sit and listen to him of this, undeniably even to him, peculiar trait.

"Cleaning up refuse is the best job I have ever had. Swear to God."

Bob and Susan exchanged a look, which Daryl had found to be a pretty common response to his admission. He knew a busboy was not an enviable position in the pantheon of the American workplace. Perhaps the fast pace and relative invisibility appealed to his demure sensibilities. The tips weren't bad, the hours flexible. What's not to like?

"That's wonderful," Susan said, only because she could not think of anything else to say that would not inhibit their attempt to extract information from this severely disturbed young man.

"A man was shot here a couple weeks ago," Bob said anxiously. "We understand you found the body."

"Oh, well…"

She stepped in before Daryl could finish. "Bob."

"What?"

"Rule number one."

"You were serious about that?"

Bob took Susan's hard stare to indicate she was in fact serious. Hands up in mock surrender, he stepped out of the way to let her ask the questions.

"Daryl, we understand you heard the shots and were the first on the scene."

Daryl muttered something unintelligible and gave the sign of the cross. He wasn't exactly a religious man, but he did not feel like taking chances. Christianity felt like a good safety net, just in case. God help him if Buddhism was the way to go and if the almighty were a chicken, he'd be taking the express elevator nonstop straight to Satan's doorstep.

"Poor guy. Ordered a corned beef on rye, walks to his car and bam! Messed up, you ask me."

"I know the police already asked you this, but, did you see anybody when you found him?"

"Nah, place was deserted."

"It was just you who heard the shots?"

"No, no we all heard 'em."

"Who is we?"

"Everybody in the kitchen that night. Henry and Chip, the short order guys, were cleaning the potatoes and having a smoke with me. Felipe and Beth were making out on the juice boxes and Cindy was reading her Cosmo."

"Why didn't they go check it out?"

"We all thought it was a car backfiring. I mean, we're on Ventura Boulevard, you know? We hear that sort of thing all the time."

"Why'd you go?"

"I had to take a leak."

"Aren't there bathrooms on the premises?"

"Yeah."

"All right," Susan responded, not really sure what else to say to that. She continued, "Did you see the man while he was inside eating?"

"No, I was on break."

"For how long?"

"I don't know, an hour, an hour and fifteen, maybe. Sally-Ann sat him down, I know, because she seemed kind of upset about it afterwards."

"Sally-Ann is…"

"The greeter girl."

"Do you know who waited on him?"

"Nah. I don't pay that much attention to what goes on inside this place, you know? I just work here."

"Is Sally-Ann here?"

"I'm going to tell you one thing right now," Bob said with declarative force. "I am never, ever eating here."

"Amen to that."

"Listen, Susan."

"You have a complaint?"

"I'm not going to just sit back while you talk to everyone. He's my father."

"This is for the best."

"You're a control freak."

"I think that's a little beside the point. You need to leave this sort of thing to me."

"What sort of thing are you referring to? Asking people whether or not they saw anybody at the scene of a crime? Gosh, gee, I don't think me can handle that tricky type question like."

"Fine," Susan said tersely. "When Sally-Ann gets here, you talk to her. I won't interfere."

"Promise?"

"You have my word, and my word is like oak."

"Like oak?"

"Strong and unyielding."

"Sorry I asked."

Hi. I'm Sally-Ann. Welcome to Jerry's. How many in your party?

Such a simple refrain, and yet Sally-Ann failed at delivering it far more often than not. It wasn't her fault, though. Her boyfriend Danny was cheating on her with the nanny two doors down from them. She was sure of it. She didn't have any proof, but it was only a matter of time before he slipped up and she caught him, and then that bastard was out the door. Maybe she would call that show *Cheaters* and make an ass out of him on national television, show everybody what she had to put up with on a daily basis.

Her rampant failure to execute her workplace duties was just so not her fault. It's not possible to cheerfully bid a friendly family hello when you just know your lover is screwing around behind your back. There was a surveillance store down on Sunset that advertised spy equipment, perhaps she could video him or track his movements like they do in the movies.

To be perfectly honest, it was a bad time for Danny to leave. She had missed her period and she probably wasn't lucky enough to be bulimic or anorexic or whatever the thinning shit is that makes you miss the ferry for the crimson river. Twenty years old and she was going to have a baby. Or an abortion. An old roommate of hers had four abortions and didn't seem the worse for wear. The last time had given rise to a nasty infection and a two-week stay in the hospital and then her mom found out and damn near put her in the morgue, but no long-term ill effects. Either way getting knocked up was probably going to screw up her life.

Sally-Ann looked at her watch. She had been on shift for forty minutes. It was high time for a break. The last thing she wanted today was to deal with people. She found the manager, Samuel, staring at her chest again. Samuel was harmless, and if letting him check out the twins made it easier for her to avoid actual work, then so much the better. There might as well be some advantage to being a woman in the workplace.

"Sam, I'm taking a break."

"Some people want a word with you in the back. If that's cool with you."

"Whatever. They can talk while I smoke."

"A man was shot here a couple weeks ago. Karl Kessler. We understand you seated him that night."

"Who are you?" asked Sally-Ann.

"My name is Robert, but you can call me Bob."

"Who are you?" Sally-Ann asked, directing the question at Susan, who was doing her best to stand surreptitiously behind Bob.

Susan stayed silent. Bob waited expectantly for a response, and when none was forthcoming, he turned to her with his eyebrows raised. She looked back innocently, unwilling to utter a sound. She did mouth the word 'oak', at which Bob gritted his teeth and turned back to Sally-Ann.

"That's Susie," he said.

"I'm on my break, so I don't really have time to yak. What do you guys want, anyway?"

"I just want to ask a few questions about the night Karl was shot."

"I don't know anything."

"Didn't you seat him?"

"Yeah, but then I booked on out to meet my boyfriend."

"So you didn't see anything that happened inside the restaurant while Karl was there?"

"Who are you?"

"I'm bad with names too. Bob."

"No, I mean, what, are you, like, a cop?"

"No, I didn't want to give you that impression."

'What are you?"

"I'm just…I'm investigating Mr. Kessler's death."

"You're a private eye? Do you do adultery cases?"

"No, not exactly."

"Not exactly? What does not exactly mean?"

"I don't have a license, or anything like that, but I am investigating."

"If you're not a cop or a snoopy, then why the hell should I talk to you?"

Bob looked to Susan for help. He might as well have asked Poland to successfully resist invasion.

"He was my father."

"Who? The dead guy?"

"Yes. The dead guy."

"Huh. Yeah, well, I don't really know anything. Sorry. I'm gonna go back inside."

Bob waited as long as possible after Sally-Ann dropped her cigarette, spun around and ambled back inside before turning to look at Susan.

"She didn't seem to know anything," he said.

"I got that. We could talk to that waitress."

"Sure. Maybe you could ask a few questions this time."

"Are you sure? Me no really good at ask questions like what?"

"Oh, I'm going to ask questions. But could you not be mute if the situation warrants it?"

"I could probably do that."

"Very gracious of you."

It was bad news from the time he opened his front door to the instant Paul pointed a .38 revolver at his head, cocked the trigger and stroked the trigger with his index finger. Knee-shaking terror fills most people at such times, but Derek had been threatened with a gun too often to go weak in the knees at the threat of death. Instead, righteous indignation filled Derek.

"What the fuck are you doing?" Derek asked, to the evident dismay of everyone in the room.

Paul thought about it, lowering his gun.

"What am I doing?" he asked.

"Yeah, what are you, crazy?"

Derek looked to Paul's lackeys, but each fastidiously avoided his gaze. *Son of a bitch is crazy, his kids know it but they're too chickenshit to do anything about it. Great.*

"I'm not crazy."

Derek narrowed his eyes. The man sounded even crazier when he denied that he was crazy. *Maybe I'm wrong*, Derek thought. *Maybe he's just acting crazy. Let's try a logical approach.*

"I owe you five-hundred dollars. Right?"

"You do."

"How about I pay you five-hundred dollars right now."

"Do you have it on you?"

"I do."

Derek took off his shoe and shook loose a roll of cash. Carefully pulling the rubber band off, Derek counted out five-hundred dollars, comprised of two hundred dollar bills, a fifty, eleven twenties, a ten, two fives, and eleven ones. Harvey noticed the total came to five hundred and one, but was not about to make mention of it.

"A pleasure doing business with you," Derek said to Paul, handing him the cash.

Paul pocketed it. He would later spend all of it on flowers for Amy, a gesture that forced her to turn the house upside down in desperate search for hidden bibles and rosaries. That she was unable to find any did not dissuade her of their existence.

Derek could not help but notice the gun did not disappear. Nobody was talking, nobody was moving. He waited as long as he could, hoping he would not have to be the one to break the silence. Total fucking nut job this guy. Only one way to walk out the door, gotta out crazy the crazy.

"Motherfucker, do you know who you're messing with? You're damn lucky I paid you that five, I could've just stepped all over every one of you and wiped off the shit left over on the next stupid fuck who thought he was something. Fuck all of you very much."

With practiced nonchalance, Derek turned to walk out. The men who had come to his door earlier stood between him and the door. Can't back down now, Derek. Lower the shoulder and pile-drive right through them.

"You idiots gonna move, or do I get to move you?"

"Step aside," Paul said from behind Derek.

Alan and Rick moved away from the door. Derek turned to give a parting shot to Paul, but stopped at the sight of the gun once again aimed at his head.

There is no sudden burst of insight or staggering sense of depression and loss that comes with the unquestionable realization that you are going to die in the next minute. This was a little disconcerting for Derek, who had always assumed the end of his life would be an exciting moment of self-reflection and epiphanies followed ultimately by catharsis and then, finally, death. Maybe you needed two minutes to die properly.

Althea did not like being a waitress. It had been marginally better when she worked at Olive Garden, but only marginally. Her feet hurt when she went home, her hair was going to smell like French fries for all eternity and not even free meals were enough to offset the damage an eight-hour shift did to her custom designed sixty-three dollar nails. But her bleak view of food service boiled down to a fairly simple principle when push came to shove. People were cheap bastards.

Jerry's Deli charged outrageous prices for every item on the menu and alcohol was available and yet despite these two happy accidents, Althea rarely took home more than a hundred dollars a day. How hard was it to leave twenty percent? People left eleven percent more often despite the relative difficulty in calculating eleven percent versus twenty percent. Not a day went by that Althea didn't fantasize about every patron in her wing choking to death on poison of her choosing. It was the only time she ever smiled at work.

"Althea?"

Althea looked for the greeter, but Sally-Ann was off on yet another break. That girl kept her job with possession of graphic, embarrassing photographs of management in compromising positions. It was the only possible explanation for a girl who did her job as infrequently and badly as Sally-Ann did. Althea hated seating people a tad less than serving them.

"Yeah?"

"I'm Bob. This is Susan."

"Hi, Bob. Susan. Would you like a booth or a table?"

"Neither, actually. We'd like to ask you a couple questions."

"I thought we agreed to avoid clichés," Susan whispered.

"I didn't tell her to make my day or anything," Bob responded testily.

"Who are you two?"

"You were on shift when my father was murdered outside."

Althea's attitude changed instantly, her face bleeding sympathy. "That was your dad? Damn, I'm sorry, man. Damn. That's a rough trip."

"I heard there was a commotion that afternoon. I was hoping you could tell me if my dad was involved."

"Yeah, of course. You sure you two don't want to sit down? Have a drink? Meatloaf is our special this week."

"No, thanks."

"Okay, well, yeah, your dad was having some attack or something, it was hard to tell. I was picking up an order when it happened, but when I heard the commotion, I took a peek and this old guy is on the floor. It was tough to see, there were a lot of people swarming around. He got up a minute later, though, so I didn't think too much about it. That's tough, man, losing your pop."

"Was there somebody near him? Did somebody catch him when he fell or check his vitals?"

"Bunch of people, I guess. Though there was this one guy. He helped your old man into a chair, looked like they spoke for a minute."

"Did this guy pay with a credit card?" Susan asked hopefully.

Althea shook her head. "Nope, cash."

"Do you remember what he looks like?" Bob asked.

"Sure. He was a good tipper. I always remember a good tipper."

Chapter 11

WEARING MAKEUP didn't bother Sean. He could not say the same for the nose. It was such a pain to keep the damn thing on right. It was always slipping off in the middle of the show. The kids thought it was hilarious, but the parents always made a big production out of it when it came time to settle the bill. Technological innovations had put men on the moon and split the atom but connecting a string to a bright red rubber nose was beyond the reach of technological innovation.

He was still reeling from yesterday's performance. The singing portion had gone well. The dancing portion had gone well. The bottle of seltzer in the eye had gone fairly well. The caricature portion had gone poorly. The birthday boy, an oversized six-year old with a scream that would curl a banshee's toes, did not see his likeness in Sean's rendering. So much so that Sean was promptly fired without pay. He would file a grievance with the union, but that didn't do much for his immediate inability to pay the rent. His excessive drinking probably didn't help matters any.

Sean answered the door in his underwear, clown makeup still plastered across his face. Bob shot Susan a look, which she consciously avoided.

"Sean, you look like shit."

"I don't feel a whole lot different. Come on in and share the joy."

The room was sparsely decorated and what little was present would charitably be described as filthy. Empty pizza boxes were the closest thing to furniture. Clothes, videos, pornography, empty bottles, half-empty bottles, books, a dead plant, wrapping paper, a postcard of Dublin and a Homer Simpson doll littered the floor.

"You want a drink?"

"Here on business."

"I heard you got shitkicked."

"Suspended."

"Whatever you want to call it. You come here to commiserate?" Sean addressed Bob. "I got shitkicked myself, you see. You the new boy toy?"

Bob raised his eyebrows in amusement, but Susan didn't see the humor. "Don't be an asshole, Sean. We're here to hire you."

"You got kids now? How long have I been off the force?"

"We need a sketch artist. The best, I might add."

"Oh, yeah? How much you willing to pay?"

"How much do you need?"

"Two hundred."

"Sounds about right."

"Did I mention how good it is to see you, Ciarelli?"

"You too, Sean. I like the makeup."

The smudged makeup coupled with the alcohol stained shirt made his bitter smile seem exceedingly gruesome.

"Everyone does."

The store was quiet, the soft hum of the fluorescent lights blending nicely with the easy-listening music. Mid-morning was always quiet, the deliveries for the day done, the commuters and their coffee fixes long since departed. Mostly kids came in, cutting school and desperate for a sugar fix. Rick perused the year-old donuts (an optimistic estimate), remembering days when knocking over establishments such as this was his bread and butter.

Rick had never given all that much thought to his employment. It came and went, good times were virtually indistinguishable from bad times. His association with Paul put an end to the stick-ups, which was probably for the best. It was only a matter of time before some Apu put a twelve gauge into his abdomen. He wasn't exactly sure what it was that he did now, but he hadn't had to use a gun in over a year, and his take home pay was more than he'd ever thought possible. There was little room for complaint.

"I'll take a pack of Marlboro hundreds."

"Lights?"

He shot the overweight clerk an annoyed glance. There was a time, my friend, when I would have stuck a gun down your gullet for much less, but that was a long time ago. To do so would risk his apartment, a spacious two-bedroom with an adjoining patio that overlooked the pool two stories below, which in turn gave a near perfect view of the plethora of ridiculously hot women employed by the adult entertainment industry who engaged in sunbathing on a daily basis. God bless the San Fernando Valley.

"Here you go, pal. Four and twenty."

"Must be karma," Rick said acidly, picking around his wallet for a quarter.

"What's that?"

"Now you miserable bastards are robbing me. Keep the change."

"A nickel. Thanks."

Rick ignored him and stepped outside, tapping the box against his thigh. He should be scared out of his gourd with what was happening. He'd never seen Paul kill anyone before. Harvey had told him there were a few back in the day, when they were getting their start, but it had been Pete that had done the deed. Paul didn't like to get his hands dirty, Harvey said. *Past tense*, Rick thought to himself. It was good to know the other guys were just as scared.

"Can I get one of those?"

The surgeon general could bitch all he wanted to about the evils of tobacco, but until he came up with a better way of attracting the opposite sex, Rick was going to keep to his half a pack a day habit.

"Sure. Need a light?"

She leaned into his lit match, her blouse opening up just enough to reveal the pale contours of her breasts. Out of towner, probably here to spend a few days at the beach, then head back to Peoria.

"Thanks."

"No problem. Tourist?"

"Is it that obvious?"

Rick shrugged, giving a little half smile. "Where you staying?"

"With a friend. Tarzana. You know where that is?"

He laughed, the girl giggling along with him. "It's two miles west of here, straight down Ventura Boulevard."

"Thanks again."

"You should get a Thomas Guide."

"You're the third person to tell me that."

"And what does that tell you?"

"I guess. I'm only going to be around for a few days, though, so I figured I'd just use the internet. You know, like everybody else."

A little sass never hurt anybody, and Rick wasn't about to let a little lip deter him. "Maybe you should have somebody show you around town, just to make sure you don't get lost and end up in Simi Valley. It'd be bad for our image if we let pretty young things from…"

"Sioux City."

Damn, he'd been close. "It just wouldn't be right if something bad happened, I'd never be able to live with myself." Rick punctuated his words by pushing up against her, his efforts rewarded when she reached out to take another cigarette, her hand lingering on his forearm.

"Well, we wouldn't want that. I'm Jessie."

"Rick. What are you and your friend doing tonight?"

He barely listened to her answer, more interested in the revelation that had come to him the moment he'd felt her ease into his touch. It wasn't the act itself, it was the power he held. All the women he'd slept with, and here he was outside a Mobile station in Encino with the insight of the century. Isn't that interesting.

It took Sean less than twenty minutes to create a remarkable likeness of Karl's killer. It had taken far longer to get him to agree to work a party for Althea's four-year old daughter. Sean was not skilled in the art of negotiating. He had once given up his sandwich, milk, and pudding to his sister in exchange for a carrot and somehow thought he was getting the better end of the deal at the time, but he was not about to get hosed with such a plum deal standing two feet away.

"I'm not working for half-pay. Fuck that."

"What did he look like?" Susan asked, trying her best to steer the conversation away from Sean's requested remuneration. She might as well have tossed a drowning elephant a life vest.

"My daughter loves clowns, but I'm not paying three-hundred dollars for someone whose breath smells like turpentine," Althea stated, quite reasonably in her mind.

"I don't need this. I can walk anytime and it wouldn't bother me a smidge."

"I don't see anyone stopping you. Idiot."

"Who are you calling an idiot, you—"

"Whoa, easy there," Susan interjected in the nick of time. Althea looked ready to break out the boxing gloves and dash Sean's face along with their hopes of putting a face to their suspect.

"Might I interject on behalf of my dad?" Bob asked, his voice teetering on the edge of anger.

Sean looked suitably abashed. "You're right, my bad. I'll do it for two hundred."

Althea was not deterred for one moment. "One."

"Althea," Susan lamented.

Althea stood firm, crossing her arms defiantly. "One."

"I'm out of here," Sean yelled, much louder than intended.

The other three people in the room stopped short at the sound of his raised voice. None made a move to stop him from leaving, and for good reason. He hadn't made the slightest motion towards the exit.

"Whom are you yelling at?" Susan asked, a bit bewildered by Sean's behavior.

"It's who," Althea interjected.

"It's whom," Susan argued. "Trust me. Me and English go way back."

"Okay. But it's who."

"What if you can cut out an hour earlier?" Bob proposed.

"He's not leaving early," Althea argued stubbornly. "He's doing the whole shebang."

"Half an hour early?" Sean asked.

"For one fifty?"

"Yeah."

"All right," Althea grudgingly agreed. "Deal."

Sean and Althea shook hands, still eying one another warily, as the vein on Bob's neck began to slowly subside.

"I'd just like to say, in cases of plural object form it is, in fact, whom." It was Susan's turn to be the object of three annoyed sets of eyes. "I'm just saying."

Chapter 12

BUREAUCRACY IS a state of mind. Susan kept telling herself this as the minutes droned on. The longer she waited, the more foolish she felt. Her colleagues were smart, dedicated people. Althea would have been interviewed, Karl's public stir examined, a dozen witness statements checked, rechecked and then corroborated. They were going to have this picture somewhere on file and be eight steps ahead of Susan and worse, she was going to get laughed at. 'Aren't you suspended?' 'Are you kidding me?' 'You need a haircut.' It would last until after her retirement party and even then, she was sure legend would grow amongst fourth-generation homicide detectives of the rogue agent who made an ass out of herself investigating a case that had already been closed and who should have spent that time visiting a salon. *Maybe I should get reddish highlights*, she mused.

The look Ortiz gave her when she finally made it into the office was beyond description. Something like the look a child gives a parent when presented with a pair of purple socks when the gift desired resembled four wheels with a foreign acronym. With a little pity thrown in for good measure. Susan pressed on, surprising herself with her recent ability to defy all reason and logic in pursuit of…well, she didn't really know what. But she was fairly certain it would be worthwhile when she reached the finish line. It had to be.

Oh, God, please let it be worth this.

"This guy has a motive," Susan stated, as if it were the undeniable, categorical truth.

"Susan, and I say this with great respect, but what the fuck are you trying to kid? Motive?"

"It's the reason people do things. Like murder."

"Oh, mercy. It is to laugh."

"Will you listen to me for three minutes? Three minutes."

"Three. But you're buying me a coke when we're done."

"Karl is playing a game. Steal the wallet. He's played it plenty of times before. He fakes a heart attack, and waits for a guy to come over and help. Karl fleeces him, but this time the guy makes him for it. Out to the lot, bang-bang. Lifts Karl's wallet to make it look like a mugging."

Ortiz appeared deep in thought. Susan's hopes were raised and just as quickly dashed.
"I think I want a Cherry Coke," he said.

"Ortiz."

"There's no indication other than the son's word he ever stole anything in his life. He did collapse, but our autopsy revealed a developing case of tricuspid atresia that would more than account for that. You're arguing sketch boy here blows away an eighty-year old man in broad daylight on Ventura Boulevard after finding out his wallet was taken."

"Run the picture."

"No. But I'll overlook the fact you're questioning witnesses in an ongoing homicide investigation if we can go get my Dr. Pepper right now."

"What will it take for you to run this picture?"

"You're not willing to pay that price. And I can say that now with as much innuendo as I like because you're not a fellow officer."

"Where's your better half?"

"No need to shout, mi amiga. Here I am." Alekhov moved

up next to Ortiz, the two forming an imposing, if mismatched pair. Alekhov's shaggy blonde hair and loose fitting clothes a more southern California look than Ortiz's close-cropped military appearance.

"Did you interview this guy?"

Alekhov barely glanced at the sketch before sitting down and putting his feet, or more accurately, his legs all the way up to his knees, up on Ortiz's desk. With practiced disinterest, Ortiz swept his desk clean of Alekhov's legs. Temporarily finished pestering Ortiz, Alekhov turned his attention back to Susan.

"No, never seen the man."

"He was at the Deli when Karl was killed. Waitress positive ID."

"Which one?"

"Althea."

"Which one was she? Uber hottie?"

Ortiz shook his head, recognizing the name. "No, she was the bitter, angry one."

"Oh," Alekhov said, disappointed.

"So are you guys going to run the picture or do I have to write more unflattering comments about you in the ladies room?"

"We'll look into it."

"That's all I ask. See you around."

Susan was out the door when Ortiz yelled after her.

"Wait, what about my Sprite?"

Bob was not thrilled. He should have been ecstatic, in Susan's professional opinion, but he most definitely was not. She had never met a detective who did not play it close to the vest when it came to a case, and she was by no means exempt from that list. Siberian wolves were less territorial than the men and women Susan had served with in robbery homicide. A 'we'll look into it' was akin to a vault door opening wide.

"So that's it?" he asked incredulously.

"That was more than we might have expected. Don't get agitated."

"We solved the damn thing. Don't get agitated? We solved it. They should give us medals and that son of a bitch's head on a pike."

"Bob, it doesn't work like that."

"I'm getting that. All right. So what's our next move?"

"Next move?"

"Yeah."

"I thought we agreed this would be it. Identify the possible assailant and take the curtain call. Whether the police do anything about it from this point is their business, not ours."

"We're making a new thing."

"A new thing."

"Yeah, it'll be great. We can call it our action plan. Number two."

"Action plan number two."

"Catchy, yeah?"

It was the slightly off-kilter grin that accompanied Bob's oddest statements that made him so appealing, Susan determined. It had to be. It simply couldn't be the merits of the debate, which, from her position, she seemed to be losing, though that seemed logistically impossible. Not that she could be blamed. How does one effectively argue with a crazy man? Let's supersede a police investigation. Why not, you ask? How do you even begin to discuss such nonsense in a rational manner? The fact that she was clearly the sane one meant precious little when it was obvious to both of them that Bob was going to get his way. Again. Susan frowned. She did not like that. Who the hell was this guy?

"How did somebody like you get into chiropracting? I really want to know."

"I needed a gig, something to pay the bills."

"A gig?"

"I graduated chiropractic college, if that's what you're insinuating."

"Mocking, really. Did you graduate real college?"

"And North Valley Wesleyan Chiropractic Night College isn't a real college?"

"Need you even ask?"

"I went to UCLA."

"Graduated?"

"Is it any wonder the LAPD has such a bad reputation? You're very mean."

"Just because you didn't graduate from a real college, doesn't mean you need to get defensive about—"

"I graduated, missy. Dean's list and everything. I real smart-like"

"So cracking backs came into the picture how exactly?"

"How many times do I have to tell you? We don't crack backs. It's simply an adjustment with an accompanying cracking noise. Not all that unusual a story, I wouldn't think anyway. Started up as a lark, a way to make a few bucks. Here I am eight years later and I can't imagine doing anything else. Of course, it's hard to imagine doing this either."

"You hate it?"

"Hate is such a strong word."

"It's often an unpleasant situation."

Bob scrunched up his forehead, thinking. Satisfied with his thoughts, he nodded to himself.

"No, I hate it."

"You can't tell, by the way."

"Tell what?"

"That you hate it. In the office, I mean. You can't tell. You do a good job hiding it."

"Thanks. I don't hate every bit of it."

"No?"

"You meet some interesting people."

"Same with my job."

"Which began how exactly? Where does a homicide detective get her start?"

"I had a deeply disturbed childhood."

Bob waited for a little more, but nothing was forthcoming. He pressed on. "So you're exorcising some demons? Righting the wrongs of the world?"

"Who can say why anyone does anything?"

"Sounds like a BA in philosophy talking."

"I told you, I was an English major. We threw things at philosophy majors when they weren't looking."

"Susan."

"Okay, sometimes they were staring right at us and we went ahead and unloaded on them. I was nineteen, don't judge me."

"Relationships are all about give and take."

"We're in a relationship?"

"I'm going to venture out on the ledge and say yes. You lie and say you like my music, I meet your parents, you help me solve a murder, I end up buying you a scone sometime in the future. That's a relationship."

"You want to meet my parents?"

"I'm willing to meet your parents. Crucial difference. And buy you a scone at some point."

She thought about it.

"We're in a relationship?"

"For my part."

"Really?"

"I think so."

"What do people do at a moment like this?"

"Well it depends."

"Does it now."

"In the fifties, they'd have a chaste hug and peck on the cheek and then the two people would retire to their separate residences."

"What do folks do in the new millennium?"

He flashed that crooked grin again. "I have no idea."

Susan felt more at ease the second time she woke up naked in Bob's bed. Not at ease, exactly, but certainly more at ease. She wasn't sure anyone was ever entirely comfortable with communal nudity the first ten times or so. Once you've hit double digits in any activity, the thrill, and consequently the unease, have long since beat a hasty and permanent retreat.

She was pleased to discover he still didn't snore. He also didn't talk in his sleep, which was a positive. She had slept with a man who spoke in his sleep, and to compound that irritant, he spoke Russian while slumbering. Susan was constantly awake, trying to decipher his babbling, whether for her own edification or for potential national security she was never entirely certain.

Reality had to intercede eventually. It was an unfortunate truth Susan had learned time and time again. It's impossible to spend all your time naked in somebody else's bed. Better women than her had tried and failed. They'd had sex twice, which clearly meant a strong move towards boyfriend/girlfriend. Susan was a rank amateur at that level. She had turned pro years ago at flirting, dating, and screwing, but the talent to tolerate a guy for extended periods of time in close proximity still eluded her. Sure she got the occasional call to come up to the majors, but it was just for a cup of coffee. No team had ever offered her a long-term contract.

She eyed Bob thoughtfully, her forehead scrunching up in curiosity.

"Bob, are you pretending to sleep?"

Without opening his eyes, Bob answered, "Yes. Is that weird?"

Susan laughed. She found herself doing that a lot with him.

Before she could stop herself, she blurted out, "I know a gal at the FBI who can run the picture for us."

"That'd be great." Bob opened his eyes, smiling. "Susan?"

"Yes?"

"You don't think I'm using you just to find out about my dad, do you?"

"I figured it was all a clever ruse to get me in the sack."

"Tell me about your job."

"What do you want to know?"

"Everything."

"Got a starting point in mind?"

"Are you happy?"

"Let's just say I dwell in possibility," Susan answered, deflecting the question with her favorite Emily Dickinson quotation.

"Do you want out?"

"I'm not sure. It's just…"

"What?"

"It's hard." She paused, ordering her thoughts. "The work, the life. It's hard. My good days involve thugs, rapists, idiots debatably human in origin. I could do without that sometimes."

"But you're not sure?"

"I'm good at it. I'm not a supercop, but I'm good at what I do. You get a charge from that you wouldn't believe and it carries you sometimes. But I just feel worn down thinking about going into the office. It weighs on you."

"How do you feel now?

"Right now?"

"In general now."

She thought about it.

"I feel really good." Susan smiled bashfully and had a hard time meeting Bob's gaze.

"As long as you don't think I'm using you for the investigation. I'm going to stop pretending now. Stay the night and don't argue about it."

How did he know she was going to leave? Was she that obvious? Susan resolved to spend less time analyzing the intuitive gentleman to her left and more time practicing her facial expressions. Blank serenity was first on the list. She practiced for ten minutes before she fell asleep.

Chapter 13

PETE DID all his best thinking before he got out of bed in the morning. Normally, it was due solely to the astonishingly comfortable pillow his mom had given him as a Christmas gift last year. Filled with feathers or down, the damn thing felt like a really fluffy cloud. It must regulate the blood flow to stimulate thought. Of late, he was sad to note, it was virtually the only time of day when he wasn't forced to endure all manner of hellish tortures, from his wife's scolding gaze to his boss's profanity laced tirades and increasingly frequent shooting sprees.

Prison was foremost on Pete's mind this morning. He did not want to go to prison. It wasn't so much that he objected to being locked up per se. He'd done three months back in his twenties. Met some nice people, slept a lot. But now? Wife who wants to cut your heart out, boss is killing people for no reason, bladder infection keeps popping up. Who has time for jail?

An explosion rocked the bedroom. Pete jerked up, his eyes wide, sure that his ticket was getting punched. *Just like in the movies,* he thought. Nina put an end to those thoughts as she punched the dormant alarm clock into submission and rolled over. Even Nina wouldn't be able to sleep through an actual mob hit.

Gaining his bearings, he slipped out of bed, donned his fuzzy slippers and bathrobe and trundled downstairs, though as soon as he hit the top of the staircase, he immediately wished he had never left the comfort and security of his pillow.

The smell of filth was unmistakable. Putrid, rotting filth. Wet, to boot. It was emanating from the dishwasher, as was a thick sludge that covered most of the kitchen tile.

"Goddammit," Pete whispered in God's general direction.

He snatched the mobile phone from its cradle and walked over to the edge of the flood. He peered at the dishwasher, which had thoughtfully placed a 1-800 number in clear view on the front of the horrid machine in case of an emergency. *This qualifies*, Pete thought, as he dialed the number.

"Yeah, hi, I need somebody to come out to my place right away. My dishwasher is leaking crap everywhere."

"All right sir, if you'll hold for a moment, I'll connect you to our service department."

"Okay."

Wisps of black smoke caught Pete's attention as the soothing sounds of Brahms filtered through the receiver. *I wonder if that's bad*, Pete thought absentmindedly. The tufts of flame visible through the cracked front raised an eyebrow and the low, dark rumbling increasing in volume did not bode particularly well, either.

"Maintenance."

"Good, I got a real thing over here. My dishwasher is on fire and—"

The explosion knocked Pete back a few steps and he covered his face as small scraps of metal floated past his head. The torrent of sewage coming from the eviscerated machine increased tenfold and he saw his annoying little problem fast becoming a force ten hurricane type disaster.

"Get somebody to my house right fucking now. My place is flooding with shit."

"I'll transfer you to service, sir."

"Who the hell are you?"

"Maintenance."

"Come fucking maintenance, then. Isn't that what you people do?"

"You have to place an order, sir."

"I am placing an order. I'm ordering you to my fucking house."

"No need for language like that sir. You have to place the order with service, and then they direct us from that point. One moment."

"Don't you dare put me on hold, you miserable little—"

He considered continuing, if only to vent his anger at the rapidly approaching seepage, but the man's grating, infuriating calm had been replaced by the soothing tones of Mozart. Pete was not, however, soothed. Perhaps if he was not being driven backwards by the approaching tidal wave, he might have taken a deep breath, shrugged, and chuckled at the silliness of it all. As it was, his path of retreat was being quickly cut off.

The blackish river had moved over the short steps leading from the kitchen to the living room like Victoria Falls. Reaching the staircase was no longer an option. Neither was the front door. Slowly driven back like an army facing insurmountable aggression, Pete vainly looked for an out. He found it atop his prized oak coffee table, purchased for four-hundred dollars at a flea market in West Hollywood a year before he met Nina. It was the only item in the living room she had allowed him to keep when she interior decorated the entire downstairs to a glossy IKEA-like sheen.

Safely aboard his life raft, he watched helplessly as the torrent swept by, destroying his fake Persian rugs one by one.

"Service."

"If you transfer me again, I will come down there and kill you."

"What seems to be the problem, sir?"

"My downstairs is flooded. My dishwasher is on fire. Send

somebody to eighteen Woodlake Avenue before I decide to name you and your family in my lawsuit."

Hanging up the phone, Pete felt very alone. This is not how his life was supposed to turn out. Bad marriage, bad job, flooded house, ruined rugs. He was almost forty for Christ's sake. For the first time, he seriously weighed the possibility of quitting the business. Nina would like that. His mom would like that. He could have medical insurance and a 401k with a real job. He and Nina could have children. He'd like children, as long as they weren't brats. The more he thought about it, and the higher the water level was rising, the more appealing the idea became. Quit the business. Why not? There would never be a better time, Pete surmised.

"Nina!"

No answer. He shouldn't have been surprised. He'd taken her to see a KISS reunion concert a few years back and she'd fallen asleep during the guitar solo. What was a mini Hiroshima and some yelling compared to Gene Simmons destroying a guitar?

He decided to call his mom and she picked up on the eighth ring.

"Hi, Ma, it's Pete."

"It's eight in the morning," his mom replied testily, sleep still in her voice.

"Were you sleeping?"

"Of course not, don't be silly. What are you doing up?"

"Dishwasher woke me up. How's Brad?"

Gloria had remarried six months after Pete's dad had died. He hadn't minded. Everybody needs a warm body and Brad was as warm as anyone in his sixties was going to be. Plus, he was a good shuffleboard player and that made his mom light up when they went on those Carnival Cruises.

"He's fine." Everybody was always fine with Gloria. Pete had broken his arm and two ribs careening off a brick wall with his motorbike at nineteen and despite lacerations that made his left shoulder look like a Halloween costume, he was deemed 'fine' not five minutes after she saw him in the hospital bed.

"How are you, mom?"

"How am I?"

"Yeah."

"I can't remember the last time you asked me that."

"I'm asking now."

"I'm fine."

"Good, I'm glad. I've been thinking lately. About stuff. You know, life type stuff."

"You and Nina fighting?"

Pete snorted. "When are we not?"

"You're not leaving her."

"Of course not, Ma."

"No son of mine is getting a divorce. No one in our family has ever gotten divorced. You hear me?"

"We're not getting divorced, Ma. We're just arguing a lot."

"About what?"

"Stuff, I don't know. Shit. That's not what I want to talk about. I've been thinking about stuff, is the thing. Maybe thinking about making some changes."

"You're going legit."

"Didn't say that. I dunno, though, maybe. What do you think?"

"Sweet Jesus and Mary, I have prayed for this day. I thought you'd never come around. Move back to Syracuse, Brad and me will put you and Nina up until you get a place and, oh, it'll just be so wonderful, and I have to tell Brad, can you hang on, I just, oh, honey, I'm so glad, I could just cry, can you hang on, or, why don't I just call you back. Is that all right? Are you going anywhere?"

He snorted again as he surveyed the situation, unbelievably but unquestionably deteriorating. He was going to have little choice but to move in with his mom after his house was condemned by the government and declared a natural wildlife preserve.

"No, Ma, I'm sticking around for a while."

It wasn't that Susan dreaded the weekly phone call to her parents. Not exactly. She loved them both very much, of this there was no question. But it was an exercise in masochism when she had news that would undoubtedly raise their ire but had to be reported if she were to remain a dutiful daughter.

The last time such an occasion arose, Susan had voted no on proposition 167F, which, among other things, required new companies to post signs in neighborhoods advertising fair employment practices for all applicants. She thought it was a waste of paper - Leland Ciarelli, ever the working class pro-proletariat soap-boxer type when he wasn't drinking an aperitif and lauding the International Monetary Fund, decried any and all opposition to the proposition as an affront to decent society. Susan had spent an hour and a half on the phone that day, and all she wanted when she called was her uncle Ben's email address. Luckily, the incident at the liquor store hadn't raised much of a red flag, probably since her parents considered every minute spent as an enforcer of the peace as one gigantic ongoing public shaming.

She had the routine down better than the high-wire trapezists at the circus, a pretty fair analogy to every aspect of conversation undertaken with her parents. A little small talk, followed by a few semi-sincere compliments and sycophantic praise for something done somewhere by somebody of which about eight people in the northern hemisphere might possibly be aware of, yet was deemed indispensable to further science, and finally the truth, which Susan uttered as quickly possible. She ended the vaudeville show by asking about the state of tenure within the Physics department and ten minutes later she was off the phone, none the worse for wear.

Today was going to be different, Susan vowed. Today was going to be the beginning of a brand new give and take relationship between parent and offspring. It would certainly be frustrating and at times excruciating, but ultimately worthwhile. She wasted no time and launched right into it.

"I'm seeing a chiropractor, Mom."

"Oh, dear lord, Susan. I'm getting your father."

"Mom, wait—"

Too late. Patience, Susan, patience. They'll be dead before you, with any luck, and then this will all be worthwhile. She could hear the phone switching hands. Once more into the breach, dear friends, once more…

"Susan, your mom is through the ceiling. What did you do?"

"She's seeing a chiropractor," her mom intoned in the background.

"No, she isn't."

"Yes, I am, Dad. It's not a big deal."

"Did he tell you your leg is an eighth of an inch too short?"

"No, dad, I'm seeing a chiropractor, as in romantically."

There was a short pause and for the briefest of seconds, Susan thought she might be off the hook.

"How is that better?"

"Can you put Mom back on?"

"Still, I suppose it could be worse. You could be seeking care with the man."

Even the daftest infantryman knows better than to step on a land mine when there is a paved walkway not five feet away. Susan, however, was incapable of rational thought where her parents were concerned.

"Well, that too…" The words just died on her lips. She could hear her father furrow his brow and gently shake his head, wondering where he went wrong with his only progeny.

"Here's your mom."

Susan rolled her eyes. At least voice your displeasure. That would at least be something. Years of pent-up frustration and anger welled up within Susan every time she tried to share anything with her dad.

"Susan," her mom intoned gravely, "do you remember what Doctor Morgan said about chiropractors?"

Doctor Morgan had been the family physician since the Ciarelli clan had first moved to the United States. He was a nice man with many, many wrinkles and a penchant for haranguing every other health care professional who was not in his Rolodex. His most virulent attacks were saved for chiropractors, who were, in words Susan remembered with alarming accuracy, "A scourge on the tumor of malpractice!" Memorable to be sure, even more so for a curious little six-year old.

"Not really, Mom. Bob is very nice, by the way."

"Have you started looking for jobs yet?"

Her mom could change gears better than most Nascar drivers.

"Still a cop, mom."

"Let me put your father back on."

"Mom—"

"I just finished Safire's last tract," her dad said. "Have you read it, yet?"

"Not yet, Dad." Susan had no intention of reading it. She found Safire audacious, but preferred the op-ed page to five-hundred pages of grammatically incise but fluidly draining prose. She'd never dare mention that to her father. That conversation would make the 'seeing a chiropractor' discussion seem pleasant and engaging by comparison.

"Here's your mom again."

She rubbed her eyes in fatigue.

"Susan?"

"Hi, Mom."

"Are you eating well?"

"I had some fruit this morning."

"Betty and Donald had twins. Isn't that amazing?"

"Wow, I'm so happy for them." Who the hell are Betty and Donald?

"You sure you're eating?"

"Absolutely."

"You're dating a chiropractor?"

"Can we refer to him as Bob from this point forward?"

"I did like Danny Aiello in Jacob's Ladder. Tim Robbins got better after visiting him."

"Don't encourage the girl," Susan's dad mumbled in the background.

"When are you coming to visit?"

"Soon, I hope. I should get going."

"Let me put your father back on then."

"Mom—"

"Take care of yourself out there."

"Thanks, Dad. By the way, how are things in the department?"

Alan looked up from his menu. "You see the Lakers last night?"

Had they not been in public, Harvey might have leapt across the table and strangled him right then and there. Instead he asked, "You know what you want yet?"

"What are you having?"

Harvey wished Rick would hurry up and get back from the bathroom. He hated eating alone with Alan. The man was incapable of conversing in an intelligent manner. Every third sentence was some nonsense about something or other. He genuinely didn't know because he'd stopped listening to Alan prattle years ago, the mere sound of his voice shutting down Harvey's ear canal. He'd have dumped him years ago, but Paul loved the kid.

The waitress stopped at their table, an exasperated look on her face at the sight of Harvey smoking. Her nametag read Leslie and was turned upside down, a pretty fair analogy for Leslie's life. He thought about putting his cigarette out, but only for a moment.

"We'll need another minute," Harvey said.

"You see any ashtrays?"

"Don't worry your pretty little head about it, Sweets. I'll make do."

Leslie wasn't about to let it slide. "I'm finishing up a double, cigarette smoke makes me nauseous, it's against the goddamned law, so do me a fucking favor and stub it out on your forehead before I bring my meathead short-order guys out here to do it for you." Leslie smiled pleasantly and switched to the sweet, dulcet tones of her workplace persona and asked, "Now, you want to hear the specials?"

Harvey took a long drag and decided eating was more important than beating the hell out of some minimum-wage wetback. He stubbed out the butt on the table and made a point of staring at the waitress's chest.

"Absolutely."

Leslie sighed inwardly, it was just her luck to be finishing up at a table like this, but she went ahead and recited the same special they'd been running for the last three years, the breaded catfish with scalloped potatoes, a combination which one December night alone had sent four patrons to the emergency room with food poisoning, yet miraculously did nothing to change the restaurant's standing with the department of health nor alter the cook's less than meticulous preparation of the dish. Leslie herself ate her meals at home.

"What's the soup of the day?" Alan asked.

"Cream of mushroom."

"Is it any good?"

"Couldn't tell you."

Harvey said, "We'll need a few minutes."

Leslie rolled her eyes and walked off to take her break. "Take your time," she mumbled. "You've only been here fifteen minutes."

Say goodbye to your tip, Harvey thought.

"Leonard nuts all over a three with two guys in his face and we lose. What the fuck?"

"You gonna get the soup, Alan?"

"Nah. What are you having?"

A fucking nervous breakdown, you idiot. *Thank Christ*, Harvey thought, *Rick's back*. He shouldn't be all that upset. It was his idea for the three of them to have dinner together, after all. Get away from Paul, who probably was having a nervous breakdown, or at least a mid-life crisis. Pete was about as bad, but at least that was understandable. That wife of his would drive any man into fits of depression. He should just beat the hell out of her and get it out of his system.

"That waitress is brutally hot, Man," Rick said. "Try not to piss her off, yeah Harv?"

Too late for that. "I'll do my best, Rick."

"Club sandwich," Alan intoned.

"Hurrah."

If Alan noticed Harvey's sarcasm, he certainly gave no indication. "I'm gonna hit the head."

Harvey watched him get up and walk away in wonder at the magnitude of some people's obliviousness. When he looked back to the table, Rick was smirking at him.

"Yeah?"

"Relax, man. It's not the secret of the century your opinion of Alan ain't the highest."

"Is that a fact?"

Rick shrugged, that same smirk still on his face. Rick had never given any indication of a thinker, but then again, he'd never been smug either. Tonight is going to be more interesting than I thought.

"You got plans after this?" Harvey asked.

"I figured me and the waitress'll head off to her place."

"A good decision. I have been to your place."

"Been kinda antsy lately. Things and whatnot."

"I reckon so."

"Been thinkin' about the future a lot."

"Oh, yeah?"

Alan plopped down next to Rick. "I think I'll just have a burger. What about you?"

"Just a salad for me," Rick said.

"A salad?" Alan asked, surprised.

"Well, I've been wanting to cut out certain things from my diet lately," Rick answered, looking pointedly at Harvey. "For my health."

There it was. A simple proposition, laid out for Harvey's approval. He'd considered leaving before, certainly the thought had crossed his mind after Mr. Point and Shoot had entered the building. He'd gone home after the last one, had some whiskey, watched some shitty reality dating show, and come to the realization that a homicidal maniac at the helm gave him hardly a moment's pause. His job hadn't changed much. The money was the same, the hours were, if anything, better. What the hell did he really care? Striking out on his own would be a gigantic hassle. Too much responsibility, one headache after another. No, Paul was fine and dandy Mr. Handy as far as Harvey was concerned.

Everyone else was another story altogether. And now Rick steps up to the plate swinging a two-by-four for my viewing pleasure. He probably wasn't looking at Paul, Rick was lazy and shiftless, two of his more reliable qualities. He wanted responsibility less than Harvey. So it came to Pete or Alan. Actually, Harvey mused, perhaps it came to Pete and Alan. Alan was a fool, Pete was not. Neither was irreplaceable. Maybe it *was* time to strike off in a new direction. He'd have to remember not to underestimate Rick again.

The waitress came back, pad in hand. Harvey gave her his most conciliatory smile and said, "Rick, I know just what you mean."

Chapter 14

THE FEDERAL Bureau of Investigations building, located at 11000 Wilshire Boulevard, was the happy recipient of a dozen or so protests a year. Today's unruly gathering was displeased at the role the United States played in the recent clash between Albanians and Turks in northern Greece. Colorful signs abounded with such choice phrases as, 'U.S. policy promotes genocide,' 'Isolationism equals inequality' and Susan's new favorite, 'Albania rules, USA drools.'

It took Susan and Bob fifteen minutes to work their way through the crowd, their obvious destination resulting in some rather unpleasant and crudely formed sentences being lobbed their way. Veronica met them in the lobby and escorted them past security and up to the eighth floor. Her cubicle was as much a shrine to Hello Kitty as it was to law enforcement. There was even a Hello Kitty stuffed animal with a utility belt, sunglasses and a baton in its paw.

Bob picked it up, turning it over in his hands, a big grin on his face. "My aunt would love this. Where'd you get that?"

"San Francisco. I honestly believe that if Hello Kitty was exported to every nation and remote corner of the world, there'd be an end to terrorism. Have you ever heard of someone suicide bombing with a Hello Kitty t-shirt and bumper sticker? You never will."

"Veronica, you said you had something for us."

"Patience, Child. Let's talk about your fella here."

Susan turned noticeably pale, her eyes shifting uncomfortably. "Oh, please, no."

"Oh, don't be a pill. He's gorgeous. Does he have a brother?"

"No, I'm an only child," Bob answered, looking to enter into the conversation.

"You told me he was adorable, but damn, no wonder I haven't been able to reach you lately."

"You think I'm adorable?" Bob asked Susan, grinning at her discomfort.

"If anybody wants me, I'm going to be outside," Susan said to no one in particular.

"No need to get touchy," Veronica said.

"She does that with you, too, huh?" he asked.

"Yeah, but if you get a few drinks in her, she loosens right up."

"I found that—" Bob started.

"Please stop talking now," Susan said, pressing her hands to her ears.

"I think you're making her uncomfortable," Bob whispered to Veronica.

"It can't be me. It has to be you."

"I don't think so."

"I'm thinking yes."

"But I'm so adorable."

"I knew this was a bad idea," Susan groaned.

Veronica's computer sprang to life and an image of Paul appeared on the screen, along with his vitals.

"Here it is," Veronica said. "Paul Costa. Just had to make sure it wasn't one of those silly classified thingees. I'll email this over to you. You owe me dinner and details. Or I could just use my imagination."

"I do owe you one, Veronica. I'll call you."

"You're leaving already? Wham bam thank you ma'am?"

"I don't recall saying thank you."

After she dropped Bob off at his apartment, ignoring his repeated requests to accompany her to the station, Susan went straight to see Ortiz.

"I've got a name," Susan said.

Ortiz grinned and replied, "You have many names around here. My favorite is-"

"Check your email. Paul Costa."

Reluctantly, he clicked on his inbox. His mood darkened when he opened the attached file. "Did you run that picture through our system? If you did, you are in serious goddamn trouble, and don't think for a second that being cute and flippant will get you out of it."

"You think I'm cute, Ortiz?"

"Only when you're being flippant," he said, calming down a little. "What's the name again?"

"Paul Costa."

"You went outside, right?"

"I did."

"You sure?"

"Everything on the up and up. My word--"

"Is like oak, yeah, I know. Call me in a couple days."

Amy should have seen it coming. Before she ever opened the front door, before the policemen in cheap suits entered her immaculately cared for neo-classical dining room with oak cabinets and a slightly uneven dining room table, and certainly before her husband proposed a second wedding in Las Vegas. All the signs were there. There was no mistaking it. Paul had lost his mind. And the problem with crazy people is, first and foremost, they do crazy things. Amy could deal with violence. She understood cruelty. But she had never been able to adapt to uncertainty.

The detectives asked to see Paul, though they declined to state their purpose. Amy led them into the living room and offered them coffee, which they declined, which was fine with her since she didn't know how to use the coffeemaker. She went upstairs to deliver what should have been dire news, especially given the recent actions Paul was about to divulge. Like everything else of late for Amy, his reaction was not what it should have been.

"There are two policemen downstairs asking for you. What's going on?"

Surprise, fear, rage or a combination of all three would have been normal reactions for her husband of eighteen years. Instead, Paul looked positively ecstatic at the prospect of law enforcement in his house, as if a head of state or long lost relative had just arrived for a dinner party.

"Are they armed?" he whispered to Amy, trying to peer over her shoulder.

"I didn't ask, but they're cops, so my guess is, yeah, they're packing. Why are they here?"

"It's not what you think, Sweets. The business is fine."

"Then why are they here?"

"Oh, probably because I've been killing people a lot lately. Don't worry, I'll get rid of them in a minute and then we can spend the afternoon together. I was thinking maybe a picnic?"

He kissed her on the cheek and headed downstairs. Amy, dumbstruck, watched him go. It wasn't until she heard his feet hit the staircase that she thought to herself, *I wonder what exactly he meant by get rid of?*

"Gentlemen," Paul said, greeting Ortiz and Alekhov

warmly, shaking hands with each man in turn. A firm handshake was a thoroughly underrated method of social intimidation. A flimsy grip denotes weakness of character and places a man in a precarious state of constant overcompensation. If one squeezes too hard, there is substantial risk of cowing the recipient and exposing your own strength at an inopportune moment. A good handshake is firm and quick, without the slightest pain for the recipient but with clear knowledge to both parties that such an end is only a false word away. Shaking hands is much like blackmail. Intimidation is only useful if the threat of violence is recognized, but once the subject is pushed too far, disaster will soon befall all involved. Paul practiced shaking hands in front of the mirror at least twice a week.

"Paul Costa?" Ortiz asked, impressed by Paul's stature. Just shy of six feet, Ortiz felt dwarfed by Paul's defensive-lineman frame.

"In the flesh. What can I do for you?"

"We're investigating a murder outside of Jerry's Deli on the fourteenth of last month."

"The fourteenth?" Paul interrupted.

"Yes."

"I was there. I had a guy come down and take a statement a couple days later. But you already know that, right? Why else would you be here, right?" Paul laughed good-naturedly. "Did my wife offer you guys a drink or something? Soda maybe?"

"No, thank you," Ortiz declined.

"We've been collecting witness statements and were wondering if you might have anything more to help us," Alekhov said. "We're at a bit of a dead end, I must confess."

"I'm really sorry, but I don't think I'll be of much help. It's just like I told the other officer. I ate lunch, not a great meal, by the way, and then I left."

"You didn't see anything?" asked Ortiz.

"I didn't see anybody get slaughtered out back, if that's what you're asking."

Ortiz studied Paul's reaction, but if the man was faking innocence, he was a born actor.

"That's awful, I'm sorry," Paul said, regret and sorrow filling his cheeks. "No, no, I'm sorry, I didn't see anything."

"Were you dining with anyone?"

"A friend, Alan, but he left pretty quick, he just stopped by for a minute."

"His last name?"

"Sumpter. He lives near Koreatown, down by sixth and Alexandria."

He made a note in his Palm Pilot and looked to Alekhov, to see if his partner had anything further. Alekhov grimaced and shook his head no. Ortiz turned back to Paul and handed him his business card.

"We appreciate your time. Listen, let me leave you our card, get back to us if anything comes to you."

Paul took the card and examined it, just long enough to feign interest.

"I sure will."

"Hey, what kind of soda do you have?" Alekhov asked.

"Uh, I think Coke and maybe a root beer."

Paul opened the refrigerator and rooted around while Ortiz glanced at his watch, more than a little anxious to be on their way. Ortiz was punctual and rigid, a little too much so, Alekhov had always felt. Tweaking him a bit by snarking a soda from some witness was just the sort of fun that made partnering with the man such a delight.

"What kind of root beer?" he asked, disregarding Ortiz and his increasingly annoyed stare. If Paul noticed, he gave no indication.

"Stewarts."

"Oh, I love that stuff. Would you mind?"

"My pleasure," Paul said, taking a bottle from the back.

Amy waited until the sound of the policemen's car had faded into the distance before coming back downstairs. So many questions on her mind, she hardly knew where to begin grouping and then ordering them in terms of importance and relevance and heaven knew how she could even broach the subject with Paul. She barely recognized the man.

Was there any way out of this mess? What sort of divorce settlement could she expect? Judges simply had to be sympathetic to the wife of a murderer. Her fake drug addiction was sure to come out, which didn't bode well for her chances. Plus, Paul was the sort of man who might view a separation as grounds for death. Did she want to be single at thirty-nine? She was still a pretty woman, but that couldn't last much longer, no matter how many times she went under the knife.

I've been killing people a lot? What the hell kind of thing is that to say to your wife? Any decent person keeps such matters hidden. Paul had killed people, Amy knew, but he had never discussed the matter with her. Were his newly attentive and homicidal nature connected? What was she supposed to think, or worse, do? She couldn't go on this way that was for sure.

She found him holding two bottles of wine above a picnic basket. He looked troubled, a frown on his forehead when Amy stepped into the kitchen with her first salvo of questions at the ready. He beat her to the punch.

"Honey, do you think red or white?"

At a complete loss, she found her mind staring down from above, watching her body standing and staring in abject despair. Amy could come up with only one question, and in retrospect, it was not the perfect choice.

"Maybe just some soda?"

"I gave the last of it to the detective."

Amy sighed.

Alan waited until the policemen drove off before calling Harvey. It wasn't that he didn't trust the other guys, they were perfectly all right fellas, but Harvey just seemed to always know what to do.

"Harvey? It's Alan."

"What can I do for you today?"

"Police just came by."

"What'd you do?"

"I didn't do anything. It's about Paul."

"Do tell."

"That guy at the Deli he clipped."

"What'd you tell them?"

"That I had stopped by to have a quick lunch with Paul that day. That's it."

"Don't wig out on me, Alan."

Alan didn't think he was 'wigging' out at all. Harvey seemed nervous, which wasn't like him at all. "What's going on?"

"Don't talk to them again."

"They're cops."

"They can't force you. You sure you didn't tell them anything else?"

"Of course not."

"I'm worried, Alan. I think Paul's in real trouble."

"They have something on him?"

"Why else would they see you? He's been a little loose lately, it doesn't surprise me the cops are looking around."

"Yeah, I guess. I mean, yeah, it was only a matter of time, I guess. What do we do?"

"Keep your guard up. Try and keep Paul from making mistakes. Don't let the police in, no matter how trivial the matter in question might be."

"Totally. Thanks, man."

"My pleasure."

The bluish tinted pill was the size of a baby aspirin, its edges rough and uneven, as if advertising the character of its content. Amy admired the power of such a small thing as she felt its complete lack of weight in her palm. A brave new world awaited her, and all she needed was a glass of water.

Locking herself in the downstairs bathroom in order to begin a Percodan addiction was never something Amy expected or desired. Her life had become complicated, and complications were not part of the overall equation. Marrying Paul had been simple. Living as a housewife with no chores was easy. Creating drama by overextending her Discover card and faking drug addiction was both simple and easy. Living with a crazy man who treated her with kindness and dignity and love was just not acceptable. Married men had affairs to satisfy a mid-life crisis, they did not ignite a comfortably stale marriage with gifts and considerate sex.

Some women marry for love. Not many, Amy surmised, but surely some. Amy was not one of them. Paul was a man of many admirable traits and most of those resided at the First National Trust on Sepulveda Boulevard. With a little luck, she had forty years of good living left. If her options were reduced to a marriage of equals between two committed loving partners, or a drug-induced haze of borderline insanity, then the choice was clear. She was going to need a glass of water.

"What's the good word?" Susan asked.

"We talked with him."

"I don't like any of those words."

"Here's the problem," Ortiz continued. "Kessler was shot and killed fairly quickly. Not one witness statement taken can account for the whereabouts of every person in the joint for a two to four minute period. Your man has a direct alibi. We crosschecked it with the other statements and we just can't place him at the scene."

"I don't like any of those words any more than the previous ones."

"We went out and confirmed the man's alibi."

"Just a pit stop?"

"Alan is a contractor out of Pasadena. He was there, he was with Paul, he had a tuna on rye. All we needed was confirmation. If something develops, we'll pursue it."

"I think a more exhaustive interrogation might be in order. You know, like a session involving more than one question involving face to face contact."

"We can't question him, Susan. And you know it."

Susan knew exactly why Paul could not be questioned. It was protocol, protocol she herself had been bound by since its inception her third year in robbery homicide. She went ahead and asked, as innocently as she could without smirking, "Why not?"

"It's not a lead. You know the city directives on manpower expenditures on—"

"It's a lead. Trust me."

"Do I even need to make a sarcastic joke about taking your word to the mayor and receiving a big thumbs up and a blank check in return? I can't do anything. Not won't. Can't."

"The guy has a record."

"Listen, I'm a believer. I really am. Something is not right with this guy, I can feel it. I don't know exactly what it is, but it's definitely something. The Susan Ciarelli ship has sailed and I'm on board. I swear. I'm just telling you what I can't do."

"What can you do?"

"Interesting question. It would be wrong of me to call a civilian and tell them on the phone the name of a witness slash suspect's alibi. But if I were to have the last name and an address on my desk, and I were to go get a soda with money from someone who had promised to buy me a soda on a previous occasion, then I fail to see my culpability in the matter. So…" Ortiz trailed off, his less than subtle exposition finished.

Susan dug in her pocket. "I don't have any change."

"They take bills, Ciarelli. A five if you have it."

The house was a short walk away. Susan took her time getting there.

"Don't be so edgy."

"I'm not edgy." Susan was indeed edgy and knew she was doing a bad job of pretending she wasn't and that only served to make her edgier. She sighed. "I'm a little edgy."

"There is nothing illegal about our actions," Bob reminded her.

"It's a gray area."

"Really?"

Susan nodded.

"How gray?"

Susan shrugged.

"I'm not quite there on reading your non-verbal signs."

Susan rolled her eyes playfully. Bob laughed.

"Yeah, that one I got, thank you, Miss Subtlety. My question I guess is whether or not you'll get into hot water over this."

"I'll be fine." Susan was not so sure that this was true, but didn't feel the need to burden Bob with that knowledge.

"Good."

She laughed to herself. "I can't believe I'm here."

"In a general sense, I can't help but agree with you."

"How about in a specific sense?"

"It's hard to imagine anything else. With this many clothes on, anyway."

Susan ignored him and knocked on the thick oak door. Her hopes for the day were threefold. First, and perhaps most important, she hoped the day did not end with her arrest, imprisonment and expulsion from high society. Second, and not far behind, was her hope that the gentleman on the other side of the door might assist in compiling a case against Paul Costa. Thirdly, she desperately wanted to avoid confronting the nagging belief that she really liked Bob and that they were headed inexorably for a serious, long-term relationship that would crush her when it ended in disaster. She really shouldn't have slept with him a second time. That was so going to give him the wrong idea.

Chapter 15

"WHO ARE you, again?" asked the thin man wearing an expensive watch. Susan might not have noticed the timepiece save for Alan's tendency to scratch his nose when nervous. It was a tic he'd developed over many years, becoming so ingrained in his behavior, he had not the faintest clue it ever occurred. If he'd known, he would have immediately had an excellent explanation for his poker losses and renewed appreciation for his wife's strenuous objections to his insistent wearing of his 1983 Swiss diamond encrusted watch, who fervently believed such displays of wealth ostentatious and elitist.

Susan said, "We're investigating the death of Karl Kessler."

Alan shrugged nonchalantly and motioned them inside. "Shoes off, okay? It's the carpet, I just had it serviced."

The thick shag was, at a lenient minimum, fifteen years out of date. It was, however, very shaggy, and the scent of lemon emanating from it was not unpleasant. Bob stepped out of his loafers and Susan removed her sandals. The feel of the rug on her feet was exquisite. Eyes wide, Susan stared at the ground in disbelief. It occurred to her she had never stood on shag carpet without shoes on. This was really quite something. She took a few steps and found each one more pliant and giving than the last. An eyesore, no question, but one can always dim the lights.

"Kessler...the old guy at the Deli?"

"Yes. You were there, we understand."

"How do you know that?"

"We have our sources," Bob said ominously.

"What would those sources be?"

Susan interjected. "You were there, right?"

"Yeah, yeah I was there. I didn't really see anything."

"Well, we're more interested in this man. You had lunch with him the day Kessler was killed. "

She handed Alan a photocopy of the sketch of Paul. He set it down with barely a glance. He stood up and walked into the kitchen.

"You guys want a drink or something?"

"No, thanks. We were just wondering if you might walk us through the day."

Alan strode back into the living room, automatic pistol in hand. Bob sat, frozen, stunned. Susan stood up and held out her hands in warning.

"I'm a police officer."

"So?"

Alan did his best to pull the trigger, but found the gun strangely unaccommodating. Like any professional, he crinkled up his nose in perplexed curiosity and raised the gun closer to his face for heightened scrutiny. If he'd had a little more time, he would've noticed the safety latch still in the 'on' position. When he retold the story to Paul, he left out this tiny little salient detail, which he was sure would have led to much harassment from his friends.

As it was, he had barely enough time to look from the malfunctioning weapon to a charging Susan. Alan had played high school football, even made second team all-city his junior year. He found Susan's tackling technique vastly superior to most starting linebackers. Still, she landed awkwardly, and he seized the upper hand as they wrestled for control of the gun. He twisted and elbowed Susan onto her back, knocking the wind out of her. Ripping the gun free, Alan managed a victory smile before the cheap knock-off vase Bob tattooed him in the face with ended the skirmish and left Alan with a nasty cut needing eight stitches to close running from his left eye down to his ear.

"What's it like when you're actually on duty?" Bob asked Susan, the shattered remnants of the vase still in his hand.

She crawled out from under an unconscious Alan and vomited all over the freshly cleaned carpet in response.

Baker was less than thrilled, a fact he made sure to express to Susan the instant she poked her head through his door. She wore the cheeky smile she saved only for her most ingratiating moments. These were usually reserved for his office, or at least he fervently hoped this was the case.

"Did you miss me?" she asked.

"Do you have any idea how much harder my life is with you in it?"

"I'll take that as a yes."

"Are you punishing me? It wasn't me that suspended you. I stood up for you."

"Really?"

"Well, I didn't say anything bad about you, if that's what your snippy tone implies."

"My tone is not snippy," Susan replied in an even snippier tone.

"I want you to go to press with this," Baker said, handing her a piece of paper with the words 'NO COMMENT'.

"Bolding it was a nice touch," Susan said, unable to repress the appreciative smile.

"Thank you. Now get out."

"Were you this terse when I was actually working here?"

"Worse. Time off has made you soft and sensitive."

Susan gave an undignified snort. Baker cracked a smile for the first time since receiving news his favorite homicide detective avoided getting herself killed fighting some idiot contractor at the same time he was fighting with the vending machine over a bag of Fritos.

"Charm school just never stops paying dividends, does it Ciarelli?"

She found Bob waiting patiently by the vending machines, eyeing the bullpen thoughtfully. It made Susan feel vulnerable, him knowing where she worked. She liked the mystery of it. When people learned how boring her work really was on a day-to-day basis, it always took the luster out of her job. Distance was crucial to maintaining the illusion that her life was exciting. Although, to be fair, she had been assaulted twice in the last month. And she had been to his place of business.

"What's the dealy?" Bob asked.

"Did you say dealy?"

"Yeah, it's like deal but with a Y."

"I'm going to be saying no comment in deference to my once and future commanding officer. You may say anything you wish if questioned."

"Can I tell people how sexy you are when you first wake up in the morning?"

"No."

"How about—"

"No."

"Not even—"

"Especially not even."

"Fair enough."

Susan eyed the vending machine hungrily.

"Buy me a Snickers, will you?"

"Anything for my girl. You really think the press is going to come after you?"

"They've probably been chomping at the bit to follow up on my last misadventure," Susan said ruefully.

"Are you Susan Cianelli?" asked the intrepid young reporter Bobbi Lang.

Four years at Sarah Lawrence and a master's degree from UPenn had earned Bobbi a grand total of three nondescript obituaries in the Indianapolis News, a now defunct newspaper. Freelancing for the LA Weekly didn't pay her anything, but it presented a genuine opportunity for advancement. I was far and away the most successful free weekly 'zine in the country. Writers had begun their professional lives in the cramped office on Sunset and ended a stellar career in such varied places as the Boston Globe, the New Yorker and the Arab News. It was even money in Vegas whether her parents would stop supporting her before she was hired by a major publisher, Bobbi herself unsure whether or not to place twenty bucks on red or black.

She'd seen the news clips of the young, blood-splattered detective with the potty mouth and figured a good story once is a good story twice. There might have been a bit more competition for the story had not a Long Beach grand theft auto rookie been caught earlier that day with his pants down, literally, and two pounds of cocaine spread around the house of a male prostitute.

"Ciarelli," Susan corrected automatically.

Bobbi checked her notes. The name didn't sound quite right. "Are you sure? I mean, of course you are, it's just...you know what? It's not important. The important thing is you're here and I can ask you some questions. If that's okay with you."

Bob made a point to scan the horizon before his gaze settled on Bobbi. He turned dramatically to Susan. "This must be the surging throng you predicted."

"Shut up infinity."

"I was wondering if you have any comment on the events that transpired earlier today?" Bobbi asked.

"I do not. Thank you."

"Are you sure?"

'I'm sure."

"I could really use the story," Bobbi said, trying not to sound too desperate.

"No comment."

"Can I give you my number?"

Susan took the proffered card and pocketed it, nodding curtly to excuse Bobbi. Bob watched his feminine namesake leave, his feelings a little bruised.

"Why didn't she ask about me?"

"She's after news."

"You're a little meaner today than usual."

"Sorry."

"You can make it up to me with sex."

"I don't really see that happening."

"We just barely survived a near death experience."

"What a fabulously awful sentence."

"We should celebrate."

"How about sleep?"

"Really?"

"Very tired."

"Nap?"

"Very nap."

"Can I at least tuck you in, grandma?"

Susan stifled a giggle.

"You can go tuck—"

"Thanks for bailing me out."

"I didn't," Paul said. "Harvey here, of his own accord, acting independently, put up your two hundred fucking grand bail."

Alan nodded glumly from the backseat. The seat belt was cutting into his waist, and no amount of squirming was helping. An irritated look from Paul brought all movement to an abrupt halt.

"I'm going to need that back, too," Harvey deadpanned. Alan wanted to laugh, but wasn't sure it was appropriate.

"Well, you want to tell us why you tried to kill two people in your fucking living room?"

"They had a picture of you," Alan said simply, as if nothing else need be said. Paul waited a few moments before pursuing.

"A picture?"

"Some printout, but it was you all right. They were asking questions about you and that old guy you plugged at the Deli."

"So you tried to shoot them?"

"Cops had just been by to talk to me, what the hell was I supposed to think? I was trying to protect you!"

"So you tried to shoot them."

"Seemed like a good idea at the time."

"It fucking what now?"

"They were fingering you for the job!"

"What are you, an idiot?"

The car came to a stop in front of Alan's house. Paul and Harvey waited expectantly for a response from the front seat.

Somewhere in the back recesses of his mind, Alan knew there was some snappy comeback about mistaking the appropriate circumstances for indiscriminately blowing people away, but he couldn't quite come up with it, which, in the end, was probably for the best. Apologizing was the move.

"I freaked out, I don't know. Fuck. They showed me the picture and I just freaked out. I'm sorry."

"Damn, Alan, it's all right," Paul said, trying to reassure him. "Relax, we're going to take care of it."

Alan let Harvey and Paul inside, reluctantly closing the door behind him. He wanted very badly to be left alone.

"What can I do?" Alan asked, trying his best to keep the note of desperation to a minimum.

"For now, nothing. Just lay low, stay put. Let things cool off for a while. Cool?"

"Yeah, no worries. Thanks Paul."

Harvey noticed the ugly stain in the carpet by the remnants of the shattered vase.

"What happened to your carpet?"

"Are you awake?" Bob whispered softly.

She didn't stir in the slightest. Whispering clearly wasn't going to get the job done. Bob prodded her gently.

"Susan?"

Still nothing. Now she was just faking. He smiled. Faking sleep to avoid a crazy person was his specialty. How dare she try and horn in on his territory. Who did she think she was? A valuable lesson must be learned.

"I was thinking about what we might do next. I think we should tail Paul. Follow him, get the dirt on him, so to speak. I'm not doing anything tomorrow, we could start then. And later, I was thinking maybe we could get married. How are you on kids? I've always thought the spare the rod spoil the child philosophy a bit too lenient. We don't want them to grow up bleeding heart liberals, do we? I've picked out matching rings and I know a guy who can marry us real legal like. I know a great place in Santa Cruz where we can grow old together and raise wildebeests."

Was that a smile? It was hard to tell with Susan. She was more expressive when she was actually sleeping than when she was pretend sleeping. He had to be a little impressed.

"You're pretty when you're laying in the bed with your eyes closed."

"Lying."

"I am not. You are one beautiful lady."

"No, dope, you're not laying, you're lying. Chickens lay."

"People lie."

"And how."

She opened her eyes with a grin. Bob stroked her hair, trying to meet her eyes with his, but it was a futile effort. She was still shy with him when they were alone. The mere fact that she was here was going to have to be enough, and Bob felt strangely elated when he realized that such a trifle, in point of fact, was.

"I was a little groggy earlier."

"I was a stallion."

"Never say that again. I'm iffy about your choice of words in general, but that one should be eliminated immediately from your lexicon."

"Do you want something to snack on?"

"No."

"Do you want to get a head start on tomorrow?"

"The rodding of our future children or the following of our prime suspect?"

"I have the utmost confidence in our ability to do both."

"Let's wait until tomorrow."

"Okay."

Susan's stomach was growling. If she couldn't fake sleeping, she might as well eat. "What do you have to eat?"

"I can make French Toast."

Susan perked up. "Ooh."

Chapter 16

IT WAS not hard to infer from the black cloud of depression that hung around the room that Paul was in a particularly dour state of mind. It was not at all uncommon for Paul, especially of late, to spend the early part of their weekly meetings laughing and joking with the boys. Today held none of that frat boy promise, and Pete had not the faintest clue as to why he suddenly wished he were anywhere else in the world other than at this place in this moment. Getting old is not easy.

Paul stood up at Pete's entrance and beckoned him forward. Harvey and Rick melted into the background, only increasing Pete's deep sense of foreboding. Paul's arm snaked around Pete's shoulder, forcing him to repress a shudder. The last time Paul held him this close, he had been 'asked' to burn down a widower's townhouse. He led Pete into the hallway, closing the door behind them.

"Pete, my old war horse. I need a favor."

"Sure, boss. What's going on?"

"I just bailed Alan out of jail. He tried to shoot a cop or something. Anyway, I just called over to his place to see how he's holding up and he's had a good stiff drink and the wife's put him to bed. I need you to head over there and kill him. The wife, too, if she sees you."

Pete wasn't sure quite how to react. He'd killed before. Twice. He certainly hadn't enjoyed it, but it wasn't as bad as the layman might think. Both nights, he had made it home before nine. Besides, two fewer drug addicts ripping off old women on the subway and the world was a better place for it as far as he was concerned. But murdering a friend and his wife? That just seemed wrong. Maybe he'd heard him wrong.

"Sorry, boss. Didn't quite catch that."

"I know it's a load to drop on you, but it's for all of us. The man squealed on us, dropped a dime on every one of us. We're all getting indicted, and if he gets into a courtroom, we're gonna be missing daylight for the next ten to thirty years. Without him, there's no case. I don't like it any more than you do, in fact, it makes me sick, but it's gotta be done. Call me when it's done."

"Couldn't Harvey…" Pete didn't like the sound of desperation that had crept into his voice, and Paul dashed his hopes with a quick shake of his finger.

"Not this time. I'm gonna be at the Bounty, and as far as anyone else knows, you will be too. We'll have a few drinks and carry on tomorrow. I owe you one on this, Pete. I won't forget it."

Pete had been to Alan's house many times, mostly because of the exquisitely cared-for circa 1953 vintage pool table with fringe trim and all the original billiard balls save for number twelve. He had played pool as a kid, but when he came to the realization that women preferred team sports heroes to people who spend eight hours a day practicing under fluorescents, his interest in playing professionally died a quick death. Alan had rekindled his love of the game after landing his wife and he was not a bad player if he did say so himself.

However, Alan was not a good player. In fact, he was astonishingly bad. It was criminal for a man to own a work of art such as he had and treat it with such abuse. It was like the man who owned an authentic, certificate of authenticity stamped Elvis Presley guitar and was unable to play a Tom Petty song. After winning seventy some-odd consecutive games, Pete was determined to throw Alan a bone. Scratching no less than four times failed to turn the odds in Alan's favor, and when he accidentally banked the eight ball in off the rail, Pete managed to claim yet another victory.

The question on his mind as he made the short trek from his Porsche up the walkway to the front door, pistol with silencer attached ready in hand, was not how he could remain undefeated at eight ball despite every effort to the contrary, but whether he would actually be able to murder a person who had no clue he might very well be the worst pool player in the history of civilized man. And his wife.

Not sure of the answer, Pete rang the doorbell.

Throwing darts is an art form. At least, that's how Charlie liked to describe it. To simply play necessitates a board and a dart, to excel requires proper technique, skill, practice, and strategy. Charlie's parents had given him a set when he was eight, its use restricted to the basement, which was just fine with Charlie. Growing up in Montana fourteen miles from the nearest kid his age, and thirty miles from the nearest gas station meant isolation in a cramped, damp fourteen by twenty-two room was less a punishment than it might have otherwise sounded. It left plenty of time to perfect the overhand two-point grip and an aggressive stance on the metal versus plastic dart debate. With age, Charlie was still of the opinion the general public was sadly lacking in proper appreciation of all things darts.

He had thought joining the police force would have given him ample opportunity to meet others of a similar bent with the time and inclination to engage in such activities, but it was not to be. Policemen, it turned out, were boring, lazy people, mimicking the general public to a depressing degree. His dartboard in the basement went unused save for the efforts of his girlfriend, Mary, who, despite a questionable interest, engaged Charlie in epic tournaments on a weekly basis. Reflecting on his relationship as he rang the doorbell, Charlie knew he really ought to marry that girl. He was never going to find someone better.

The double homicide awaiting him inside turned his attention elsewhere.

The Bounty was a squalid little bar on Wilshire Avenue, not far from the hotel where Robert Kennedy was assassinated. Locals favored it for its lack of pretension and cheap shots. Paul liked it for the dark lighting, kitschy décor and potently deep fried cuisine. He sat as still as he was able, given the circumstances, huddled in a corner booth with Harvey. Drinking with Harvey, who clearly did not share his appreciation of the bar, was growing increasingly tiresome.

"He should have been back by now."

"Ease back a little, Harv."

Harvey grunted noncommittally and lit up a cigarette. Paul blanched at the sight.

"Put that out, would you?" Paul asked.

"They don't enforce it here."

"I don't give a shit, I want you to put it out. It's bothering me."

"Since when?"

"Do you have any idea what you're doing to me?"

"To you?"

"Your cancer stick there is worse for me and every schlub in here than it is for you. Go outside and get some fresh air while you prematurely age."

"What the in the hell are you on about? I've seen you smoke fucking stogies the size of a gator, for Christ's sake."

"That was then. I'm trying to be healthier. Cut out all the

toxins. I had a protein shake today at Jamba Juice."

Harvey did his best not to snigger in contempt, stubbing out his cigarette instead. He had enough on his mind without getting in a pissing contest with fucking Jane Fonda next to him. He checked his watch and grimaced.

"I could give him a call, if you'd like."

"Either he comes, or he doesn't."

Harvey took a long drink and did his best not to mock Paul's newfound sensibilities, just saying diplomatically, "Good to know."

His breathing got a little easier ten minutes later as Rick ambled in through the western style saloon double doors. His pulse rate evened out, watching Rick say a quick hello to the bartender. It must have gone well, Harvey reasoned, since he took his sweet time walking back to their booth, his interest more in the aging bartender's rack than in reporting the news. Man chases too much goddamned tail.

Rick sat down, spreading his arms over the back of the booth. "It's done."

"Good. I made the call five minutes ago. What was it like?"

"Which one?"

"Alan."

"Didn't say a word. Just stood there with his mouth open all shocked."

"And her?"

"Had some unladylike things to say."

"How many times you shoot 'em?"

"You're not supposed to ask questions like that," Rick said, frowning. "Like asking a woman if she had an orgasm."

Harvey nodded his agreement, draining the last of his bourbon. "Rick's right. It's gauche."

Paul shrugged. "All right. You guys want a beer? I'm buying."

Nina greeted the desk sergeant with open disdain, less for her aggrieved wife status than for Sergeant Harper's close approximation to a seventh-grade bully who had existed for the sole purpose of introducing Nina to the harsh realities of life without the protection of her parents.

"I'm here for my husband, Pete Morell. Where is he?"

"Mrs. Morell, I presume?"

"One in the same."

"Just a moment, please."

Sergeant Harper picked up his phone and punched in a few numbers with a disturbingly fat pinky finger. He spoke in hushed tones, and since it was obvious to Nina she wasn't going to be able to eavesdrop, she took in her surroundings instead. It had been quite a while since she had been in a police station. The last and only time had been at the tender age of twelve over a misunderstanding involving an older boy, a pond and a large quantity of illegal fireworks. The whole event might have been funny save for the dead frogs that floated by the elementary school during recess as a result of her tomfoolery. The detective questioning her had felt bad when she broke down in tears (genuine, because of dead frogs and second graders) and let her go with a not so stern warning.

Nina tapped on the counter impatiently until Sergeant Harper hung up. "When can I get him out of here?"

"Usually there's not any bail set on capital cases, Ma'am."

"I'm sorry, I was clearly talking to myself a moment ago. Maybe you can help me. When can I get my husband out of here?"

"There'll be an arraignment, you'll be notified when. You've got an outside chance at that point, but I wouldn't get your hopes up."

"Thanks."

Nina took a seat on a hard wooden bench near the exit,

staring across the room at a blind man with an overbite. Police officers trudged around in view, some holding files, others cups of coffee. An irate man yelled at Sergeant Harper for a minute, then stormed off in mid-tantrum. A prostitute, or what she hoped was a prostitute given the state of the woman's attire, was rudely pulled into the station. The stench she carried with her was indefinable, probably accrued over a lifetime of misery. Over the next twenty minutes, traffic of the sort moved back and forth languidly, Nina finding herself lost in the gentle monotony of human suffering. Working here must really suck, she surmised.

Two men walking purposefully towards Nina snapped her out of her trance. A mismatched pair if she had ever seen one, she steeled herself and tried to remember the dead frogs, should tears once again be necessary to secure freedom. She should tell them to stock the waiting room with magazines, too.

It was obvious to Nina she was in an interrogation room. She was seated in the only chair, the two detectives flanking her. One stood in the back corner smoking a cigarette, looking to Nina as if an episode of the X-files was being filmed. The other, the shorter, less attractive one, Nina noted, perched on the corner of the cold, metal table in front of her. A large mirror allowed Nina to watch herself while she waited for the detectives to speak. I wonder if somebody is watching me back there? Do they videotape these things? I wish I would've put on some makeup before leaving the house. At least some lipstick. She shifted in her chair impatiently. All right people, let's get this show on the road.

Deciding to break the silence and set the tone for the duration of their time together, Nina asked, "What the hell am I doing here?"

"We wanted a quick word with you," Ortiz said matter-of-factly.

"I want to see my husband."

"He's being brought up, but it'll take a couple minutes."

"Would you like something to drink?" Alekhov asked kindly from the corner. She wondered offhand if they were playing good cop/bad cop.

"I'd like to see my husband."

"May I call you Nina? Great," Ortiz continued without pausing for a response. "Nina, your husband is being charged with two counts of murder, possession of an illegal firearm and was found at the scene of the crime covered in the victim's blood and all of that is just the death penalty portion of the iceberg. I'm guessing there's another ninety percent under the water."

Nina cleared her throat and said, "My husband is innocent." She thought it sounded pretty persuasive, given the circumstances.

"That's not what I'm asking, Mrs. Morell. I don't want you to condemn your spouse. I was just wondering if you can you account for your husband's whereabouts last night?"

"Am I under any obligation to answer that without my lawyer present?"

"None whatsoever."

"Good. As long as the record is clear on that. I wasn't with him, so no, I can't account for my husband's whereabouts."

"Then how do you know he didn't do it?"

It was a very reasonable question. The simple answer was that she did not know whether her husband had shot Alan and his wife in the head. She had been home, taking the new dishwasher for a spin. It was entirely possible that Pete was guilty of every charge levied against him. It was, in fact, likely. The nice officer who called her down to the station had divulged to her that Pete had been caught exiting Alan's house, a gun had been found on his person, blood on his clothes, two dead people inside. He had killed people before, Nina knew. What was the mob line? All part of the business.

She could tell them that Pete left her at ten till eight. She knew he was armed, though that was not in question. He had told her he was going out to 'take care of business' or some such hackneyed phrase that would surely pop up at trial as the smoking gun, no pun intended.

Still, as much as Nina was tempted to send Pete to the gas chamber for being an inconsiderate husband, she just couldn't bring herself to do it. It seemed wrong somehow. Better to play the outraged, aggrieved wife and let matters play themselves out.

"My husband is not capable of doing something like this. It's as simple as that."

"Ma'am, if he confesses now, we'll recommend he gets life with the possibility of parole. That's as good as it's going to get, and barring a phone message from the Pope or President, it ain't likely to get that good again."

"You want me to get him to confess? For his own good? Can I have a toke of what you guys are smoking, or is that frowned upon during business hours? I'm hazy about what the police are allowed to get away with these days."

"Ma'am—"

"Pete and Alan were friends, there is just no possible way. You've got the wrong man." She leaned forward. "Do me a favor, will you? The next time you want to waste your time, go out and get somebody else to try and send my husband to a shithole for the rest of the millennium."

Nina leaned back in the chair and gave Ortiz and Alekhov her sternest, most irate glare. Inside, she was turning cartwheels, barely able to control her glee. Obstructing justice, protecting a murderer (maybe) and doing it all in a way that would make Meryl Streep green with envy. Was it wrong to enjoy moments like this? Surely not. Why else would anybody get married?

"I didn't do it, babe."

"Really?" Nina asked.

"I swear. Paul had me go over there to do it, but he was dead when I got there. I walked in and, yeah, I had the gun, and yeah, I thought about it, but I just couldn't do it. I hate shooting people."

"You do?"

"I never wanted to tell you. I thought you wouldn't think as much of me."

"Why'd you even go over there?"

"I don't know. I think to warn him. The moment I stepped inside and saw the pool table, I knew I couldn't plug him. I found the bodies upstairs."

"That's how you got blood on your clothing?"

"How'd you know about that?"

"The police questioned me."

"What did you tell them?"

"Nothing. And not just any nothing. Fucking brilliant nothing. I was all angry and disbelieving. I'm going to be a great defense witness. Have you talked to the police?"

"Waiting for the lawyer."

"I'll have somebody by tomorrow. I can't bail you out, we don't have enough money."

"Don't worry about it. It'll be harder for them to get to me in here."

"Paul?"

Pete glumly nodded.

"Why'd he want Alan dead?"

"He said it's because Alan squealed on us, but that's horseshit. I don't know the real reason."

"So, you weren't going to kill him?"

"No. I got there and I couldn't go through with it."

He looked sincere. Pete never looked sincere. He occasionally looked sexy. He often looked dumb. She could only remember one occasion when he did look sincere, and that was when he vowed to love honor and obey her. And he had. The realization struck Nina as funny and she let loose a little laugh. Pete reached out his hand to touch the plexiglass. He never cheated on me, he never hit me, he only threw me in the pool once, and that had been a lot of fun. Sure he was obnoxious, insensitive, loud, crude, and boorish but, but…there must be a but in there somewhere. At least a however.

It hit her like a hurricane. She loved him. That was the however. She wanted to laugh, but kept a straight face for Pete's benefit. When this was over, though, she was going to drink a pitcher and a half of something eighty-proof. If the situation were any different, Nina would have moved heaven and hell before admitting to her husband she loved him, but the man was facing a death sentence. He could use the pick me up.

"I love you, Pete. We're going to get through this." The relief on his face was audible and he closed his eyes to keep from crying. "I'll be at the arraignment tomorrow."

"Don't go home. Go straight to a motel. Check in under a different name."

She felt scared for herself for the first time since he had called her from lockup. She'd been so busy contemplating Pete's future, she hadn't even considered there might be repercussions for herself.

"What are you telling me?"

"I don't know. I don't know why Alan was killed, I don't know why Paul set me up. I'm still working it out, and I just don't know. But if Paul's out to hedge on his bets, you don't want to be seen. Better safe than sorry. Promise me."

Stay away from a murdering psychopath with his sights set on lovable little Nina? No problem.

"I promise, Pete."

Chapter 17

"THAT'S A pretty nice house," Bob said in a more envious tone than he would have wished.

Bob and Susan looked out the rolled down driver's side window of his Honda Civic at the Spanish Stucco monstrosity before them. The real estate agent had persuaded Amy it was the house for her by pointing out how much nicer the house was than any other within a two block radius. Paul hadn't been bothered by that fact, either.

"Can we sneak in and look for stuff?" Bob asked.

"Don't make me thump you on the back of the head."

"I was just asking. If you'd rather, we can sit here and talk about your personal life and how we feel about each other."

Susan smiled. "Nice try, but we're still not going in. Why don't you break out the coffee."

"I could do that."

Quiet silence while stalking his father's alleged murderer was not really how Bob envisioned spending his time. Pointless chit-chat with his girlfriend, all the while stalking a potential killer, was much more to his liking. It was obvious she wasn't exactly one hundred percent in favor of action plan number two. That she was there at all was a miracle. Perhaps antagonizing her was not the best road he could take at this particular moment, but sitting around drinking coffee was an even less attractive alternative.

"I think I should be armed."

Susan did her best not to hit Bob over the back of the head. "No."

"I think we should discuss me being armed."

"Have you ever shot a gun?"

"I have not."

"Held one?"

"I had a cap pistol when I was a kid. It didn't work very well, but it looked really cool."

"Well, you know the most important part then."

"All I'm saying is I feel a little dependent. That's all I'm saying."

"I'm not armed either."

"But you're very tough. You clobbered that scumbag like he was a rag doll. That was very cool, by the way."

"I'm not sure that's how I would have described it."

"Well, I meant the beat-em-up portion, not so much the hurling all over the man's carpeting afterwards."

"Thank you. You did hit him with a vase."

"That was neat, wasn't it?"

"Yup."

"Thanks. How long do you imagine we'll have to wait here?"

"Oh, the best part comes when we follow him to places where we will also sit and wait. Waiting is the thing. Hurry up and wait."

"I'm getting that."

"Are you antsy? We've been here ten minutes."

"I'm impatient."

"Tell me about it," Susan said, irritation floating to the surface.

"So I should drink my double mocha caramel thing and hush."

"Yes."

"All right."

Nina opened her book on criminal procedure, bought on the way to the courthouse at a Barnes and Noble with a ridiculously good looking cashier for eighteen dollars and twenty-four cents, and flipped to chapter eleven, The Arraignment Process. The arraignment process, she read with rapt attention, is a relatively simple procedure, in which the accused is presented before a judge and the charges against him made public. The accused enters a plea. The judge then decides whether or not to allow bail and if so, in what amount. A trial date is set. A more simple process is difficult to imagine in the overcrowded, excessively litigious contemporary climate.

She closed the book, satisfied. *That doesn't sound all that bad*, Nina thought. The inept young attorney who was willing to work on a thousand dollar retainer might even be able to handle it.

Checking into the Crazy Eight motel was not the high-point of her life. It wasn't the lowest, either, though that was not cause for celebration, and if anything, reason to lament a number of extremely poor choices and run-ins with alcohol and boys at an early age. The old man who took her cash without question informed her of the fascinating history of the motel, including the origin of the name. It seems a semi-wealthy man of ill repute purchased the land in the early part of the twentieth century and did nothing with it. His heirs, however, sensing the vast profit making potential of an acre of land in the middle of nowhere, opened a hotel. It took Los Angeles a good sixty years to move in around the Crazy Eight, and by that point, the original owners had long since taken hold of their senses and sold to a mildly unbalanced retiree from Fresno who dubbed the motel the Crazy Eight for his place in the order of birth amongst his ten siblings. It was clean, it was out of the way, and like everything else of late, it was going to make a good story down the line. Though not enough to take her mind off recent events, it was a small consolation for the forcible abandonment of her life.

Glenn Thompson had spent eighteen years as a premier defense lawyer in Sacramento before the black robe was made available. Accepting authority over Los Angeles criminal court room two-thirteen was the worst mistake he would ever make, and this included wife number three, a noticeable black mark in his five-marriage run, the current incarnation of Mrs. Right a petite young real estate agent with a penchant for licorice and a talent for handjobs.

It wasn't the cases, it wasn't the hours, it certainly wasn't the pay, for money had ceased to be important since an obnoxious uncle with a good insurance policy had a boating accident and made Glenn independently wealthy before he was thirty. It was living in Los Angeles. Sacramento had been a paragon of virtue compared to the cesspool of filth he was forced to wade through every day, inside the courtroom and out. Homeless people constantly accosting decent citizens, smog that could choke a Chernobyl survivor, traffic that made the blood boil, pretentious arrogant schmucks in pretentious arrogant sushi bars, all of which might have been bearable if it were not for the genuine belief of its citizenry that L.A. was, indeed, the City of Angels. For some bizarre reason, every able-bodied man or woman seemed to shrug their shoulders and smile vacantly past him when the subject was broached. It wouldn't have been so bad if he just had someone to commiserate with on the subject. As it was, all he had was the satisfaction he took from his bumper sticker being read on his commute to work, 'The refuse of the country slides down westward'.

Glenn would have quit ages ago except for the enormous pleasure he took deciding the fates of degenerate low-life scum.

Outside of vacationing for three weeks every year in Puerto Vallarta, it was the only portion of his life that didn't contribute to his constantly escalating blood pressure. A docket with the most wretched refuse ever to grace God's green earth was all that kept Glenn from hitting the snooze button on his alarm clock each and every morning. It was his reason for living.

Glenn took one peek at today's docket and smiled. Today was going to be a good day.

"All rise," said the plump, bored bailiff. "Criminal court part two is now in session. The honorable Glenn Thompson presiding."

Glenn loved making everyone wait. It went back to a childhood fixation on rock candy that was never indulged without the extraction of endless hours of manual labor in the backyard. His mother would taunt him with it, tease him until he could practically taste the smooth surface and delicious center. Then he would end up shoveling mulch for an hour.

"Be seated," he finally said.

The defendant was a hulking monster, guilty as hell in all likelihood. Still, had to maintain the appearance of impartiality.

"Mister Morrell, are you aware of the charges before you?"

Pete stood, bravely, thought Nina, and looked the judge in the eyes.

"I am, sir."

"How do you plead?"

"Not guilty."

Nina reached around the table and grabbed Pete's hand as he sat down. His hand was sweaty and shaking. She squeezed it tight.

"Very well. Mister Prosecutor, your thoughts on bail?"

"The state opposes bail, your honor."

"Yes, I thought it might. Defense?"

"Your honor, my client is an esteemed, vital member of

society—"

"Who happens to have a criminal record and is currently charged with a double homicide. If you're trying to make me laugh, by all means, please continue." Glenn paused, savoring the public defender's discomfort. Poor schlub gets stuck with a double, probably on his first day out of law school from the look of that peach fuzz on his chin.

"No? We'll deny bail, then." Glenn turned to his clerk. "Chuck, what's open?"

Chuck scanned the calendar, wishing he could work for a judge who was just a tad less bitter. It was especially hard on his wife, Tonya, who was subject to a daily rant on the bastardization of the American judicial process. God bless her temperate soul, though, for he would never have the heart to sit through another day without her at the end of it. Maybe I'll bring home a pizza tonight, Chuck thought, as he scanned the calendar.

"We can do the twentieth of next month," Chuck said.

"The fun starts on the twentieth gentlemen. Next case."

Susan came up behind Bob's car, quickly getting into the passenger seat. He handed her a bottle of water, a reward for doing reconnaissance in the hot sun.

"What's he doing?" Bob asked.

"He's still feeding the birds."

"Still?"

"You're bored, aren't you?"

"We're watching a man feed birds," Bob answered, clearly bored. "For forty some odd minutes now."

"We're watching for incriminating behavior."

"Doesn't mean I can't get antsy."

"So you've never been on a stakeout?"

"I wish it was old hat."

"It's my first, too."

"Really? You've never been on a stakeout?"

"What is it exactly that you think I do?"

Bob chuckled, happy for the respite. Watching Paul was crushingly monotonous, and he was going stir-crazy, the result of two days of completely useless espionage. Recounting the past forty-eight hours was migraine inducing, the day to day behavior of a psychopath proving relentlessly dull. Driving to the park to feed the birds was emblematic of the man's bizarre behavior. Running down his mental checklist, Bob wondered if maybe there was a pattern to be found. The man had spent the first day in his house, save for emerging in the early afternoon to throw a bunch of pills out the front door and take his Trans-Am to the car wash.

The following day, he had gone to lunch, alone, seen a movie, a romantic comedy no less, alone again, left his car at the car wash while he went to Starbuck's and then went to the park to bond with pigeons over moldy white bread. What conclusions can be drawn from this? He likes birds and movies and Starbucks. And cleanliness, since he did have his car washed and waxed twice. What can you say but the man loves his car. Bob looked up sharply, a wonderful idea appearing before him in bright and shiny Technicolor.

Bob turned to Susan and said, "I'll be right back. Honk the horn if he gets close."

He was out the door before she thought to question him. She would never make that mistake again.

Paul's father had brought his four-year old son to the park to feed the birds on a blustery August day. They sat in silence and tossed breadcrumbs to pigeons for an hour. On the drive home, his dad stopped off and got a giant bucket of chicken for dinner. It was the first concrete memory Paul could recall, and it was a most pleasant one at that.

Reliving the past turned out to be less than thrilling. It was cold, and his overcoat did little to shield him from the biting gusts of wind. The pigeons were greedy little disease factories, and Paul would have rather shot them than fed them, but it didn't seem to be in the spirit of the day. If he didn't need some time away from everything, he would have left two minutes after sitting down.

Having Alan and his wife killed and then sticking it to Pete was bothering him. It just felt wrong for some reason. Harvey and Rick had been very convincing, their arguments structured and logical. With the outfit's new image, he could less afford a large contingent of hoods, especially ones that tried to kill police officers with pictures of him in their hands. The dead bodies piling up were bound to attract attention sooner or later, and Pete clearly didn't have the stomach for what was to come. As Rick had made clear, it just made sense to consolidate his troubles into one convenient solution, but it left a bad taste in his mouth. Feeding the ducks was not helping, though Paul knew it had been a long shot from the beginning.

He was about to call it a day when the faint sound of a car alarm caught his ears. His car alarm, as it were.

Chapter 18

PAUL STARED in shock and outrage at the indignity that had befallen his beautiful, beautiful car. The driver's side window was smashed, the seats covered in sludge and wet leaves.

"Son of a bitch."

People were everywhere, so it came as no surprise to Paul that not a single person had seen anything. Witnesses to petty vandalism were about as common as a perfectly cared for vintage Trans Am, and now he was standing on a sidewalk with neither, only a bag of breadcrumbs in his hand. Standing and staring in outrage was not really the most productive thing to do, but Paul couldn't help himself. The world could be such a cruel place sometimes, he mused.

He wished Pete wasn't rotting away in jail on a murder beef. He didn't want to admit it, but he was feeling worse and worse about the whole debacle. It was the right thing to do, he was sure of it. Pete had been getting downright fidgety. You can't run a successful business with fidgety people around. A decision had to be made and he had made it, personal feelings be damned. He hadn't been happy doing it, that was for certain. Pete and him went way back, had shared a lot of good times, made a lot of money. It seemed wrong somehow to end a friendship with a double cross and a trip to the gas chamber. It was funny, Paul had to admit to himself, that he felt far worse for screwing over Pete than for having Alan and his wife murdered. Life's a funny thing sometimes. The sludge had already seeped into the fabric of the bucket seats. He was going to have to have the whole damn interior overhauled. If only he could have the son of a bitch's heart on a pike, it might actually have been worth his car getting soaked with mud in the first place.

He took out his cell phone and dialed up Harvey. "Hey, I need you to come pick me up, I'm at Griffith Park," Paul said, hanging up the phone as quickly as he had taken it out.

Might as well get started with the workday, Paul thought to himself. He surveyed the damage to his car one last time and shook his head sadly. It was a tragedy, a dyed in the fucking wool heartfelt tragedy for such a beautiful thing to suffer such an indignity. Walking away, he tried to focus on the job at hand. After all, killing Nina isn't going to happen by itself.

The two sat in silence a long time before Susan finally said, "I'm not sure how to feel about this, Bob."

"We just struck a blow for justice."

"You broke a window and dumped a bucket of mud into a man's car."

"It's a brave new world."

"What does that even mean? What are we, petty vandals now?"

"It was a big bucket. I don't think petty is the right word."

"I'm invoking rule number four. All actions undertaken by either party, which really means you, mister bad seed, will commence only upon mutual agreement, which pretty much excludes you."

"Let's say we never catch him doing anything, and the police never find any evidence against him. Real possibilities both."

"At least you will have desecrated his car, is that it?"

"Hearing it out loud does make it seem a bit childish."

"Yes."

"I'm sorry."

"Everybody is entitled to one act of childish aggression. I'm just glad you didn't shoot the guy in the kneecaps and then kick him while he was down."

"It was either that or the mud bath?"

"You made your choice."

"We're still going to follow him, right?"

It just occurred to Susan to ask, "Wait, where'd you get the bucket?"

Harvey was happy to drive in silence. No sooner had Paul sat down in the passenger seat than a thirty-second outburst of profanity poured out, followed by fuming silence, then a brief period of exposition, and then another bout of expletives, the overall effect much like listening to an excerpt from *Scarface*. This most recent example notwithstanding, the past week had been a marked improvement in Paul's erratic behavior. Gone were the outbursts and bizarre requests. He had even taken the time to go over the books and complain about a fourteen percent decline in this month's revenue, an almost daily activity the past few years until the recent unpleasantness. Maybe things were going to return to normal of their own volition.

They were only a few miles from the motel. Nina was a strange gal, but he had never thought he would be ten minutes away from plugging her. He wouldn't take any pleasure in it, but it was a smart move. It surprised him when Rick brought it up, but it only made sense. If they were going to the time and trouble of axing Alan plus one, and setting up Pete in the process, there was no need to take any risks by letting the wife run around all willy-nilly. It was an open secret that Rick wanted to fuck Nina ten different ways from Tuesday, so introducing her to Mr. Coffin was about the last thing Harvey expected when Rick had bought him a cup of coffee.

All of which brought an unpleasant train of thought pulling into the station. Rick had never demonstrated much aptitude for anything other than thug-like intimidation, certainly not for problem solving and long-term strategic planning. *I wonder if I might have to take precautions*, Harvey thought. Don't want to end up on the bottom of the food chain looking up. Still, that sort of thing could wait for another day. As long as Paul was around, and Rick wasn't ambitious or crazy enough to make a move on that particular part of the pecking order, his position was secure.

He pulled into the parking lot across the street from the Crazy Eight. It had been quite a month, one bizarre day after another. Today was shaping up to be no exception. When this was all over and done with, maybe a vacation was in order. The more he thought about it, the more enticing a prospect it became. A little time away from Paul and Rick and Pete and dead people was exactly what he needed. It was the best idea anybody had come up with since the day before lunch at Jerry's when Pete had mentioned how nice it would be if they could order Chinese food once in a while during meetings. I say goddamn, Harvey my man. All in all, I might be the only sane one left.

Griffith Park, located at the northernmost corner of Hillhurst Avenue and stretching out to the mighty Los Angeles river, is a sight to behold. Stretching out from the Santa Monica Mountains, it covers 4,310 acres, has three golf courses, an amphitheater, a merry-go-round and the Hollywood Sign. Hiking around the unkempt trails was hugely popular with the nearby hipsters and retirees alike, and a most enjoyable way to spend an afternoon, the size of the park enough to create the impression that L.A. was far in the distance. To reach a truly desolate part of Los Angeles, however, one need only drive south down Hillhurst from the park for two miles until fear or cascading objects force your car into a hasty U-turn. Such dichotomy made L.A. anything but boring, though at the moment Bob wished very much he were driving north on Hillhurst to the park rather than away from it.

"This is good."

"Is your door locked?"

"Relax, Bob. Jesus, get out of the Valley now and again, would you?"

"Your door's locked, right?"

Susan ignored him and focused her attention on the Trans-Am with the broken driver's side window in front of them. She had been on the brink of forcibly planting Bob in a chair and telling him she could no longer participate in a venture that consisted of following a man from one distressingly dull locale to another without any discernible sign of criminal behavior or intent. Then came a trip into a part of town decidedly different from one a man of Paul's stature should be visiting.

"Where do you think he's going?" Bob asked for the umpteenth time.

Susan did her best to answer without betraying her urge to give his forearm a nasty Indian burn. "I don't know."

He took the hint, or perhaps became more interested in the homeless man urinating on a mailbox. Regardless, she was glad for a little quiet as they continued driving into downtown L.A.

The day had not gone particularly well for Nina to that point. It started when she dressed poorly for the occasion. Thinking subterfuge more than practicality when she was planning the escapade, Nina chose her most conservative attire, a black skirt and white blouse, in the hopes she would blend in with the locals. The heels were the worst part, and her face burned red when she remembered her sneakers were back at the motel, and as it turned out, breaking into a man's house to search for incriminating evidence is not as easy as television would have you believe.

First, you have to case the joint, as the industry experts call it, or at least as the industry experts on television call it, and that is no mean feat in modern day cattle-farm housing projects that have overtaken suburbia. Those lousy suburbanites have no jobs and spend all their time watching one another's houses. A housewife with nothing to do except pry into other peoples' affairs came onto her porch to water her plants every five minutes, scanning the street for any good gossip to report to her book club on Sunday. Eventually, she found a window of opportunity and a way in through the back fence by climbing over the top with the aid of a tricycle stacked on top of a barbecue grill. This whole process took the better part of an afternoon and proved rather tiresome.

Second, there was the matter of evading the alarm system. This Nina managed to do less successfully, but in fairness, this was only because she did not know Paul had an alarm system. Certain to be a victim of a massive coronary, she was frozen in place as the alarm beeped at an obscene volume in her ears. Only a miracle in the form of Mrs. Costa, staggering down the hallway in a drugged stupor saved Nina from incarceration or death. It should have comforted Nina's sensibilities that patients who take a few too many Vicodin manage to retain memory and basic motor function, but her interest was less with Amy's severe medical issues than with the possibility of springing her husband from prison.

A third issue sped to the forefront as she began poking through drawers and sifting through coat racks. Pete had told her to look for a big handgun that looked like a slightly smaller version of what Dirty Harry carried, but she had no idea where to look for it. Pete always kept his gun in her lingerie drawer, but Amy had nothing but underwear and a very scary looking vibrator.

Two hours had gone by and Nina had nothing to show for it but an appreciation for the valuable contribution to personal health and society in general drug rehab centers provide. Grumbling to herself, she walked out the front door, said hello to the surprised postman on her way out and drove home in a very dark mood.

Her mood did not improve when she glanced in the rearview mirror and realized her sunglasses made her look like Mamie Van Doren. She resolved to change clothes immediately upon return to her motel.

"Who is that?"

Susan looked up from her flat Dr. Pepper in time to see a blond woman with ridiculous sunglasses exiting her car and walking surreptitiously to the office. Every third step was followed with a nervous look this way and that.

"So what," Susan answered.

"That doesn't strike you as odd?" Bob asked. "Someone dressed like that in this place?"

Susan shrugged. "It's L.A."

"So?"

"Par for the course. If it were normal, then I'd be worried." Susan shook her soda, hoping maybe that would set the taste to right. "Is your soda all right?"

"She's coming out of the office."

"She's having an affair, she came here to get a room."

"She wasn't in there long enough to get a key. She's here to see somebody."

"Like Paul."

"It's a possibility," Bob said. "Don't you think?"

"So we wait and see," Susan answered, mildly impressed with Bob's investigative instincts. Her attention quickly returned to her soda. "Seriously, I think mine is just liquid syrup."

It was Paul's inability to handle Harvey's smoking that enabled Nina to avoid being shot multiple times in the head. At the time, Paul was only concerned with the bleak possibility of spending endless hours waiting for Nina to return to her unrepentantly filthy motel room with Harvey's black tar cigarettes infecting every fiber of his being.

"Harvey?"

"Yeah?"

Paul gave him a cold look as if his meaning was obvious, but Harvey just shrugged, feigning ignorance.

"Could you, please?" Paul said, spelling it out.

"I'll step outside," Harvey grumbled.

"Thanks."

He closed the door behind him, his lit cigarette hanging limply from his mouth. *Sometimes that man can just be impossible*, Harvey thought. *It's a fucking cigarette. Son of a bitch acts like I'm taking a cattle iron to his mom.*

The shadow caught his attention a second before the purse impacted his face. The shock as much as anything sent him crashing to the ground. His first look at Nina was her expensive yellow high heels getting smaller and smaller. *Dammit*, Harvey thought. *Paul's really gonna be pissed off now.*

"Paul!" he yelled.

If she knew the cause of Harvey's presence outside her room the moment of her arrival, and were she not struggling to run in Carl Lewis type fashion, in two-inch heels to boot, Nina would have enjoyed the congruence of Paul's fear of deadly secondhand smoke as her own personal salvation. As it was, she could only firmly resolve to purchase a pair of sneakers if and when she was no longer in extreme and immediate personal danger.

In case anyone had been looking for her car, she had the forethought to park three blocks away behind a Jack in the Box, but there was no way she was eluding multiple gun-toting thugs for three blocks in two inch heels. *Maybe if I can make it someplace public they won't risk it*, she thought. Her best bet looked like the nail salon across the street. It might work if oncoming traffic didn't do Paul's job for him.

The roar of a Honda Civic's engine coming to life didn't even register to Nina until it came to a screeching stop next to the staircase. The passenger door flew open.

"Get in!" Susan yelled.

Images of her mom threatening abandonment and starvation should she ever get into a stranger's car were all Nina could think of as she practically dove into the backseat, her cheek impacting heavily with the seat belt clasp.

"Go, go, go!"

Nina wasn't sure if she had uttered those words aloud, but the car obligingly sped off in a blur regardless. She poked her head up to see Paul's stunned face fading quickly into the cement jungle behind her.

"Are you all right?" Bob asked, Nina catching his eyes in the rearview mirror.

"Thanks to you. Johnny on the spot there."

"It's what we do," Bob answered, the adrenalin still coursing through him.

Susan rolled her eyes and took a long look at the road behind them. No one seemed to be following.

"Lucky for me," Nina said, still catching her breath. "Where are we going?"

"The police," Susan said, as if it were obvious.

Nina's eyes went wide. "I don't want to go to the police."

"Bob, pull over. Listen, I don't care if you're a hooker—"

"I'm not a prostitute."

"I don't care if you are."

"But I'm not. Do I look like a prostitute? Who the hell are you?"

"I'm a chiropractor," Bob answered happily. "I just quit, actually. She's a suspended police officer. Bob and Susan."

"Nina. I'm a housewife. I only sell my body every other weekend for spending cash."

"Sorry, it's just your ensemble and the hotel in the middle of the day…"

She waved off Susan's apology. "I can appreciate your thinking I'd want to go to the police. I just can't."

"Why not?"

"Those men back there. They framed my husband for murder. If I report them for chasing me a little, what the hell good does that do?"

"Chasing you?" Susan asked, chiding Nina for her interpretation of events. "They go to jail for attempted murder and conspiracy to commit murder. If they really did frame your husband, we can tie that to them once they're in jail."

"Oh, why didn't I think of that? And then, afterwards, we can all go out for custard with unicorns."

Both Susan and Bob shot her a look, and Nina did her best to ease back on the throttle. "I'm sorry, that was harsh, you did just get done saving my life. It's just that trying to bust them for something petty that they'll make bail on twenty minutes later isn't going to get Pete out, it'll probably just make it harder."

"Why were they after you?" Bob asked.

"Loose ends, I guess," Nina answered. "Why were you two at the motel?"

"Oh, that Paul guy murdered my father and we're following him in an attempt to uncover incriminating evidence against him and his cohorts. Nina, you said?"

A wave of cold washed over Nina. "Uh-huh."

"It's nice to meet you."

The drive home was unpleasant. After searching Nina's hotel room and finding nothing but a strong predilection for turquoise tank tops, the three turned off the lights and left. Paul insisted Rick and Harvey accompany him back to his house for a strategy session. The forty-seven minute ride should have provided ample opportunity to make any and all necessary decisions. Instead, the time was spent haranguing Harvey for his mind-boggling ineptitude, a charge that hurt him all the more for its strong resemblance to the truth. To his equal chagrin, Rick had become a brown-nosing little sycophant, echoing Paul's every sentence with choruses of assent.

Harvey was thrilled when they finally walked into Paul's kitchen to find Amy unconscious on the floor. Any distraction was a welcome distraction, and judging by the pallid color to her cheeks and extremely faint pulse, the whipping boy hour was coming to an abrupt end.

Rick picked up the telephone.

"What are you doing?" Paul asked him, stooped awkwardly over his wife.

"Calling an ambulance," he answered, suddenly uncertain.

"Are you kidding?" Paul asked in genuine surprise. "Harvey, help me get her into the john. Rick, there's a medical kit in the cupboard, above the peanut butter. Let's move it, people."

A month after Amy had popped her first pill, Paul felt it prudent to call up a local medical supply company and purchase adrenalin, hypodermic needles, gauze and a stomach pump, items for which he was only forced to part with three hundred and seventeen dollars, a bargain in his eyes. The only surprise was it took so many years before he needed to take his little toys for a test drive. Her arms kept slipping from his grasp as he and Harvey did their best to get her into the bathroom with a minimum of bruising. *I wonder if adrenalin goes bad after a while*, Paul thought.

Rick dumped the kit on the ground and all three men looked back and forth between the black monstrosity and Amy. The principles of a stomach pump were simple enough, as Paul had always imagined. The application of those principles proved a bit less so.

"Is that all of it?" Harvey asked.

"That was everything in the cabinet," Rick replied crossly.

"I read the instruction manual when I bought it," Paul said.

"When was that?" Harvey asked.

"It has been a while. But I remember it being really easy. I think this part here extends out and then we shove that down her throat and press this button."

All three had their hands on their hips, eyes cast seriously at the pump. Harvey pursed his lips thoughtfully.

"You suppose it runs on batteries?"

"No," Paul answered, shaking his head. "We have to plug it in."

"Where's the cord?" Rick asked.

It took four minutes to finally plug the pump in, three minutes to extend the tube and thirty seconds to open Amy's mouth and start pushing the tube down her throat. The day, and only because everything before it had gone so calamitously, was finally taking a turn for the better.

Nina knew the answer before she asked the question. "What was your dad's name?"

"Karl Kessler."

"Paul shot him," she said, bracing for his reaction. He didn't look like the violent sort, but this was the sort of news that could unsettle even the steeliest of competitors. "My husband, Pete, he was there when it happened."

Bob didn't say anything for a long time. "I'm really sorry," Nina added, feeling impossibly pathetic for offering such a lame apology.

There it was, finally, and it didn't feel at all like he expected. Bob sat down heavily. It shouldn't have had any effect on him. He had convinced himself Paul was the man behind the gun, but he just wasn't prepared to hear it said aloud by someone other than himself. It made everything so much more final, his father's death more real, more immediate. Bob felt like crying for the first time since the funeral.

Karl had not been the model for the father of the year award. He meant well, and he was overwhelmingly charming through most of Bob's childhood, but he was rarely present for any great length of time. Bob's mother, Gail, never legally divorced her husband, but she and Karl ceased being husband and wife when Bob was eleven. It didn't change the father/son dynamic much. Karl saw his son four or five times a year, for major holidays and birthdays mostly. It never bothered him as much as it might have other kids. His father was just too much damn fun to be mad at for any length of time.

Upon reaching adulthood, if not maturity, Bob kept in regular contact, his father always happy to regale his son with magnificent exploits and deeds of daring. When his mom died, it was harder for Bob to slough off his father's excesses and eccentricities. They still talked, but there was a sadness permeating their conversations that never fully disappeared.

"Why?" Bob asked.

"Pete told me about it. It was at Jerry's Deli. Your dad lifted Paul's wallet. So he shot him."

"Just shot him."

"I'm sorry."

"So your husband, he saw this live and in color. He just stood there and watched."

Nina opened her mouth to answer, but nothing came to mind. He made a fair point. Her husband was not a good man, not in any real sense of the word. He had killed, was culpable in any other number of violent crimes. How do you defend such actions?

"He didn't pull the trigger," was the best Nina could muster. "I'm sorry, I really am, but the man you should be angry at is Paul."

"I am, don't worry about that. And I say this next part with all due respect to you, but fuck your husband. He can rot in jail for all I care."

"It's that simple, isn't it?"

"Yeah, it is."

"He didn't do it. So he was there. Should he have done something? Of course. How easy is that to say here and now? You're a chiropractor, a square little goody two shoes if I've ever seen one and you have no idea what you're talking about. He's a career criminal, you don't just have a change of heart in the middle of a homicide in progress."

"So he's had a miraculous transformation now that he's facing the chair?"

"Lethal injection in California," Susan interjected. Bob and Nina barely noticed.

"I don't know. But he is sitting in a prison cell facing the death penalty. Does that sound like the punishment fitting the crime?"

"As a matter of fact..." Bob trailed off snidely.

"I can't apologize for him, and if I could, I could never apologize enough. I am really, though, really sorry for your loss."

Bob had nothing polite or bereft of profanity left to say, so he walked out the door. Nina and Susan enjoyed the quiet for a few minutes.

"Pete works for Paul?" Susan asked.

"It's an even split, but Paul runs the show. Been that way for a long time."

"Neither of you kept any dirt on him, I don't suppose?"

"It does seem kind of dumb in retrospect."

"How did he set your husband up?"

"Paul sent him to kill one of the other guys, Alan, and his wife, and when Pete got there, they were already dead. Paul probably tipped off the police, so they found him standing over the bodies. Bad luck there."

"He sent Pete to murder the people who had already been murdered."

"Yes."

"So he was framed for a murder he was going to commit anyway."

"He wasn't going to go through with it."

"Hm."

"He wasn't. Besides, it's a moot point. You can't be sent to the gas chamber for thinking about killing people."

"Lethal injection."

"He didn't do it."

Bob came back a few minutes later with a box of donuts. Pastry was the only thing he could think of to improve his disposition. It wasn't helping so far, but then he'd only eaten one. He didn't really expect any improvement until donut number four was on its way down his gullet.

"What's the case like? Is there evidence against your husband?" Susan asked, continuing with her questioning as if Bob had never left.

"Some," Nina admitted.

"What is some?"

"There was a little of Alan's blood on him when he was arrested. Like I said, he was standing over the bodies, which can't look good. With the murder weapon in his hand."

"So it's circumstantial at best," Bob said, his mouth covered in honey glaze.

"Listen up, Mister and Missus Sarcastic. I know my husband, and despite how naïve and idiotic that sounds, especially since I know he has killed people and has stood by while others killed people, I know he didn't kill these particular people. I'm not saying this well."

"No," Bob agreed.

"Let me try it this way. I can help you with your thing."

"Is that a fact?" Susan asked skeptically.

"I need evidence that Paul framed Pete," Nina said, plunging ahead. "I can't imagine there'll be a whole lot, but if we can get anything at all, the whole case will collapse. It has to, because he's innocent. If you guys help me find it, I'll convince Pete to turn state's evidence in exchange for accessory charges against him being dismissed. Paul and his cronies go to jail."

"Except your husband, who goes free," Susan felt compelled to add.

"It's a big W all around. All things considered."

Susan was about to answer when she turned to Bob, who was chewing blankly on a donut. This wasn't like a normal situation, in every possible interpretation, and it meant her normal instincts might need to be tempered. She simply couldn't automatically agree to something without his approval; this wasn't a police investigation, she wasn't a detective and it wasn't her father who was buried in the ground, though it struck the law and order side of her as an excellent proposition. The entire criminal court system was predicated on plea bargains, a harsh reality that thrust itself into Susan's life so long ago she'd ceased to contemplate the moral implications of it. Everything would grind to a sudden and brutalizing halt if every single criminal case was actually prosecuted in court, but watching Bob eating his third glazed cake in quiet contemplation of the offer on the table made her remember just how soul crushing the prospect was for the victim's family.

It was exactly this sort of thing that made the idea of returning to the police force such a nebulous proposition. It was just as terrifying to imagine any other career scenario, but it put into perspective much of what she'd lost, namely the sort of perspective a normal person has when confronted with moral compromise. Not that she'd term Bob normal, but still, it gave one a moment for pause.

"I suppose it couldn't hurt to have you on board," he admitted reluctantly. "We all want to see Paul's head on a pike. Susan?"

"I'm not making any promises about your husband," Susan said to Nina. "If we clear him in the process, then so be it. Any deal afterward has to be made with the police."

"But you'll try to make it happen. And you're a cop."

"She's suspended," Bob said, a bit too automatically for Susan's tastes.

"Why are you suspended?"

"I will do my best," Susan said, avoiding the subject of her current hiatus. "You have my word."

What other choice did she have, Nina thought. "Okay."

"So what do you know?" Susan asked.

"I don't know anything," Nina answered honestly.

"Where should we start?"

"I don't know what to look for, and I'm not at all sure where to begin looking for it."

"We should begin, then."

"Yeah, you're going to fit right in, by the way," Bob said, multi-colored sprinkles dotting his chin in truly absurd fashion.

Chapter 19

BRANDON DROVE a 1993 Ford Mercury Sable, with a 3.6 liter engine, power locks and windows, air conditioning that didn't work, and the faint odor of apples sunk deep into the upholstery, the result of a visit to an orchard in a failed effort to impress a waitress from a great restaurant in the bad part of Pasadena. To say he drove it, however, would be to underestimate the importance 'Betty' (Grable which rhymes with Sable) played in his life. Brandon lived for his car. It was his identity and aside from his long-time friend Winston, it was the only thing he cared about. This was for three reasons, to which he had given a great deal of thought and written down on a slip of paper he kept in his glove compartment in lieu of up-to-date registration. The paper read:

1. A man's car is his castle.

2. Betty has saved my life six-and-a-half times. This is six more times than my family has and two of those idiots are responsible for one of the unsuccessful attempts.

3. The best sex I will ever have took place in the front seat of Betty.

3. A car will never betray someone who truly loves her.

The first number three on the list was no longer applicable since he spent two days in bed with a high school dropout named Shirley who was convinced that the sun rose and set in his pants.

She had later tried to rob and kill him (homicide attempt number five), but Betty had come to the rescue once again, allowing him not only to escape a gun-wielding maniac, but providing an opportunity to watch the woman by whom all others would be judged shrinking in the rearview mirror while bullets embedded themselves in his trunk. He had come up with the new number three on his way to break into a vet's office for some antibiotics. It was much better than the old number three, Brandon felt, but he was way too lazy to cross the former off the list.

Despite his adoration, Brandon was forced to part with his beloved once or twice a year, sometimes for up to two months at a time. Betty was unregistered and Brandon was not technically the owner. He had bought her for an even grand on the up and up, but had lost the pink slip during one of his botched 7-11 quickie jobs and the DMV was resistant to providing registration without proof of ownership. He wasn't about to part with Betty, but sure enough, about a year after his tags first expired, L.A.'s finest impounded his baby and refused to let him bail her out since he could provide no proof the car was his. This was a low point for Brandon, but fortunately it was short lived.

The impound lot put a lien on his car and within a week, it was at auction. Brandon had slept outside the lot and followed her as she was towed to the police auction. His only competition for Betty bowed out at two hundred and twenty-two dollars. As far as the auctioneer was concerned, he had never laid eyes on the car until that day and as such, was not forced to pay the exorbitant impound fees. Brandon drove off with his car, pink slip in hand.

This should have been the end of it, but Brandon was not a man to take on the yoke of responsibility when a shortcut was so readily available. The night he had sprung Betty, he made a few calculations. The impound fees came to a total of three hundred and ninety-seven dollars and eighty-two cents. The ticket the cop gave him was a hundred and five. Registering a car in L.A. would cost a minimum of two hundred and sixty-three dollars, which he would have to pay every year.

Thus was born an idea.

He would drive the car without proper registration. In the eventuality he was pulled over and the car taken from him, he would simply buy the car back for less than the cost of registration. Since the car would always change ownership once it went to auction, he'd never have to pay for any tickets he received or any fees incurred due to impounding. Plus, as an added bonus, he got to give a gigantic middle finger to the system.

Betty was temporarily taken from him seven times over eight years, and each time, he bought her back for a pittance.

It was a good plan, minus the few weeks he often had to wait while Betty was shipped off for sale. Competition was always scarce for a car with over two hundred thousand miles on it and a seemingly equivalent number of dents and dings, and the most Brandon ever shelled out for Betty was two hundred and seventy-five dollars. He kept the multitude of pink slips in the top drawer of his bedside table. It always made a good story at the bar, and Brandon got a lot of mileage regaling anyone within earshot of his exploits with Betty.

Terrified of doctors, Brandon refused to see anybody about the severe pain in his stomach despite the increasing difficulty in carrying out even the simplest of physical tasks. He didn't know it was cancer, but he wouldn't have been surprised at the diagnosis, and he instinctively knew his time was coming to an end. To insure his precious car from falling into the wrong hands, Brandon wrote down instructions and placed them inside a sealed envelope, to be opened upon his death. Brandon passed away a few weeks later in his sleeping bag, twenty yards outside the Encino branch of Andy's Anytime Towing.

Winston learned of his friend's death and in accordance with his last wishes, broke the seal on Brandon's last will and testament. Reading through the carefully handwritten two pages, Winston felt a sense of foreboding spread slowly and inexorably through his body.

There were explicit instructions.

Amy's condition stabilized around midnight. The worst of it had passed several hours earlier, which enabled Harvey and Rick to politely excuse themselves from a thoroughly uncomfortable situation. Rick went home and called Theresa, a skinny blonde with low standards and a yen for chocolate pudding. Harvey made a beeline for the nearest bar, which turned out to be an ultra-trendy former beauty parlor that ditched the manicure stations but kept the large swivel chairs and pink pastel wallpaper. Despite the tacky décor, he was pleased to find that cheap whiskey tastes the same the world round.

Paul was left with a comatose lump in the guise of his wife. He had a pretty good idea what his friends were doing and would have given all his future fortunes to trade places with either man. As it was, he patted down Amy's forehead with a washcloth for the umpteenth time and gritted his teeth in impotent rage. Killing someone was what he needed. Either that or sex. Perhaps sensing her husband's desire to kill and/or fuck someone, Amy rolled over and burped loudly, putting an end to his interest in her, homicidal and otherwise.

No longer concerned with his wife's immediate health, Paul took out a pen and sheet of paper from the bedside table shaped like a lumpy watermelon (a particularly horrid wedding gift from Amy's hippie sister) and decided it was time to make a list. People had been making lists Paul's entire life and they had to be doing better than he was at this moment. Maybe they were on to something.

Top priority simply had to be sorting out his business affairs. Nina not dying and then running down the stairs and diving into a car was vexing to say the least. She would have to be taken care of, and quickly. The longer she was bouncing around in the free world, the more difficult it was to envision long-term growth and viability for his business interests. Long-term growth was a priority, to be sure, but it paled next to the more pressing issues of the moment. Paul underlined long-term growth and numbered it two.

He sat back, reflecting on the list so far. Maybe the reason companies fold so often is a lack of perspective. If a CEO is always fumbling around with the hassles of day-to-day business, when will he have time for big picture issues? The Nina situation would resolve itself sooner or later, Paul reasoned. *The big picture is where I'm the most valuable,* he thought. To that end, he switched numbers on the list, Nina's unnatural end now occupying the second position.

Delegating authority came next, followed by an increased focus in security on all transactions exceeding ten thousand dollars. Number five was finding a high interest mutual fund with a solid twenty-year track record in order to maximize everyone's retirement fund. Killing at least one new person a week was number six. Paul would have gotten much further, but Amy was stirring next to him. He patted her arm affectionately, resolving to make Amy's health and happiness lucky number seven on his list.

At no time did it occur to him to try and track down the Honda Civic that saved Nina's life.

It took Susan, Bob and Nina less than ten minutes to share every pertinent piece of information at their disposal on Paul and his henchmen who were not dead or in prison. It would have been less, but Nina spent three minutes explaining the interpersonal intricacies between Paul and his men, information mostly gleaned from Pete's monosyllabic complaints. Susan was less than impressed, a fact she didn't bother to hide and was only too happy to share.

"You came straight from digging around his house to the motel."

"Pretty much, yeah."

"What does that mean?"

"I stopped for a smoothie."

Susan's gaze was drawn to Nina's feet. "You searched his house in heels?"

Nina hoped her face wasn't turning red, but she considered it doubtful the universe was in the mood to do her any more favors on the day.

"I'm new to the whole breaking and entering thing. I'll do sneakers next time."

"What were you hoping to find?"

"A gun, maybe. I don't know, really."

"And what were you going to do next?" Susan asked, rubbing her eyes in an attempt to make everything simply disappear.

"I hadn't gotten that far," Nina answered sharply. "In my defense, you know, I had a lot on my mind."

"I have a suggestion," Bob said.

The look of doubt on Nina's face was understandable, perhaps even to be expected. After all, she didn't know him from Adam. But the exact same look from Susan was less than Bob might have hoped for.

"He's killed quite a few people so far, exactly how many we can't say. Right? These other two idiots that trail around after him, well, my thinking is they're how we get to Paul. They're probably witnesses to most of this nonsense, maybe we can get them to roll over on him. From there, we can clear your husband, and then go after Paul."

"How would we do it?" Susan asked, idly scratching her forearm. "I mean, it's a good thought in theory."

"They're not likely to be forthcoming to me," Nina said.

"Maybe we could blackmail them?"

"With what?" Susan asked.

"A fair question."

"I don't know enough about them to hang something over their heads that could bump a murder charge," Nina said, thinking out loud. "Rick's always wanted to sleep with me, if that helps."

"Perhaps your husband would know something," Bob offered.

Pete might not be too happy about her admitting his guilt in a capital crime to complete strangers, one a former police officer no less. Nina crumpled her brow in reflection. Actually, he'd always been an ends justify the means sort of guy. It was perhaps the defining characteristic of his life, from threatening the minister at their wedding to the ill-fated time he'd tried to get his money back after walking out of *Moulin Rouge*.

He'll probably love this, Nina thought. Besides, she concluded to herself ruefully, she certainly wasn't breaking any records on her own in this race.

"Visiting hours are from three to six."

Cops are cops are cops the world over. Some idiot sold Pete a clearly real and obviously stolen Cartier watch a few summers back, but not before spending five minutes regaling him with the details of a recent and harrowing brush with the law that nearly ended in an arrest despite valid receipts for said watches. The story was likely a poor attempt to discover whether Pete was an undercover officer, or maybe just an unnecessary reassurance that the merchandise was above board, and it went on well past its expiration date, but still, fifty dollars well spent.

Wife number two had been astonished he would risk purchasing stolen goods out in the open. 'What if he'd been a cop?' she had asked, her voice rising in pitch with every passing syllable. Pete just shook his head, wishing he could make her understand. It was impossible to explain with words, but somehow he just knew. Frankly, her real focus should have been on the man who was able to find such a bargain, but her mind didn't work that way and she was never one to appreciate his finer qualities, just another of the many reasons he didn't miss the woman.

Pete knew the axiom to still be true as he stared through the filthy plexiglass at the stranger in the ugly blouse next to his wife. Something about the air of entitlement, or maybe just the inevitably condescending tone of voice, but it was unmistakable. Alan had told him once that cops and criminals share the same attributes, the same basic DNA as it were, and with the LAPD's propensity for outrageous acts of casual violence with no repercussions and seemingly little to no regret, the assessment was unlikely to be too far from the mark.

He asked the woman anyway, just to be civil.

"So who are you?"

"My name is Susan Ciarelli. You witnessed a shooting outside Jerry's Deli a month ago."

"You're a cop, is what you mean."

"I'm on temporary leave right now. But, yes. I'm a cop."

Pete's eyes flashed to Nina, who did her best to calm him down with hand gestures, a skill she was slowly perfecting with every visit to the state penitentiary. She especially disliked the thin layer of grime that was stuck to everything, from the door handles to the chairs. She shifted in her seat at the thought of what was happening to her skirt, Pete's favorite and her most expensive article of clothing, the two details likely going hand in hand.

"It's all right, Pete. She's going to help us. She's just a little bit abrupt."

Susan ignored Nina's not-so-subtle suggestion to take it down a notch and instead leaned forward dramatically, her face close to the plexiglass. "I've agreed to try and help you and your wife. In exchange, you'll testify to what you saw in the parking lot that day."

"What are you talking about? Who the hell are you?" he asked in hypothetical incredulity.

"I can't do it by myself," Nina said. "I need help and where else are we going to turn?"

"I don't want you getting involved in this."

"It's a little late for that, Sweetie. Paul has already tried to kill me, I don't really see the harm in trying to make him stop, however bizarre this particular option might be."

He wasn't the slightest bit happy about it, but the attempt on his wife's life did not go unnoticed. "I'm glad you're all right."

"Maybe we can get Rick or Harvey to roll over on Paul. If one of them admits to Paul killing Alan, or ordering it, or whatever, anything, we can link him to it in some way, and you're off the hook."

"I don't know," Pete mumbled skeptically. It sounded like a shit plan to him, but then his brain hadn't been much use to this point during Paul's murder rampage and he sure as hell wasn't in much of a position to help himself at the moment. What choice did he have but to trust his wife? Maybe this was his cosmic reward for marrying a smart chick.

"It'd be Harvey, if you could make it swing. He's smart enough not to take a dive for anybody, doesn't matter no matter, you know? A big if, though."

"Is there anything we might be able to use against him?" Nina asked. "Leverage? Anything?"

"He's cleaner than any of us. Smart, like I said." The more Pete thought about it, the more far-fetched the whole idea sounded, and the more depressed he felt. "I just don't know."

"Let's go back to Paul," Susan said. "You all worked for him, right?"

"Right."

"Maybe we're over-thinking all of this. All of your illegal activities," Susan paused for a moment, appreciating Pete's nervous flick of the eyes to the guards at the word illegal, "went through Paul. He ordered, guided, coordinated in some fashion, everything."

It took him a long moment to reply, "Yeah."

"Harvey never went outside the family?"

"No, he was a real straight arrow. As far as these things go."

"Anything else you think might help with this guy?" Susan pressed. "I mean, hookers, gambling, something dark from his past?"

Pete sat back, staring hard at a point in space. He shook his head grimly.

"Nothing specific, no. I never expected…" Pete trailed off.

"Enemies? Anything?"

He shook his head again, getting visibly frustrated. She tried a different tack. "Let's look at it through Paul's eyes then, maybe we're coming at this the wrong way."

"Paul? He's got enemies now," Pete said, laughing out loud. "That's for damn sure. He's got enemies coming out of his ass. That's what happens when you turn psychotic."

"*Turn* psychotic?"

"He wasn't always like this. He used to be all about money, like any normal person. Then, I don't know, he just lost it and started blowing people away. Weirdest fucking thing. The thing is," Pete continued, "he's not going to stop either. He's just going to keep going.

Pete let that sink in before saying, "You know what I do, right?"

"Basically."

"He's going down the list of people who owe us money, and it's a long fucking list, and he's just bringing them in and then bang-bang cross another name off the list. He's not going to stop."

"You have a few names in mind? Who might be next?"

"Get me a pen and paper."

"You didn't answer me earlier," Susan said, holding Pete's gaze.

He looked back hard.

"Lady," Pete growled, "you save my wife's life and I'll do anything you want. You have my word."

Susan sat back and shrugged her acceptance. "It'll have to do."

"I should have come with you."

"No."

"I'm just a little unclear on how exactly this is going to help us."

Susan dug in deeper with her thumbs, trying to reinforce her point by pulverizing Bob's shoulder muscles. It was bruising her ego that he hardly reacted to her touch, and she had moved progressively from gentle, sensitive massage to the intentional infliction of pain, neither of which caused more than the occasional sigh, which might very well have been the result of Susan's retelling of the day's events.

"We know people he's killed, and now we know people he's going to kill."

"Yeah, I got that part," Bob sighed, as if on cue.

She changed her rubbing motion. "How's this feel?"

"A little to the left. We're going to do what now?"

"When it happens again, or if we're lucky, and I suppose if the guy on this list is lucky, before it happens again, we can tie that information back to his past victims. Pete thinks this Harvey guy is the weak link. We'll use what we know to force his hand."

"Sounds complicated."

"It is." She left out any commentary on her opinion of the likelihood of success, instead asking, "Does this hurt?"

"You can go deeper."

Susan could not go any deeper. Her fingers were killing her.

She turned Bob around to face her instead.

"What's going on with you?"

"I know I've been a pain lately," Bob admitted. "This new, dark side of me. It's sexy, right?"

"That's not how I would have described it."

"Mysterious? Intriguing, perhaps?"

"It's all right, you know. It's all right to be angry. You don't have to pretend everything is hunky dory."

"So it's okay that I've been sulking and biting your head off a bit? And throwing buckets of mud at murderers?"

"Absolutely. Of course, some people find it helpful to talk about feelings."

He knew she was right, and not just about the value of spending a little time verbalizing everything he was going through. Balling up his emotions into a tiny ball of rage and then forcing that ticking time bomb into the deepest and darkest crevices of his psyche was fine for college, but it didn't bode well for those poor souls trading on the futures market of his sanity. Every time he felt like exploding was an exercise in futility, a countdown to liftoff with no ignition.

He wondered though, if the inability to actually get angry and vent was less to do with 'being another dumbass guy' as his instructor at chiropractic college had charmingly suggested right after he told her he didn't think it was such a hot idea they continue sleeping together during finals, and more that he simply didn't have it in him.

Karl had never been much for imparting life lessons, valuable or otherwise, but Bob did manage to get a twenty-minute lecture on the meaning of life one night during a car ride back from Costco, a gigantic vat of mayonnaise far too big for Karl to manage on his own resting temporarily in the trunk, the contents of which would soon be racing to their final destination somewhere in his father's vascular system, probably with a lot of tuna in tow.

He had been trying unsuccessfully for years to get his dad to visit his mom's grave, something Karl had pointedly never done, and this late in the game Bob simply queried out of habit rather than with any hope of success. Instead of the usual polite demurral, Karl smiled softly and patted his son on the knee. Life, Karl opined with typical dramatic flourish as Bob did his best not to look at his watch, was really only a series of moments. Each one to be taken in kind with a sort of relativistic flourish, never getting too high or low since one really wasn't better or worse than another, simply the next in line.

"Like a conveyor belt," Bob suggested.

Karl didn't let Bob's snide tone slow him down.

"No point getting hung up on the past, since it never actually happened the way we remember it and wasn't ever really gone anyway, and no point making plans for some better life down the road since the future is a creation of the past. Life doesn't work that way. The reason people are unhappy is because they don't understand how destructive a force memory is in our lives, destroying our future to preserve a false narrative based on future expectations. We aren't our memories. We aren't who we want to be. We're the people we are in this moment. That's all we ever have. There is no past and there is no future, and as such, cemeteries are at best a pointless endeavor and at worst a destructive force in our lives."

Bob listened in distracted skepticism, his attention more on the idiot tailgating him for the last mile or so and the likelihood that he'd left the office unlocked, which he concluded that he had not and discovered the next morning he most certainly had. "So why bother with your son," Bob had asked. "If we have no connection to the past, then what's the point of you and me?"

Karl grinned broadly and clapped him so hard on the shoulder Bob was worried he was about to run over a squirrel. "I needed a ride to Costco," Karl answered. "And I'm savoring it, the same way you should."

Bob had no idea what he was feeling or what he *should* be feeling or why the most fun he'd had in as long as he could remember was throwing a bucket of mud into a car, he only felt relatively certain that his dad would probably approve of little if any of his existential angst save for the bucket of mud.

Actually, Bob figured it was also very likely that Karl would have approved of Susan. His dad never bothered much with his occasional romantic entanglements, probably because most didn't last all that long and the few times he had met the young women, they singularly failed to impress. She might yet still fall into the first category, but boring would never be one of her flaws, and the joy his father would have taken in riling up someone who gets animated over the proper usage of commas was probably enough in and of itself to get the parental thumbs up on future grandchildren. She even put up with his moodiness and penchant for 1980's metal ballads in the car. He really should do everything to try and keep her happy, and not antagonizing her with his moodiness and fluctuating desire for revenge would be a good start. Still, he couldn't resist a little jab, just for the fun of it.

"Something about a pot and a kettle springs to mind, Susan."

She ignored him, annoyed at how close to the bullseye that one hit, pressing on. "It doesn't have to be right now, either. For future reference."

"I can handle that. Your turn?"

Thank God, she thought. "Uh-huh."

Susan sat down in front of Bob and let his hands find the knots in her neck. It didn't take him long.

"Wow," Susan exhaled softly.

"Good?"

"Did it take long to learn this?"

He thought of his instructor at chiropractic college,

realizing it had been so long he had no idea if her name was Alice or Allison, but confident it was one of the two. He settled on Alice. "It's a work in progress," Bob said, gently slipping Susan's bra strap off her shoulder to get underneath her shoulder blade.

"It's progressing nicely. You know that new Kobe beef that's all the rage? The cattle farmers hire people to massage the cows. If you're still looking for job ideas."

Bob smiled, the feeling starting at the corners of his mouth and spreading through to his core, far faster than his mind could process, and he was not at all sure if it was the image in his mind of a man rubbing a cow with the cartoon caption 'You Guide Me, Buddy' that started it, or the way Susan felt when his hands were on her, or the ease with which she could relax with him, something that would have been impossible just days earlier, but for one of the few times in Bob's entire life, he didn't stop to analyze any of it, he simply closed his eyes and smiled, letting the feeling wash over him, forgetting all about Alice, his father, his work, his life, and simply enjoyed the moment, as simple and beautiful a one as anyone could reasonably hope for in this life.

He pressed down hard on a particularly nasty knot, effectively ending the conversation.

Nina was staring at the door, standing just inches away from it. This went on for almost one full minute. Bob was going to say something, but he was curious what she was thinking about and how long she could keep it up without blinking. Nina was in fact imagining all the many ways she might die an unnatural death this day. Gunshot wounds seemed the most likely, or maybe a blunt object to the side of the head followed by dismemberment, at least she hoped that would be the order. After some reflection she thought her money was probably strongest on stabbing, but she figured that estimation was likely because the prospect scared her so much more than being shot or getting her skull caved in. It probably took a long time to die from a stab wound, unless it was right into the heart, which was way worse and made her want to rub her chest, but that impulse only made her feel more exposed knowing Bob and Susan were watching her stare at the door like a mad woman. Maybe it was all the television she watched, but getting shot never seemed all that bad. A lead pipe to the noggin brought back memories of playing *Clue*. There was also the possibility she might die in a car wreck on the way to being murdered, and that thought was almost enough to force a smile to the surface.

"My money's on the door," Susan said, growing impatient and not sharing any of Bob's curiosity.

Nina dropped her head, rubbing her eyes and feeling for all the world like a total collapse was imminent. Susan sensed her attitude wasn't helping, and she avoided catching Bob's eye to verify that hypothesis, instead deciding to bring the car around. She stepped past Nina and was out the door before Nina looked up.

"You ready for this?" he asked gently, coming around and forcing her to make eye contact.

Nina took a deep breath. "No."

The easy smile on Bob's face did a lot to ease her nerves, but it was his decision to turn her around and rub her shoulders that took all her tension out to the woodshed for a stern talking-to. She was too startled to protest, and her eyes quickly rolled back in her head in a mixture of ecstasy and relief.

"Wow."

"Your neck is like steel. Are you stressed out about something?"

"A little to the left," she whispered, ignoring Bob's attempt to be funny. No need to burden the nice stranger with her petty gripes and worries about an untimely death.

"You're going to do great," he reassured her.

"And you're basing this on what?"

"Instinct."

"Good luck with that."

Bob pressed in deeper and Nina worried that she might start crying it felt so good, and heaven help closing the floodgates once they're opened. She'd resisted the urge to so much as stop and take a breath since Pete was arrested, and if she stopped now there was a decent chance she might not get up off the mat for the full ten count and then some. Risk of utter emotional and physical collapse or not, there was simply no chance she was voluntarily removing his thumbs from her body.

"I've been meaning to say thank you, by the way."

Nina resisted the urge to swivel around in disbelief, and if the massage weren't enough to get her off her game, sincere gratitude and decency was going to send her off the deep end, every emotion spinning around now like they'd been chopped up and tossed into the blender.

"You don't have to thank me," she said, a bit too forcefully for her own taste.

There was no answer, but Nina figured he couldn't be too offended since his hands didn't miss a beat. What she'd meant to say was 'please don't thank me', but the words spilled out before she had a chance to get them right. Guilt was only used as an offensive weapon and she wasn't used to being on the receiving end of it.

"It must be hard," Nina said softly. "To be around me, I mean. I know it can't be easy for you."

"You're going to do great today."

Susan walked back in, car keys in hand. She nodded *it's time* to Nina, who swallowed hard in aching expectation, like the next kid in line to see the dentist.

She stepped away from Bob's grasp, her muscles immediately angry with her for such a stupid decision. It was time, though. My life isn't going to work itself out with a back rub, Nina decided.

"After you," Nina said.

Nina had never been to Harvey's apartment. There had never been any reason, certainly the two were not close, even by the standards of a blatantly casual second-party workplace relationship. Their interaction had always been on the surface, neither party interested in moving beyond pleasantries (Harvey) and flirting (Nina). A give and take of anything and everything bereft of meaning and importance. She'd never felt bad. It struck Nina that this sort of relationship was perhaps the norm more than the exception.

Knocking on the door, Nina felt that if the ensuing encounter went at all well, she would offer some sage advice: an unlisted number is probably the way to go in certain lines of work.

It was comforting to see Susan and Bob in the parked car across the street. The bright sun and green shrubs covering the exterior of the apartment were equally reassuring that a severe act of violence against her person was not forthcoming. She was less optimistic when Harvey opened the door and smiled the most impossibly wide smile she had ever seen, rendering her the proverbial deer in the headlights.

"You want to come in?" Harvey asked, breaking the silence.

"Yes."

He stepped to the side. Nina remained motionless. Harvey was a tough bird to read under normal circumstances. The smile had shrunk, but hadn't left his face and, if anything, was even more disconcerting. He didn't smile much. He never looked…happy. That was it. *Dear God in Heaven above*, Nina thought, *the man looks happy*. She imagined it might be the same sort of smile a lion has when a gazelle wanders into view nursing a swollen ankle. Then she pictured her old grade-school visits to the zoo and tried to remember if she'd ever actually seen a gazelle.

"Well?" Harvey asked politely.

"Things were flashing before my eyes," Nina continued bravely, "and to be perfectly frank, I'm not quite ready for those thoughts to be the montage of my life."

"Nina, I know exactly what you mean. Come on in and have a drink with me."

She was here. What else could she do?

"Okay."

Chapter 20

"What can I get you?"

"Whatever you're having."

Harvey proceeded to make two Harvey Wallbangers, the irony of which did not resonate with Nina until many days later. She took a sip. It was decidedly excellent. She relaxed. There was not a single moment throughout human history when a drink this good was served before a barbaric atrocity, of which her murder most certainly qualified. It simply could not be so.

"Thank you," Nina began, not really sure how to proceed.

"Easy as can be."

"I meant more the not killing me part."

"That's what I meant, too."

"I was thinking we might dispense with the pleasantries and get right to it," she said acidly.

Harvey chuckled. "Absolutely."

"I want Pete out of jail. Somebody's going to have to burn, and I figured there was no earthly reason it shouldn't be Paul."

"A year ago, you could have bet me anything, and I mean absolutely anything, that we would not be here today."

"I know the feeling."

"It was Rick, by the way, that did Alan. His wife, too."

"Paul ordered it, though, right?"

"With a little encouragement. But yes."

"And you?"

He looked questioningly at Nina for the first time, as if she'd taken her first misstep. "What are you looking for here?"
It would have been easy to misconstrue her question, she realized. Tact was the word of the day, and asking a man of illegal means to incriminate himself was probably in direct opposition of that agenda.

"It was a dumb question," Nina agreed.

"I'd like to help."

"But…"

"I've made some questionable choices, Nina. Especially of late. I'm almost fifty. I don't want to die in prison. I'll help. But I'm not going to start over from scratch."

Money. Of course he wanted money. Upon second thought, it didn't seem so crass. Harvey had put in a lot of years, prime earning years at that. Every executive deserves a golden parachute, why settle for less.

The real burning question then became how much would he accept and where the hell she would get that kind of money. Nina almost laughed out loud when her first idea was to steal the money. Perhaps theft was not the best way to extricate her and hers from a criminal lifestyle. She had a bank account. Liquid assets. She'd been dying to pawn Pete's golf clubs for years. Perhaps this wouldn't be such a terrible way to progress.

"You'd like to help," she said, effectively opening negotiations.

"I want out," Harvey intoned. "I'd like to help very much."

Very much, Nina mused, is probably a low-to-mid six figures phrasing. She might be able to swing that. A few hundred thousand dollars to free an innocentish man and revive a marriage? Cheap at the price.

"You'll come with me. Tonight. You'll make a statement, in

which you admit no guilt on your part in the involvement of the most serious offenses, and you'll agree to provide information on other crimes to which you will be granted immunity."

"In exchange for…"

"Let's work something out," Nina resolved, feeling pretty good about herself.

At the exact moment when Rick's life was taking a sharp downward descent, a nosedive in fact from which he would never recover, he was having a fantastic time trying to bed down a Hooters waitress and, he thought with no small measure of pride, doing quite well. She was a transplant from Ohio, an actress (of course), and the poor girl was just getting over a bad breakup with a verbally abusive parking lot attendant from Long Beach. The fact that the beau lived below Anaheim was cause enough for ending the relationship in Rick's opinion, but he sympathized at the appropriate moments as she unloaded her most common and pedestrian sob story. A well placed 'uh-huh' and a sympathetic nod was doing the seduction equivalent of two shots of tequila and a Valium. Lunch had even been tasty.

"I'll be right back with your check," Cindy purred.

"Take your time," Rick replied.

In point of fact, he did not want the afternoon to end. Hitting on waitresses was one of his favorite activities, and a welcome respite from the hurly-burly hustle and bustle of work. It wasn't the normal, everyday responsibilities that had him down. Killing Alan and framing Pete had been quite the lark, and the rush of power he felt for helping to orchestrate the whole scheme dwarfed the momentary thrill of pulling the trigger.

Excavating the boss's wife's stomach, however, had been a freaking nightmare. Not for the first time, Rick wished he got paid overtime and/or hazard pay. Dealing with Amy's shit definitely qualified. This is why union membership is at an all-time high, he figured, even with corruption and excessive dues and behemoths like Wal-Mart. Can loan sharks organize? He could be the president. Jimmy Hoffa without the unpleasant ending under Giant's Stadium.

His train of thought was derailed by the return of waitress dream girl.

"Here you go. I left my number on the back."

Rick flipped the bill over and immediately noticed three things. First, the young lady had indeed left her number, minus the area code, which, in Los Angeles, essentially meant the first three digits of her number were 555. Secondly, she had miscalculated the bill, and by quite a large margin. Eighteen dollars for a side of fries? That seems a tad high, he mused. He was hardly likely to argue over a few dollars when sex was on the line. Perhaps that was the plan. Overcharge the sucker and pocket the difference. The thought of such a cold, calculating ice-in-the-veins woman was dispelled when he noticed she had misspelled the 'please' in please call me. He looked up and smiled. All in all, he might very well be in love.

Rick would think about this particular afternoon often. Doing eight years at a spic populated shithole north of La Jolla necessitated endless escapist fantasies, though not in the literal sense. Fond memories of youthful indiscretions and adult recreation of moments like the afternoon with Cindy, the lovely and dumb Hooter's girl, became one of two pleasures in his life, the other being chicken patty night at the commissary.

His days passed in rigid conformity to the rules (written and otherwise) of California's third largest state prison. Up at eight AM, mosey down to breakfast at nine. Some free time, which Rick used to hide in his cell was followed by lunch and mandatory 'yardwork', the inmate-coined phrase for outdoor activities. Rick was bored, but not enough to risk playing basketball or lifting weights with some truly scary motherfuckers. Visiting hours were available before dinner, but he never had to worry about that. Dinner and lights out before you could blink. Structure was the name of the game for convicted felons, and Rick adapted with relative ease.

Falling asleep at night to the rhythmic snoring of his cellmate, one thought would invariably come back to him night after lonely night. Prison is not fun, but it sure beats the hell out of working.

Nina was not happy.

"No. Definitely not. Out of the question. No, no, no."

The promising start had become muddled down in increasingly antagonized tones. A smarminess she had not expected from Harvey had risen with the force of a tsunami, and she was ill equipped to combat it. Her only defense was to stand firm, not to give a single inch of ground.

"It is quite the reasonable offer," Harvey continued smugly. "If I do say so myself."

"I'm not writing you a check for three quarters of a million dollars," Nina said, exasperated. "It's idiotic."

"I know what Pete made. I know every dollar of every year."

"We don't have that. We spent money on useless extravagances like a mortgage and Porsches."

"Which is why I don't want it all."

Negotiating skill, in general, was never something Nina aspired to acquire. In school, whenever a classmate had wanted to trade lunches, which wasn't often thanks to her mom's sandwich making prowess, she had never bothered to fight very hard for the upper hand. It seemed tiring to try for the ham and cheese with mustard when the turkey on rye with mayo was almost as tasty. Why argue when I can be eating was Nina's lunchtime mantra and as time passed, this particular personality trait solidified, erasing any chance of working in sales.

Unfortunately for Nina, Harvey was not only a shrewd negotiator, he took perverse pleasure in winning an absurdly good deal for himself, regardless of the stakes. Arguing over Pete's future was, for Harvey, essentially the same as two children arguing over the last chocolate chip cookie after consuming several dozen. That she had unbuttoned the top two buttons of her blouse and was still nowhere near a manageable figure was starting to unnerve her.

"Harvey, let's come back to reality. Okay?"

"Nina, this is reality. You can tell because I'm still living in the fucking Valley."

"Three hundred and fifty thousand. It's my final offer," Nina said, surprised at the firm tone in her own voice.

It was said with strength and purpose. Less powerful words had been uttered many times before for far more important purposes. He looked genuinely intimidated. A strain of pride ran through her veins. Hope had been renewed.

Harvey took a loud bite from an apple, chewed thoughtfully, and said, "Nope."

He was very, very bored. Time spent watching Amy sleeping had moved past interesting and become earth-shatteringly boring, his state of mind completely bypassing husbandly concern along the way.

Catching the rhythm of Amy's breathing was soothing at first, like a lava lamp. A glimpse of normality, or what passed for normalcy in Paul's imagination, floated like a breeze through the room. What might have been had he gone to work everyday in a shirt and tie to a cubicle with Dilbert cartoons tacked to the wall. It was a pleasant sensation.

"Knock it off, idiot," Paul said to himself, much louder than he had intended. It didn't seem to bother Amy, leading him to the inevitable conclusion that his presence near her was no longer necessary.

It felt wrong to just up and leave, but it didn't seem to be benefiting Amy and he was about to enter his own personal coma if he spent another minute in the pseudo-hospital room his bedroom had become. Daydreaming about another life wasn't going to do anything for anybody, that was for damn sure.

Why was he even thinking about that sort of thing? Where was that list? Going over the list would help get his head back on straight, Paul was certain. Of course, the search for the list opened up another can of worms. He had never been able to find big things. His car keys were always where he left them, his bottle opener remained in the kitchen, but he had once managed to lose his gun and car on the same day (the car he eventually found in an employee-only parking space at a frozen-yogurt stand). The recently written to-do list qualified as a big thing, and for the life of him, he had absolutely no idea where it might presently lay. Somehow, he always managed to find the item in question, but not before the rapid rise of his blood pressure. Any doctor worth his salt would have been concerned had Paul's BP been measured at that particular moment and the list would not be found for another three days, when, in a fit of desperation, a rejuvenated Amy would clean the guest room for the first time since Reagan was in office.

Fortunately for Paul and his health, he abandoned the search when he remembered the first and most important note written on the list. Kill more people. Damn straight. Pondering whom to kill, Paul realized he was feeling a little alone. He should call Harvey, say hello, see if the old guy wanted to get out of the house for a little while.

Susan was not a happy camper, of this Bob was certain. It was, sadly, the only thing he was certain about, a fact that left him feeling on the whole discombobulated. He was trying hard not to think about the stakes involved just a few hundred feet from his car, and failing miserably he was forced to admit to himself. He was sweating, he was nervous, and his girlfriend was not a happy camper.

The day can only get better, Bob thought. Knock on wood.

Maybe a compliment would shake her malaise. It wasn't easy to say nice things to Susan. A normal person, when confronted with positive affirmation, would smile, say thank you, perhaps even a kiss on the cheek if the situation and relationship warranted it. In this respect, and many others he noted wryly, Susan was in no way normal.

"You look very pretty today," Bob said.

"Shut up."

It was a poor attempt at flattery, to be sure. He should have said something nice about her shoes. An insincere smile didn't seem to be asking too much, though.

"I'm edgy and nervous," Bob said. "You should be calming my nerves. And you do look pretty today."

"It'll happen or it won't."

"Great," he said, fighting the urge to audibly sigh and further antagonize Susan.

"It's just another step," Susan said, trying to placate Bob. She should cut him some slack, he was having a rough day. Betting so hard on a mobster's wife was probably not going to bust the house, but it was a step in the right direction. "If it goes well, then yippee. If it doesn't, we try something else. We've got names, we've got places to go. Relax, okay?"

"You make all of that sound reasonable."

"It is reasonable."

"It sounds that way."

"That's because it is."

"You do look pretty today."

"I was thinking of having Thai tonight."

"Okay."

"There's a new place on Virgil, down by that Peruvian restaurant you liked."

"You liked."

"That's what I meant."

There was a tone to her voice that Bob couldn't quite place. She wasn't pissed off but it definitely wasn't a happy tone, an edge to her jokiness. Subtle inquiries were out the door with Susan. She would see right through the attempt and then, with moderate cause, be more than a little annoyed he hadn't just come out with it. It was not easy to break Susan out of a funk. The direct approach was the best option.

"What's going on?" Bob asked.

"In general?"

"With you," he replied, ignoring Susan's snippy response. "Right here, right now."

"These are trying times."

Bob sighed audibly. He couldn't help himself. "That's your answer?"

"I know I'm…I don't know. But I know. It's just this sort of thing, that, I can't really, or rather I can't really say right now. But it's not a big deal and it's not anything bad to do with you."

"I wasn't thinking that at all."

"Good."

"Until now."

"Bob."

"I'm the only one of us that can be weird and awkward right now. Level with me."

"I did. I leveled."

"Right."

"Later. At the Thai place."

"Okay. As long as we get it out. Only one weird and awkward. Do you understand?"

"I understand."

"You do?"

"Why were you rubbing her back?" Susan asked bluntly.

"Ah," Bob answered, relieved, everything immediately clear.

He felt so much better.

Susan did not. "That's your answer?"

Bob reached out and rubbed Susan's head affectionately. She glared at him to stop. He tweaked her nose in response.

"I think it's endearing that you're jealous," Bob said. "But there is no need, little one. I only have eyes for you."

"Could you be any more patronizing?"

"I sure could, Kitten."

Susan tried hard, but couldn't suppress the giggle.

"Bob, you're an unbelievable dope."

Negotiations were breaking down. Everything was breaking down. Harvey was growing irritable and Nina tired. Something had to give, and both parties were noticeably relieved when the phone rang. Harvey answered it.

"Yeah."

A long pause ensued. A very long pause. This much silence had perhaps never before in the annals of human history stretched for such an interminable period of time. Not for one second of the phone conversation did he remove his gaze from Nina. The combined effect was, all in all Nina thought, swallowing nervously, more than a little unnerving.

Wanting to look away, she instead forced herself to watch Harvey closely, looking for some sign of emotion to betray the nature of the conversation, but none was forthcoming. The quiet stretched to epic proportions and Nina briefly wondered if perhaps the caller on the other end of the line had long since hung up.

Harvey looked away and mumbled, "I'll talk to you then."

He put his dead eyes back on Nina, his posture intimating a readiness to resume and dominate their wheeling and dealing. But something was different. It was subtle, but something was most definitely different. His demeanor had lost some of the arrogant confidence that so fully defined his personality. It was almost as if he was trying, and trying hard at that, to create the *appearance* of himself.

Nina thought suddenly of Stanley, that little twerp of a salesman who fleeced Pete for the Porsche, despite taking a severe beating in the process. He wouldn't be denied, it didn't matter what obstacles rolled his way because deep down he knew he was in control the whole time. Stanley always had the ace up his sleeve, he possessed something the suckers wanted, and wanted desperately at that.

Harvey is just like those poor bastards shopping at the car dealership. Hours spent haggling take the toll of a lifetime's labor for men and women who only want to drive home in a car that doesn't smell of day old donuts. It was no wonder car salesmen occupied a rung of society not far above numerous life forms not yet capable of speech. For the truly astute and/or cheap, the same techniques can be employed against the dealership. She doesn't just have the aces, she holds all the cards. Now it's just a question of will, and it was with certainty, clarity and conviction that Nina knew for a fact her will was stronger than his.

He's breaking, she realized. He's falling apart at the seams. Don't lose the momentum, Nina, you've got the man on the ropes. What in the hell do they do at the dealership at this point? Do I badger, cajole, threaten to get up and leave? Offer a financing option? Her eyes widened, and Nina had to physically resist the urge to yell 'Aha!'

Pounce, idiot, pounce!

She took out her checkbook and placed it on the coffee table.

"I'll write you a check right now, Harv," Nina said, blatantly emphasizing the word check. "Two hundred and eighteen thousand dollars. It's yours, cash it, deposit it, stow it away for a rainy day and you can walk away in five minutes and be free and clear to start your retirement. Two hundred and eighteen thousand dollars. And zero cents."

Her eyes locked with his and she could see her read was dead on, for the first time recognizing wholly the desperate straits he was in, the big picture laid out before her in Technicolor. He wanted out, badly, and he knew what would happen should he stay. He needed her, way more than she needed him. Now, stay calm, Nina. Pick up the checkbook and slowly move it back into the purse. Harvey's eyes predictably followed and she did her best not to stand and shriek in jubilation.

"Well?"

"Goddammit," he grumbled in defeat.

"Should I start signing?" Nina asked, unable to resist twisting the knife a little.

"What the hell happened to you? Didn't you used to be a shameless little tart? And not five years ago. Five minutes, I'm talking."

"The world keeps spinning, Harvey. We don't notice it, but every now and then things are bound to change."

Nina thought it an impressive line, but Harvey snorted and rubbed his eyes in disbelief, waiting impatiently for her to finish signing the check. She handed it to him, the paper crisp and new. He folded it once and slipped it into his pants pocket. Two hundred and eighteen thousand dollars.

"That was Paul a few minutes ago."

"Was it now."

"He's feeling a bit edgy, asked if I would like to come out with him and kill someone."

"You're kidding."

"His exact words. He went on to say a lot more, but yeah, his exact words."

"Did he give a name?"

"As a matter of fact, he did. Winston Mcleroy."

"When?"

Harvey looked melodramatically at his watch.

Chapter 21

THE PHONE rang on Ortiz's desk, and despite the soothing tone of the ringer Ortiz had paid money from his own pocket to install, a feeling of dread flooded through him. His instincts rarely let him down, and he was convinced it was this sort of intuition that made him a great homicide detective, if a sometimes unhappy husband. He briefly considered leaving early for the day, but picked up the phone anyway. It was his job, after all.

"Ortiz," he answered cautiously.

"It's Susan."

He almost hung up the phone right then and there. Susan's voice seemed to anticipate this very move, and escalated in urgency before he had the chance to reconsider.

"I need a favor and I need it now, don't screw around with me, just do it and trust me."

"What is it?" Ortiz sighed.

"I need a four-one-one on Winston Mcleroy. Last known, whatever you can give me. He'll have a sheet, I need it quick."

"Tell me why."

"Ortiz—"

"I need a reason. Lie to me, tell me a story, but I have to have something."

"He's going to be murdered in a few hours, maybe less. The

man responsible for this crime of the future is also responsible for six or seven murders in the last month, not to mention countless others in his twenty some odd years of criminal activity. In addition, he is responsible for the murder of Mr. and Mrs. Alan McKinnon, for which he framed Pete Morell, currently incarcerated and awaiting trial. So if I could get that information, I'd be most appreciative."

He thought about it. She had clearly lost it. Still, he had asked for a story and the lady delivered. It'd be rude not to reward the girl for spinning such a high quality yarn. He entered Winston's name into his computer and related the material to Susan.

"I'll send a unit over as well. You can thank me with a gift basket."

The line went dead so quickly, Ortiz wondered if she had gotten the address. He was particularly disappointed that he didn't have a chance to give her his closing barb. It was a good one, too.

To say it was a bad neighborhood would create a false impression. It was an irredeemable, vile street, filled with miscreants, filth and Calcutta-like sanitation. There were three sights that stood out and vied for Bob's attention as Susan drove along slowly. Far too slowly in Bob's estimation.

First off, there was a dining room set in the street. Not the nicest, mind you, and missing a few place settings, but a perfectly respectable collection of chairs around a table, still with the accompanying napkin holders. By the damage inflicted from the sun and wind, he figured it had been resting in the street for a few weeks shy of his lifetime. It had been, in fact, only five weeks.

Secondly, there was a man pacing about and ranting, loudly, in something vaguely resembling a language. This was disconcerting, but Bob had seen crazy people before. He had once played a set of tennis while a man three courts over lectured the sky about the evils of stock car racing. What was truly unsettling about this particular instance of public insanity was the woman around whom the crazy man was pacing, calmly reading a very thick book. If Bob had looked closely, he would have seen that the book was *Watership Down* and that the jacket was upside down. This would have made sight number three slightly easier to digest.

The apartment building, Winston's home, was a dilapidated pile of bricks that had somehow managed to avoid a visit from the Fair Housing Commission and/or a strong breeze. A three-story structure (the second floor completely burnt out — cause unknown) in between an abandoned Korean grocery mart and a vacant lot. Bob genuinely felt living in the vacant lot might well be preferable.

Bob checked the lock on his door for the sixth time and felt relieved that Susan had driven. He also felt, for the umpteenth time, enormously guilty for such thoughts.

"Should we park?" he asked, somewhat hoping that she would instead drive to Disneyland.

"Never been to this neighborhood before, Bob?"

"Regular haunt?"

"This was my beat for two months back in ninety-four."

Did he hear that right? Did she mean 1994?

"Wait, what?" Bob asked, confused.

"It looks worse than it is," Susan said reassuringly.

"I find that very hard to believe. Did you see Crazyman McGee back there?"

"You mean Larry?"

He was so wound up and she said it with such earnest innocence it took Bob a few seconds to realize she was teasing him. He smiled in spite of his best efforts not to. "You're a funny, funny woman, Ciarelli."

"Just easing the tension."

Sneaking into Andy's impound lot was ridiculously easy for

an establishment with no less than eight signs warning of attack dogs on the premises (untrue) and barbed wire fences (true). A ladder and a pair of hedge clippers took care of the fence and from the time Winston parked two blocks away, unloaded his equipment, scaled the fence and came face to face with Brandon's beloved Betty, a mere eleven minutes had elapsed.

What had not been easy was getting the gasoline. He didn't have a standard, Shell oil approved container to fill with gasoline. The attendant, an annoying middle-aged woman bitter beyond her years, refused to let him fill up Brandon's souvenir Milwaukee Brewers Baseball novelty helmet, a monstrosity that both Winston and Brandon could attest held up to three gallons of alcohol at a time. He had been forced to wait until she went to the bathroom, then went ahead and inserted his credit card, punched in his zip code and began pumping premium (again, Brandon's request). He had almost finished when he heard the police siren. The bitter attendant had apparently passed on urinating and decided instead to phone the police about the man with the oversized novelty hat lurking in the shadows.

Sheesh, Winston thought, *it's not as if I didn't pay for it.* Fucking people are the worst.

He dropped the pump and ran like hell, sloshing gasoline as he went. A lesser friend would have dropped the helmet, but Winston held onto it for dear life. By the time he dove behind a thick grove of bushes a block and half from the gas station, he had lost all but a few ounces of gas.

The second gas station he visited was much more accommodating, its attendant a college kid in a fraternity who looked as though he could not wait to go tell his buddies about Winston's mission.

It never occurred to Winston to wait until he reached the impound lot to put the gasoline in the helmet, a simple matter that would have made his night much easier. Moving expeditiously from point A to B was never really his forte.

As per Brandon's instructions, Winston covered Betty from bumper to bumper with premium gas, placing the novelty helmet on top of the hood when he was done. He took out his lighter, a cheap gift from his step-brother he was happy to part with, and almost set Betty aflame before remembering to say the words.

It had taken Brandon a week to write Betty's eulogy, and its importance was highlighted with a yellow highlighter in the document Winston now held before him. Certain the moment he opened his mouth the law would collapse upon him, Winston went ahead and readied himself as best he could, clearing his throat and taking a deep breath.

"I welcome you all to this happy occasion. We are here tonight to honor Betty, beloved nineteen ninety-three Ford Mercury Sable with power windows and locks and broken air conditioner. A true companion all her life, she will know no equal in this life or the next. I hereby commit her memory to the wind. Ashes to ashes, metal to metal, dust to dust."

He flicked the lighter, tossed it onto the car and inadvertently burned down half a city block. Brandon would have been thrilled.

Never in her adult life had Susan knowingly and wantonly committed a crime. Breaking into Winston's apartment was a painful experience, and only partly for the nail that nicked her wrist as she pried open the door with Bob's rusty tire jack, itself finding use for only the second time ever, the first being a brutalizing occasion in the pouring rain outside Santa Cruz when an impulse to play savior forced Bob to spend most of an evening with an unpleasant coed finding it difficult to contend with her ex-boyfriend's frequent phone calls and the flat tire stranding her ten miles outside of campus.

Once inside, he stood behind Susan expectantly. She was not leaping into action, contrary to Bob's expectations upon hearing her suggest entering another's premises without permission. Standing in the doorway motionless was probably not the best idea.

Bob leaned over Susan's shoulder and asked, "What are we looking for?"

"I don't know. We'll know it if we find it. I hope."

She was stalling. The moment she stepped over the threshold was largely symbolic at this point, given she'd forced the door and was still holding the tire iron in her hand, but it was a line the pit in her stomach did not want to cross.

"Should we start looking?" Bob asked insistently.

"Sorry. Yes, you take the kitchen."

The kitchen, if tiny room with a sink and a broken hotplate can be called a kitchen, was in disrepair. Aside from a sudden urge to have every childhood inoculation verified and perhaps retaken, Bob suddenly felt very nervous about the repercussions of sorting through another man's refuse. Susan noticed his trepidation and instantly felt better, gratified she wasn't the only one with butterflies.

"Should we worry about fingerprints?" Bob asked.

"In this place? I think we can relax."

Bob peeled a banana, or the remains of something he fervently hoped was once a banana, off the counter. "Any suggestions on where to start?"

"Maybe a phone message, I don't know. A clue, anything at all."

"How about a map?"

Bob held out a napkin (from Kung Pao Bistro on Fairfax; stolen, along with an order of the house crispy beef) with a crude sketch of East Los Angeles, stretching from Alameda to Sixth Street. A big ink dot was soaked through a section that remained clearly marked as C. Chavez Avenue. Bob and Susan shared a look.

"Should we call the police?" he asked.

That was absolutely the right course of action, though she was surprised to hear Bob suggest it. She tried Ortiz first, but he wasn't answering his landline or his cell, the result of his kid's piano recital and a promise to his ex-wife to be a better father. Alekhov was next, but his phone was turned off, going straight to voicemail, the result of forgetfulness. She thought about calling 911, but it would undoubtedly come back that she came by the tip via illegal activities, and that was not likely to make Baker a happy camper.

"Ortiz said he would send a car."

"When?"

Good question, Susan thought, her mind racing.

"Let's go ourselves," she said. "Just to look."

Taken as a whole, Susan did not enjoy her maiden intentional felony. Guilt pangs stuck with her for several weeks.

It was a first for Bob, too. He enjoyed it a great deal.

A short man with expensive clothes and a skinny blonde way out of his league stood before Detective Alekhov. The man kept casting his eyes about the room, and Alekhov's first thought was to check the database for outstanding warrants.

"I'm looking for Detective Ortiz," Nina asked impatiently.

Alekhov was having a good day. It had all begun when his girlfriend of two years moved her aerobics machine out of the bedroom and into the heavy trash bin. She used it a grand total of four times, the fourth and final time for less than three minutes. The damn thing just sat there, month after month, gathering dust and resentment. And now it was gone.

Then came breakfast. His girlfriend of two years forced him to eat breakfast, every single day with the relentless will a tyrant would envy. She was constantly harping on the importance of eggs, which would not be so bad were it not for the absence of bacon, or sausage, or something recently deceased and fried. But it was always just eggs, lonely, lonely eggs. Arguing only made matters worse, namely egg whites, so Alekhov ate quickly and tried not to think about it, which, not surprisingly, only made him think about it more. Today there were no eggs, only pancakes.

As if these two momentous events were not enough to leave a smile on his face for the entire day regardless of the number of murderers, rapists, thugs, thieves, arsonists, felons from every shade and walk of life and the various assorted jerks that floated through his professional life most weekdays, his favorite song was played on the way to work. Twice.

The two people standing expectantly before him were an easy read, even if he didn't know the exact reason they were here to see his partner. If there was anything he had learned from his partnership with Ortiz, it was the man's intense dislike of frivolous absurdities. Ortiz was a man of rigid order and discipline. Two people coming in off the street, looking all the world like the rejects from the real housewives of something or other, was exactly the sort of nonsense that drove him to work through a bottle of Advil a week.

Normally Alekhov was happy to play gatekeeper to Ortiz's sanity, maneuvering the most difficult sorts to a different department, or at least giving a little warning before unleashing the public upon him. It was the least he could do given at some point Ortiz was probably going to save his life, and this would balance out the cosmic scale well in advance. Every once in a while, though, he just couldn't resist having a little fun.

"He's over there, he just got in" Alekhov said, trying not to grin in the process, pointing to the small cubbyhole Ortiz had carved out for himself to avoid the waking world. "Go right on over."

He'd pay for it later, but tomorrow was tomorrow, and sending Nina and Harvey to Ortiz was only going to make a great day better.

"Should I get a lawyer and come back?" Harvey asked melodramatically.

Ortiz was doing his best to disregard the impending migraine. "My balls are sore enough, can you cut me some slack?"

"I was thinking a very similar thought, Detective."

Alekhov held back a smirk, admiring the man's grace under fire. *This is one cool customer*, he thought. He'd thought the man nervous at first glance, but now he could see it was more amusement on Harvey's face, his eyes soaking up all the sights like Dillinger strolling through the police station in the 30's and enjoying the view of his Wanted poster up close.

Eavesdropping on the conversation had brought Alekhov quickly into the fold. It was obvious from the look Ortiz gave him that he would rather have suffered through this particular indignity thrust upon him by Susan alone, but there was no way Alekhov was missing out on a bust this big. Plus, it was always fun to watch his partner get increasingly hot under the collar.

"You want full immunity from charges we haven't levied. You want full immunity against crimes that technically do not exist. You understand my reticence?"

"Your friend sent us here," Nina interjected, not used to playing the voice of reason of late. "You have her word."

"She's not my friend. And your interest is fairly obvious, Mrs. Morell. If it were my significant other on death row, I'd say just about anything. You know what I mean?"

"Doesn't mean it's not the truth."

"Too true. Which is why we're still speaking."

Ortiz turned his attention to Harvey, and he would have given anything to have a little more ammunition in his pocket to wipe the smugness from the man's face. "Now, Harvey, if you don't mind me calling you Harvey, if you'd like to confess to crimes you were directly involved with, and name your co-conspirators, I'd be happy to float the offer of immunity to my superiors."

"I have a friend," Harvey began, shifting in his seat. "Can I have a cigarette?"

"Sure."

"This friend," Harvey continued, getting comfortable, "he's a material witness to dozens of heinous crimes, including murder in every degree possible. Determined to mend his evil ways, for the greater good, he comes to the one honest cop in the hopes of an equitable trade. But this friend of mine? He's not an idiot."

"And I'm the one honest cop in this tell-tale little fable?"

"Susan trusts you," Nina said. "So we trust you."

It took a moment for Alekhov to realize the look on Ortiz's face was abject despair. Despite the likely end result of making a front-page bust, he was going to live with the knowledge it came with the help of Susan Ciarelli.

This day, a day to end all perfect days, has reached its zenith. It can get no better, Alekhov decided.

A headache of epic proportions was rising quickly behind Ortiz's temples. It had begun while listening to his daughter butcher Brahms an hour earlier, was spreading quickly, and no amount of aspirin would make even the slightest dent. The look of glee on Alekhov's face did nothing to lessen the impending migraine.

Chapter 22

PAUL MADE a mental note. Timing is everything.

He had arrived at Winston's apartment just in time to spot Winston exiting with a gigantic novelty hat. In retrospect, he should have walked over and shot the man in the head right then and there, but he couldn't bring himself to end the man's life without knowing just exactly what was happening.

By the time Winston flicked open his lighter, Paul decided he had heard enough to satisfy his curiosity. Stepping out, gun raised high to announce his presence, he shouted to Winston, the force of his booming voice completely lost in the ensuing fireball, which spread with shocking speed from the 1993 Pontiac to the pile of tires soaked in diesel fuel and 10W-30 and then speedily to the functioning gas pump nearby, which in turn shot a plume of fire into the night sky.

The truly bad luck came when the wind picked up at precisely the right moment to carry the flames across the street to the A&C Corporation, Ltd., which made, among other things, cardboard boxes. The boxes were the first, but by no means the last, to go, but owner and operator Anthony Clark, as if anticipating exactly such an event, had recently upped his fire insurance to more than cover the cost of such a loss, and despite heavy pressure from the upper brass of Lincomb Insurance, the investigators could find no possible trace of arson. Mr. Clark happily retired to Colorado not long after.

It didn't take long for the A&C to act as kindling for the abandoned warehouse to the left and Able Body Storage to the right. From there, the old Los Angeles Department of Water and Power building, in the process of being renovated and turned into overpriced lofts for twenty-somethings with little to no sense of the real estate market in the city's overall downtown revitalization efforts, caught fire and the domino effect was well and truly underway.

Barbara Cornel had placed the sum total of her husband's worldly possessions in storage, including his baseball card collection with signed Mickey Mantle, prized childhood collection of Scrooge McDuck comic books, furniture, clothing, driver's license and all family photographs and memorabilia. Barbara's husband, finishing a two-year stint as an E-7 Chief Petty Officer in the navy, was scheduled to return a week before Able Body Storage burned to a cinder, but was held up by a medical quarantine, itself a mistake instigated by a low-level technician failing to file proper paperwork during a routine maintenance effort on the ship's air purification system.

Afraid for her life, Barbara delayed informing her husband of the unfortunate end to his things, and instead employed a strategy of misdirection by preparing elaborate meals, ceding all control of the remote, dressed in binding underwear and smiled pleasantly until her cheeks ached from the effort. This worked for eight days. On the ninth day, Barbara could smile no more and was forced to reveal the truth, but predicated it with a fax detailing the payment Able Body Storage had authorized as 'a small token of our sincere regret for your loss' in the hopes of avoiding a lawsuit they were sure to lose given the ancient and substandard sprinklers in the building. As it turned out, she could have avoided spending so much time in the kitchen had she greeted him at the airport with this information. They spent the next three weeks in Puerto Vallarta.

Others were not so lucky.

Mr. Amberson, walking his ill-tempered but loyal terrier Lena, received second-degree burns on his arms and face when he turned the corner of Adams Boulevard at precisely the wrong moment. About one-third of Lena was set on fire, but caused little permanent damage except to alter the color of her ears to a darker shade of brown. The neighbors agreed, in secret, the traumatic event went a long way toward soothing the beast's volatile nature.

Walter Parker spent two weeks at St. Joseph's ICU, treated for third-degree burns and smoke inhalation. Carrying no insurance, Walter's case sparked enough public sympathy to earn an exemption courtesy of the mayor, a board member at the hospital. Walter took advantage, ignoring the recommendations of his doctors and spending an extra two days in the hospital, determined to get the home phone number of a petite nurse with strong hands on the third floor. It was not to be.

Claire Tanner lost most of the hearing in her left ear as a result of the explosion. Eddie Marshall, a fireman called to the scene, slipped in a puddle and landed awkwardly, slipping a disc in the process. As a result, he was forced to leave the fire department and find work as a jewelry salesman, working for his younger brother, whom he grew to truly loathe. Todd Jones, a machinist on his way home from a particularly grueling sixteen-hour shift, got caught up in the fire and lost his truck. The truck was unregistered and when the police recovered the remains, Todd was dumbfounded to discover the city was demanding almost four-hundred dollars in penalties for a vehicle that no longer ran and barely even resembled its former self.

Ryan Newble, homeless for two years since an unfortunate incident with prescription Xanax and an unforgiving landlord, barely escaped suffocation in his sleeping bag. He did not escape the destruction of his underpass that was ravaged by the fire. Devastated, Ryan spent the next few years trying to recreate the environment, with no luck. It was a real shame, he felt. He had just gotten comfortable.

Miraculously, not a single soul perished as a result of Betty's demise and the destruction of her final resting place. It was commonly accepted, though, that the high hopes for economic development in the area were laid to rest when the last of the flames was finally put out.

All of this was yet to come. At that particular moment, Paul was more concerned with the birds engulfed in the flames now falling from the sky in droves. Avoiding burnt crisps of pigeons proved to be very difficult.

The smoke was becoming thicker. Paul wiped the tears from his eyes, trying his best to find his bearings. It was obvious to him that the fire was spreading quickly, and his position of safety, the covered doorway facing away from the inferno, while getting comfortably warm, would soon become extremely inhospitable. Good sense dictated a hasty withdrawal, but he was going to be good and goddamned if Winston was going to be allowed to live after this nonsense. Simple public decency demanded an execution, and in this instance, Paul would have had a groundswell of support from all sides.

Carcasses no longer falling from the sky, explosions becoming background noise, he turned his full attention back to Winston, visible a short distance away through the smoke and ash.

Winston remained on the ground, burned badly, his hair all but gone, replaced by vicious third-degree burns. He was a mess and Paul was unsure whether the man could survive without the aid of a machine for more than an hour as it were. The pain must be unimaginable.

The fact that he was laughing made the image all the more disconcerting. The idiot was actually laughing.

If Paul hadn't seen it, he wouldn't have believed it.

Walking across the lot with trepidation, as much for the slight twinge of fear that had popped up in his stomach from the insanity growing steadily closer in the form of a half-dead giggling idiot as for the flames themselves, he felt only slightly comforted by the weight of the gun in his right hand.

Bob and Susan arrived at the impound lot four minutes before Caroline Meade's storage unit melted, destroying, among other things, one hundred LP's of various country and western artists from the 1940's, a signed photo of James Garner on the set of Maverick, a leather chair, three bowling pins and a brand new, never before touched G.I. Joe action figure (Snake Eyes), still in its original packaging. Due to a small clerical error, it would be three years before Caroline would receive compensation, and eight years after that before the lawsuit was finally settled, in her favor, the judge citing the substandard sprinkler system as the deciding factor in the case.

Too late to stop the blaze, they were the first to report the disaster to the 911 operator, Gabrielle, who would go on to grant eleven interviews on the subject to various news outlets in southern California. Her hopes of appearing on the Oprah Winfrey Show were never realized.

"Nine-one-one, what is your emergency?" Gabrielle asked.

"There's a huge fire here," Bob said matter-of-factly.

"Where is here, sir?"

"I don't know. Susan?"

"Andy's Impound Lot."

"Andy's Impound Lot," Bob repeated dutifully.

"It's on Hope Street," Susan continued, distracted.

He let the irony pass, repeating the information. "On Hope."

Susan grabbed Bob's arm, hard.

"It's Paul. He's armed."

"It's Paul. He's armed," Bob repeated, unaware he had even done so.

"Who is Paul, sir?"

Bob could see him now. He was moving slowly across the lot. A gun was clearly visible in his hand, and it looked as if his arm was on fire.

"Send a lot of firemen, send a lot of police. Please hurry. Thank you."

Bob hung up and looked to Susan for direction. Part of him wanted her to behave reasonably. Wait in the car, Bob. Police will be here soon. Let us let them handle the matter. When she took out her pistol, which looked dark and greasy, nothing like the sleek automatic weapon he had expected from the world of television and motioned for him to follow her from the car, he breathed a sigh of relief. It would have been hard to look back on everything knowing he passed up an opportunity to confront and apprehend his father's murderer. Prudence be damned.

"What in the hell are you doing?" Paul said.

Winston was about to respond when a serious case of the giggles overtook him.

"What?"

"Dude, your sleeve is totally on fire again."

Paul looked down and saw that the fire had indeed leapt up with renewed energy.

"Goddammit," he sighed.

Preoccupied with stripping off his jacket, Paul didn't notice Susan and Bob coming in behind him.

"Put the weapon on the ground and turn around slowly," Susan said, loudly and with practiced authority.

Her voice was dulled greatly by the raging inferno growing stronger with every passing minute. There was no denying her intent, though. Her gun was raised, her feet slightly apart, in perfect balance, a position born from years of practice.

Paul obliged a portion of Susan's demand and turned to face her. He paid no attention to Bob, who knelt over Winston, shocked at the sight before him.

"Jesus, are you all right?" Bob asked.

Winston's case of the giggles returned with a vengeance. Bob reached out uncertainly, completely at a loss about how to help this man who, in any sort of decent world, would have passed out from the agonizing pain he was surely suffering.

"Stay where you are," Susan barked.

He raised his hands in mock self-defense, continuing to back away. Susan stepped forward, doing her best to intimidate Paul. Judging by the ever-expanding smirk on his face, it was not going well.

"Sir, I am a police officer. If you do not stop moving, I will be forced to fire. Do you understand me?"

Paul turned and ran. Susan contemplated shooting him in the back, but felt given her circumstances, that might not be the best course of action. She begrudgingly turned her attention to Bob.

"How is he?"

"Judging by the laughter, I'd say he's in severe shock. What's the emergency response time?"

"In this part of town? Ten minutes."

"I don't think he's going to live that long."

"He's gone."

A distant cousin had imparted advice on Susan's sweet sixteen birthday party, a hapless affair that cost just under two-thousand dollars and made no less than four small children and one adult cry. Susan had been more than happy to skip a celebration of any sort the following year. Unlike every other minute of the affair, which was burned into her mind for all time, somehow the advice had not stuck. It would have served her well.

Never utter famous last words, Antonia the distant cousin had whispered to her in lieu of a gift. Never utter famous last words, because they could very well be.

Paul, storming back through the smoke, firing indiscriminately at the three surprised, soot-covered individuals inspired a wave of nausea in Susan, but no memory of the useful, albeit a bit premature, words of wisdom.

"Get down!" she yelled, shoving Bob into Winston, trying to shield them from the bullets that were, despite Paul, being not far away when he began shooting and moving ever closer, nowhere close to them.

Paul's shots, hampered by the smoke in his eyes and the uneven ground under his feet, managed to hit two tires and a light pole. A fourth shot was fired, but the bullet was never recovered. Bob went back and looked for it a few weeks later. It would have been nice to have a souvenir.

He ended up within five feet of Susan when he fired his last errant shot. It looked to her as if his expression were apologetic, or at the very least, appropriately abashed. Out of ammunition, Paul tossed his gun to the ground.

"Are you gonna shoot me this time?" Paul asked defiantly.

She hesitated for a moment, long enough for him to crack a smile, and just long enough for Bob to grab Susan's gun and shoot Paul in the foot.

Bob had never held a firearm before, let alone pulled the trigger. It wasn't quite what he expected. The recoil was sharp and abrupt, jolting his entire body. The acrid smell was dulled by the smoke surrounding them, but not completely obscured. The sound made his ears ring. All of which he anticipated, and as a result, his aim was superb for a first timer. He had been aiming for the other foot, but he was still pleased with the results.

He hadn't anticipated how good it would feel to shoot

another human being. It was a lot more fun than he would have thought.

Winston was unable to enjoy the moment, having finally and blissfully passed out at some point.

The wailing of sirens in the background signaled the arrival of L.A.'s finest. Susan reached out and gently took the gun back from Bob. She kept hold of his hand, though, squeezing ever so slightly. Eyes watering, they both enjoyed the sound of Paul moaning in pain, audible even amongst all the destruction, and waited for the ambulance to arrive.

There was no hurry, as far as Bob was concerned.

Chapter 23

THE DAMAGE to the house was severe, the floor completely ruined. The water had drained away, but the smell lingered with ferocity. The very first thing Pete did was call for an estimate. Upon hearing the news, he sat down heavily on the only piece of furniture left untouched by the flood, a not particularly comfortable wicker chair that was a gift from his late uncle George.

"I've unpacked," Nina said quietly.

Startled, Pete turned around. "That was quick."

"There wasn't that much."

It was probably not the best time to begin an important conversation about their marriage and overall prospects for the future. She couldn't help herself.

"What should we do?"

"I made a call. Should have somebody out by tomorrow."

"I meant in a general life sort of direction. Where do we go from here?"

He had been out of prison for less than twenty-four hours. The prison authorities had been kind enough to inform him another man was being charged with the murder of Alan and his wife. They seemed appropriately embarrassed when informing Pete it would take two days to process his paperwork and secure his actual release. It hadn't bothered him in the slightest. He'd needed the time to think.

Paul was done for. Harvey must have squealed, which meant it wasn't likely the two of them would be spending much time together in the future. Pete didn't have the head for business nor the energy to lead a criminal syndicate. Save for Nina, he was certain every aspect of his old life was dead and gone. Maybe Los Angeles should be included in that list. He could certainly do without the traffic. Nina might like to experience seasonal change. A fresh start in a new town might just be the ticket.

It wouldn't be easy to just pick up and move to a strange city. There was an alternative he had been considering, but was more than a little scared to discuss with his wife. There was no use putting it off forever. He braced himself.

"We could stay with my mom for a while," Pete ventured. "She'd like that."

Her gut reaction was to argue, and strenuously at that. More than that, she wanted to say no, but she was too tired to get into a gigantic argument so soon after driving him home from prison. Then again, maybe she wouldn't mind a little time away from everything. Even if it was with her mother-in-law.

"Let's talk about it later," She decided. "I'm really tired."

"You want anything?"

Nina gave it some thought. "I'm a little hungry."

"You want me to make you a sandwich?"

"I really, really do."

Amy had managed to keep solid food down for two consecutive days and her doctors were confident that the worst was over and a full and complete recovery was only a few short days away. Paul was incarcerated. None of her friends had come to visit her since his arrest. Her attorney was adamant that the sum total of Paul's assets would remain unavailable for several years, tied up in legal limbo. Insurance would cover most of her hospital stay. She was forty-one years old, in good health, and the mere thought of taking a pill, real or imagined in the near or distant future, made her stomach turn.

Never in her whole life had she felt so lost or been so depressed.

It was the uncertainty of it all that really rankled. Another day or two at the hospital and then the future became impossibly murky. Her head began to swim whenever she contemplated the coming days.

Work was out of the question. A loan seemed unlikely, the possibility of paying it back even more so. Life seemed very hard. Normally she would retreat into fake addiction, but with the absence of a support network, it seemed rather pointless.

Doctor A. Monroe came into the room, barely concealed disinterest and clipboard in tow.

"How are we doing today?" he asked.

"Depressed."

"You're eating all right?"

"Yes."

Their conversations, such as they were, never strayed beyond such trivialities. She was honest and forthright, though it hardly seemed to matter. It was impossible to tell if he ever heard a word she said. As per usual, his head was bowed, buried in paperwork. His left hand played idly with a pen, perhaps an obsessive act left over from his days in medical school.

Amy hadn't noticed the above average tan before, especially impressive for someone stuck under fluorescent lights most of their life. He must go to a salon, though it didn't conceal the pale band of flesh on the ring finger of his left hand. It was at this moment that her interest level in Doctor Monroe increased exponentially.

"Doctor?"

"Hmm?"

"What does the 'A' stand for?"

"Adam."

"Adam. That was my first boyfriend's name."

He smiled politely and went back to perusing her file. She gave him a good once-over.

Recently divorced. Completely wrapped up in his work, which, while perfectly acceptable, was not nearly as important as a tendency to find interest in anything and everything that wasn't her. Comfortably wealthy. Not unpleasant to look at.

That's a thought, Amy mused, a smile coming to her face for the first time in weeks. Maybe the future isn't so bleak after all.

Rick was arrested at half past two in the morning in his apartment. He had just fallen asleep, his last conscious thought before the pleasant recurring dream of Mike Schmidt hitting home runs was whether or not he should leave town. The possibility he might be in way over his head was only just starting to sink in, but Rick was more concerned with moving up the food chain, imagining a life where he gave the orders, than he was with the potential repercussions. He wasn't surprised when his door burst open, but he couldn't help but feel a little disappointed. It would have been nice to learn what he was capable of accomplishing.

At the same time Rick was lamenting lost opportunities, Harvey was celebrating his good fortune with a glass of Chivas on the rocks. The thought of testifying in open court against Paul was an increasingly pleasurable prospect. It would be eight months before he got to see the look on Paul's face, but it was well worth the wait. Harvey could practically feel the hatred coming off Paul while detailing the many, many atrocities that occurred during their time together. He made sure to show up for sentencing as well. Harvey felt it important to see the fruits of his labor.

It had been a full week since Bob had shot Paul in the foot, a week which had brought no life-changing revelations. Escaping death and avenging a loved one did nothing to alter the due date on credit card payments, let alone indignities like rent and food. Lounging on Susan's comfortable green sofa did nothing to alleviate the cold hard truth of the matter. He was going to have to find gainful employment. He decided to say as much.

"Susan?"

"Yes?"

"I can't lie on your couch any longer."

"About time."

"I'm sorry, it's driving me crazy doing nothing all day."

"Ditto."

Bob pressed on. "Plus, my bills are adding up and I'm slowly depleting my savings. You're not cheap to date and I like cable television. I need money and I see no other option. Well, almost no other option."

"Meaning?"

"I haven't completely ruled out the possibility of going on the dob."

"The what?"

"It's British slang for welfare."

"That seems unlikely, Bob."

"So not a good idea?" he asked, refusing to argue the point with an English major.

"You're asking a recently reinstated public servant to comment on your milking the public for their hard spent tax dollars."

"Yes."

"I think you'd be very bored."

"That's what I think. I just wish I had some sense of what would make me happy, some kind of helpful hint on where to go."

"The future isn't any more certain than the present," Susan said, trying to be helpful but butchering Walt Whitman along the way.

"I suppose."

"So definitely a no on chiropracting?"

"Well, never say never. But there's just got to be something else to make my life's work. Something meaningful and substantive. Like what you do."

Several of her fellow officers had been more than a little cold since her return. The department had taken a tremendous amount of flack during her suspension, the call for her dismissal reaching a fever pitch after the local news broadcast footage of her in the back of an ambulance near the impound lot. Her inability to stay away from trouble or refrain from bringing that trouble into the office at seemingly every opportunity did nothing to ingratiate her with those who did not want to give people one more reason to give the LAPD a hard time. She had come perilously close to losing her job with yet another piece of bad publicity.

The saving grace was a flattering portrait in the L.A. Weekly that made Susan out to be something of a hero, despite her on-the-record protestations that she hadn't actually been the one to shoot the man later charged with nine murders. She'd caught wind about rumors circulated among the higher-ups calling for her dismissal, but it was a hard sell to dump the 'courageous officer who fights for justice' as Bobbi Lang's article tagged her in its opening paragraph. The piece was picked up briefly by the AP and was such a success, Bobbi was invited to give the commencement speech at her undergraduate alma mater the following year when the school's first and second choices cancelled at the last minute, a triumph that did not forgive her student loans, but brought about a grudging level of acceptance from her parents and, more importantly, continued financial support.

Susan had never been all that worried. After all, as she was quick to point out whenever the subject was broached, it's not as if she'd killed anyone.

The first day back had been difficult. A note was left on the two-foot pile of folders stacked ominously on her desk. It read simply, 'Welcome back, ye who makes life so much more difficult than it need be for the rest of us'. Susan felt certain it was from Ortiz, what with the 'ye', though no credit was taken. She couldn't remember exactly when her English degree pedigree came to light, but it was unusual enough within the ranks to merit a fair amount of mockery.

It could have been worse, Susan figured. At least it included 'welcome'.

Sidelong glances, whispered gossip and a few cold shoulders were the order of the day. Baker had been curt, the natural fallout from having to deal with an officer involved shooting from a suspended police officer, but that didn't stop him from greeting her return with a staring contest. She lost fair and square.

Susan immersed herself in her work to avoid thinking too much about her fellow officers. Kidnapping, two suicides, an apparent homicide involving a large mackerel and an obese apartment manager from Cerritos and a botched robbery of a recently renovated Applebee's made her return to active duty the proverbial blast from the past. It was exactly the sort of nonsense that had precipitated her malaise pre-suspension, but somehow it felt different.

Bob's kind words revealed the truth. She was rejuvenated, her batteries recharged. She wanted to provide the same sort of help to him. He clearly needed it.

"I think you can do anything you set your mind to."

Bob was not impressed.

Susan took a deep breath and gave it another try. "Well, maybe it'd be helpful to think long-term. Where do you want to be in a year or two?"

"Well, it's not down on any map, that's for sure," Bob said. "True places never are."

"You've read Moby Dick," Susan beamed, not quite believing her ears.

Bob nodded, grinning cheekily. He was excessively pleased with himself for nailing the line, but she couldn't fault him for gloating a little. She reached out for his hand, drawing him closer. It occurred to her this was the first time a guy ever quoted Melville to her, and while their evening might have been better spent discussing the future, Susan decided to put such thoughts away for a less interesting time.

ACKNOWLEDGMENTS

THE origins of this book began several years ago, born from my time cracking backs, um, pardon, I meant to say making minor adjustments to patients and their spines, as an unlicensed physical therapist in the San Fernando Valley. If this book provided a few laughs, intentional or otherwise, then I rest happy in the knowledge of time well spent on the peripheries of the health care industry.

An early draft sat huddled and alone on an old laptop for quite some time, lying mostly dormant during my spells of amassing massive debt at UCLA and writing for CBS, and it only reached the general public thanks to the gentle prodding of my parents. My sincere and heartfelt thanks to them, in this, and in all things.

I also want to thank my sister, Helen, and Julia Tyler for providing invaluable assistance editing the manuscript and lastly, Christopher Whittier, who designed the cover with little more to work with than my helpful suggestion to "make it cool and stuff".

Copyright

Cover art and design: Christopher Whittier

www.ingramcontent.com/pod-product-compliance
Lightning Source LLC
Chambersburg PA
CBHW020556180626
46810CB00007B/2526